Someone was .... was focused on the gaping front of her nightshirt, which rose and fell with her terrified breathing.

"Hannah, it's me—Rook."

"You almost scared me to death!"

Rook's calm smile was infuriating. "We've got to hurry."

"Hurry? What are you talking about?"

He grinned. "To see the sun come up, remember?"

"But I thought you meant stay up all night. You know, like normal people."

"Honey, in Kansas, normal people who want to see the sunrise get up early."

"No one sane would get out of bed at this hour!"

"You're right. Why waste time out in the cold when we can be absolutely *normal* right here in bed?"

"Stop where you are!" she warned. "All of a sudden I have an uncontrollable urge to see the sun come up over the prairie."

His smile tilted rakishly. "Ah, yes, those uncontrollable urges. Aren't they the damnedest things?"

Dear Reader,

Welcome to the Silhouette **Special Edition** experience! With your search for consistently satisfying reading in mind, every month the authors and editors of Silhouette **Special Edition** aim to offer you a stimulating blend of deep emotions and high romance.

The name Silhouette **Special Edition** and the distinctive arch on the cover represent a commitment—a commitment to bring you six sensitive, substantial novels each month. In the pages of a Silhouette **Special Edition**, compelling true-to-life characters face riveting emotional issues—and come out winners. Both celebrated authors and newcomers to the series strive for depth and dimension, vividness and warmth, in writing these stories of living and loving in today's world.

The result, we hope, is romance you can believe in. Deeply emotional, richly romantic, infinitely rewarding—that's the Silhouette **Special Edition** experience. Come share it with us—six times a month!

From all the authors and editors of Silhouette **Special Edition**,

Best wishes,

Leslie Kazanjian,
Senior Editor

JESSICA ST. JAMES
The Perfect Lover

Silhouette Special Edition

Published by Silhouette Books New York

America's Publisher of Contemporary Romance

This book is dedicated, with love,
to our husbands,
Don Varner and Clint Hoy.

SILHOUETTE BOOKS
300 East 42nd St., New York, N.Y. 10017

ISBN: 0-373-09561-9

First Silhouette Books printing November 1989

JESSICA ST. JAMES

is the pen name for a Kansas-based writing team. Friends since high school, the two women began writing together about four years ago. They have published two historical romances set primarily in Scotland and England, where they enjoyed doing hands-on research. *The Perfect Lover*, their first contemporary novel, is also their first set in their home state, and they welcomed the opportunity to show readers that Kansas can be as romantically inspiring as Europe. In addition to writing and travel, the authors share a love of books and cats.

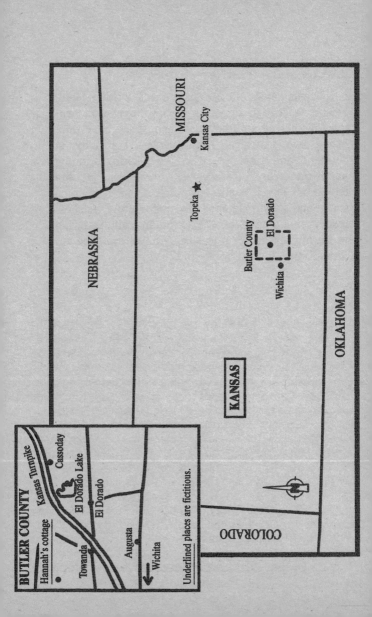

BUTLER COUNTY

Hannah's cottage
Kansas Turnpike
Cassoday
El Dorado Lake
El Dorado
Towanda
Augusta
Wichita

Underlined places are fictitious.

NEBRASKA

MISSOURI

Kansas City

Topeka

Butler County
El Dorado
Wichita

KANSAS

OKLAHOMA

COLORADO

Chapter One

Damn and double damn!" Hannah Grant swore softly. Now what?

She frowned at the shiny new padlock on the wooden gate, then gave it a vicious yank. As she had suspected, it wouldn't budge. Beyond the barrier that blocked the only entrance to the property, the narrow track beckoned enticingly, wending its way past crumbled stone foundations, an old barn and a windmill creaking in the early-April wind.

With a sigh, Hannah returned to her battered Mustang. She got in, backed up, then parked along one side of the tree-lined gravel road. Locking the doors, she tossed the keys into her shoulder bag. As she skirted the car, she glanced at the New York plates—she hadn't driven all this way just to be defeated at the end of the trip.

She congratulated herself for managing to climb over the gate with fairly good agility for a city girl, then hitched her purse onto her shoulder and set off. To the right, she could see the vine-covered remains of an old farmhouse, and realizing that members of her own family must once have lived there, she paused. But curiosity about the piece of property

she had come to see soon urged her on. The lawyer's written instructions clearly stated that the cottage was located in
the middle of an entire section of ground. Hannah wasn't
certain just what a section was, but she guessed it to be a
much larger area than this old farmyard.

Beyond the noisy windmill, the road came to an abrupt
end near a small lake, its shores densely wooded on all sides.
Someone had constructed a minute sand beach, and there
was a picnic table as well as a swing beneath the trees. It was
a lovely, secluded place and yet Hannah knew that not more
than a block away—it was habitual for her to figure distances in blocks—there was a blacktopped highway.

Thin tire tracks led away from the official end of the road,
disappearing in the knee-high prairie grass. As she walked,
Hannah forced herself to conjure up an image of the cottage so her mind couldn't dwell on thoughts of the creatures that might be lurking in the tall grass.

*The cottage was smothered in roses—roses that ranged in
color from dark scarlet to delicate pink. Roses that clam-
bered up the stone walls to cover the eaves and overhang
deep, mullioned windows. A curving flagstone path led
through a forest of blue lupine and ivory baby's breath to a
studded oak door, which stood open in welcome. The yard
was enclosed by a white picket fence, an arched trellis at the
gate dripping with purple wisteria. And falling away on
every side were fields of yellow daffodils, dancing in the
spring wind.*

Looming before her, nearly hidden by an oasis of overgrown trees and bushes on a desert of grass, was the real
cottage. A sagging wire fence enclosed the lawn, keeping its
wildness from escaping to the smooth folds of prairie that
fell away on three sides. Hannah swallowed deeply. Where
were the roses? The lupines?

She put out an unsteady hand to push open the rusted
metal gate. The path, stepping stones choked with weeds,
ended at a wooden door covered with flaking green paint.
It was neither open nor particularly welcoming.

The cottage was built of fieldstone, with wooden eaves
and a shingled roof once painted a dark forest green. There
was a screened porch along the front side and Hannah

pressed her face against the screen, shading her eyes to peer inside. She saw a painted wooden commode, a stack of lawn chairs and a folded daybed, swathed in plastic.

She could tell the door to the porch was bolted from the inside and didn't waste time trying it. Instead, she unzipped her purse and searched through it for a small brown envelope containing a door key—a key that fit the brand new lock on the front door. The lock clicked loudly, and, closing her eyes, she gave the door a shove.

The homey scent of lemon furniture polish and vanilla candles greeted her, inviting her into the cozy room. Warmed by a fire crackling in the stone fireplace and lighted only by an assortment of candles on the mantel, the room was perfect. Hannah gazed with pride at the polished plank floor, covered by a burgundy-and-blue oriental rug. A burgundy Victorian couch and two blue wing-backed chairs were arranged in front of the fire. There was a bowl of pink roses on a cherrywood table. Next to the roses was her collection of family photos in ornate brass frames. Each of the mullioned windows was covered with swagged draperies in blue velvet....

The odor was ghastly! Hannah's hand instinctively covered her nose and mouth, as her eyes flew open.

Lord, this place must have been shut up for years, she thought, trying not to breathe the stale air rushing at her.

There was a heavy mustiness—the dank, fetid, malodorous smell of disuse. In contrast, there was also the dry, acrid smell of dust and dirt. And, with a certainty based on years of experience with low-rent city apartments, she recognized the unpleasant aroma peculiar to mice, those indiscriminate little rodents with such nasty habits!

Trepidation assailed Hannah, but she forced herself to take a good look at the room. She sagged against the door frame—she had come all this way... and it was awful!

The walls were rough stone, like the outside, but festooned with cobwebs and a hornets' nest or two. The stone fireplace of her fantasy did exist at one end of the room, but its blackened hearth was badly in need of cleaning. The couch in front of it was an ugly brown, made even more disreputable by a layer of gritty dust; it was flanked by a broken-down armchair and a spindly, high-backed rocker.

Hannah ventured farther into the room, the sound of her footsteps echoing against the concrete floor. With a disappointed sigh, she bade a silent farewell to the mullioned windows of her dream cottage—the ones she was looking at were quite ordinary. At the far end of the room, behind a scarred wooden table and chairs, there were four long windows in a row, but they were so filthy she could barely see out.

On one side wall was the doorway to the screened porch, and on the opposite, two doors with a shelved cupboard set between them. At some time, someone had seen fit to paint it a hideous mustard color.

She poked her head through the first door and was somewhat reassured to find a pocket-sized kitchen, with cupboards and a stone sink under the single window. It was obvious the cottage was wired for electricity, for there was an electric stove and refrigerator, though nothing happened when Hannah flipped the light switch. Even in the gloom, she could see the refrigerator, whose door had been propped open with a large crock, contained what she suspected was a nest belonging to some sort of animal. Built of twigs and shredded cotton, it covered the entire bottom shelf, spilling out onto the floor. With a shudder, she backed away, unwilling to explore further.

The other door led into a bedroom, which was larger than the kitchen. It had two big windows and a good-sized closet, stuffed with odds and ends. There was a bed, its striped mattress tightly wrapped in clear plastic, like a giant sandwich, and an old dresser with white china drawer pulls.

Hannah turned back to the main room and, for the first time, gave in to depression. So this was Gran's cabin—her hideaway—the refuge which she had mentioned so often in the final years of her life. What could there possibly have been about this derelict pile of stones that had caused her to recall it with such fondness?

Despite the dust, Hannah dropped onto the couch and buried her face in her hands.

My God, she thought, what have I done?

In the space of one short week, she had given up everything—job, apartment, friends—to make this trip. She had driven halfway across the country to her grandmother's cottage in Kansas, certain she could find what she had been missing for so long...quiet contentment, peace of mind and the hope there was something more to living than dull routine.

A dreamer, Hannah had never attempted to act on her dreams. Since her grandmother's death nearly a year ago, she had led a confused, unhappy existence, not knowing exactly what it was she wanted. When her grandmother's lawyer had called to inform her he had received an offer to sell the cottage, it had started her thinking. The offer was more than generous for the lakeside cottage and ten acres of land, and God knew, she could use the money. Still...Gran had loved the place enough to hold onto it, even though she had been forced to sell the rest of the farm property. Finally, it came down to the fact that Hannah couldn't just sell the cottage sight unseen. She made the decision to see it first, perhaps spend the summer there; and then, if she approved of the buyer, sell it and return to New York.

Her journey was an idealistic search for something that had gone out of her life, a search that had begun the day she loaded her few possessions into the car and started west. Now she feared it might end in dusty, cobwebbed reality.

"Damn it," she muttered, "things weren't supposed to happen this way."

Back in the city, coming out here had seemed such a good idea. But at this moment, Hannah was beginning to think she must have been a borderline idiot.

Glancing about, she silently amended the thought. Maybe not so borderline....

"Crud, why can't things ever go right?" She gave the couch a vicious kick with the back of her heel, nearly choking in the resulting cloud of dust.

She realized the cabin must have been some sort of symbol to her, a symbol of the ultimate human dream—a cozy cottage in the country, needing only someone special with whom to share it to make it perfect. Discovering the awful shabbiness of the symbol had been a shock.

Why wasn't anything ever the way she saw it in her mind? As she so often did in moments of stress, she turned to her familiar daydream that always had the power to soothe her.

Just one look into the man's deep blue eyes was enough to assure her he was intelligent, experienced and incredibly sensitive. He seemed at ease in the candlelit room. He stood before her dressed in casual tweed, one arm resting on the mantel, the fingers of his right hand wrapped about the bowl of a pipe. In the left, he held a book bound in elegant leather. His hair was thick and lustrous, dark chestnut in color, faintly silvered at the temples. His handsome features were aristocratic; long-lashed eyes with faint laugh lines at the outer corners, aquiline nose, firm jaw. And she loved his perfectly sculpted mouth! It seemed his lips curved in subtle invitation each time he opened them to speak. . . .

"Who the hell are you?"

The startlingly masculine voice shattered her reverie and brought Hannah to her feet in shock. She found herself confronting a very grim-looking young man who stood in the open doorway, legs straddled belligerently. He seemed enormously tall in the low-ceilinged cottage, and the size of his shoulders was exaggerated by the plaid flannel shirt he wore. The shirt's sleeves were rolled up, and it was unbuttoned far enough down the front to reveal a hairy chest. Cradled across that chest, in muscled arms, was a very businesslike shotgun. Hannah's frightened eyes flew upward to his face.

With a thumb under the front brim, he thrust the felt cowboy hat he wore farther back on his head and returned her stare. His face was lean, stopping attractively short of boniness, with prominent cheekbones and an aggressive chin and jaw. His eyes were nearly black in their intensity, matching the raven's wing hue of his hair. When he spoke again, she caught a glimpse of straight, white teeth . . . but he wasn't smiling.

"I asked you a question, lady. Who the hell are you?"

"What do you intend to do with that gun?" she asked, taking a step away from him.

"That depends . . ."

"On what?"

"On who the hell you are."

"I'm Hannah Grant," she stammered.

"Why are you trespassing?"

"I'm not. This..." she waved an airy hand "...lovely establishment belongs to me."

His dark eyes narrowed. "You're the granddaughter? The romance editor from New York?"

"That's right."

Though he didn't actually smile, one corner of his mouth twitched noticeably, lessening her apprehension. "Somehow I expected you to look and sound a little tougher."

"Sorry to disappoint you," she said, shortly.

"Oh, I'm not disappointed. In fact..." This time he actually grinned. "So you're the granddaughter. Well, I'll be damned."

"Yes...I would think so," she replied. She intended to let a slightly insulting look travel up and down the length of his body, in an effort to put his obvious arrogance to the test, but somehow her eyes couldn't get past the flat expanse of waist and hip, clad in tight denim jeans and dissected by a low-slung leather belt with the most god-awful belt buckle she had ever seen.

"Why on earth would anyone wear a belt buckle with a cow's head on it?" she asked abruptly. For some reason, all fear of being alone with a stranger in this isolated spot had fled. Despite the gun he carried, he seemed far less menacing than many of the people she was used to facing on the subway every day.

He was insulted. "It's not a cow head," he protested. "It's an Angus bull."

"Oh? Some sort of rural fashion statement, I take it?"

"God, are all women from New York bitches?"

"Are all men from Kansas...cowboys?"

They glared at each other for a long moment. Suddenly she laughed—she couldn't help it, he looked so disgruntled.

"What do they call you?" she asked. "Tex? Slim? Snake-eyes?"

He finally grinned again. "Actually, they call me Rook."

"Rook? That's a strange name...."

"No stranger than Hannah."

"What's wrong with my name?" Now she felt defensive.

"Isn't it a little countrified for a hotshot female from the Big Apple? I thought all you city women had tough-sounding masculine names like Stevie or Morgan."

Her chin went up. "And I thought all midwesterners were slow-witted and wore bib overalls." She shrugged eloquently. "It's nice one of us was right, isn't it?"

"At the risk of sounding rude," he said cuttingly, "I'd like to point out that I'm wearing jeans...not bib overalls."

"Ah, at least you made no effort to defend your mentality. And anyway, even if you're not wearing them now, I bet you own a pair of overalls, don't you?" Hannah challenged.

"What if I do...?" He looked momentarily sheepish. "Oh, all right, so I own a pair. I promise to wear them for you sometime, just so you can gloat and feel superior."

"What makes you think I need to wait until you're wearing overalls?"

"Damn, you've got a sharp tongue!" he growled, shifting the weight of the shotgun he held. "I think I'll get back to work. It was a hell of a lot more pleasant than conversing with you."

Curious, Hannah asked, "What kind of work were you doing?"

"Gathering cow chips for the boss's flower beds."

She just barely managed to stifle the giggle that threatened to break forth. "Even a city slicker knows it isn't flattering to come off second-best to cow manure!"

It was Rook's turn to shrug.

"However, I didn't know cow chips were so dangerous they required the gatherer to be armed. I suppose my life in the tenements was just too sheltered."

His almost-smile faded rapidly. "As I came across the pasture, I saw the door to the cabin standing open and decided to investigate. The gun seemed a good idea—we've had a considerable problem with thieves lately."

"And I was under the impression the Wild West was a thing of the past. How could I know the first person I met would be a gun-totin' cowpuncher?"

"You really are a little snot," he snapped.

She laughed aloud, unable to curb her mirth even though she knew he was glowering at her.

Rook momentarily allowed himself to hide behind his anger, his mind preoccupied. He thought her laugh was wonderful—rich and full-bodied. With disgust, he likened his mental process to a coffee commercial, but knew immediately how appropriate it was. Her laugh had the same effect as a first cup of coffee in the morning: it warmed and stimulated and left him feeling very satisfied.

It didn't take long for his practiced eye to roam her slender figure from head to toe—there simply wasn't that much of her. He'd wager the top of her tousled brown head would only reach his shoulder. Her hair was shortish, about collar length, and very dark. It was neither straight nor wavy, more...curved, swirling and winging about her face in fascinating animation. But the most interesting thing was that it appeared to be sun-streaked, and though he didn't know for sure, he was fairly certain New York hadn't had much more sun than Kansas this early in the spring. Yet, the golden highlights adding such sparkle to the darkness of her hair didn't look artificial. He made himself a promise to find out about those streaks later.

The woman had great eyes, he decided judiciously. They were an incredible silver-green color, heavily lashed and so wide open they gave her an innocence that had to be deceptive. They made her appear much younger and more inexperienced than her age, which he knew had to be mid-to-late twenties.

Or perhaps it was the heart-shaped face that made her seem so young, he conjectured—or the soft, sweet mouth that disguised the acidity of her tongue. Or the tip-tilted nose that, at the moment, had a smudge he suspected came from rusty screen wire.

He hated her clothes, especially the pleated, baggy-legged jeans that tied at the ankle, though the sloppy sweatshirt that read Property of the New York Yankees wasn't much better. He squinted his eyes, trying to picture her in tight western jeans—with a "cow head" belt buckle, he added with a silent chuckle.

Something about his contemplation began to make Hannah nervous, and she coughed politely, drawing his attention.

"I...uh, thought you had to get back to work."

"Huh? Oh, yeah...I do. The boss will have my hide, otherwise."

"Your boss...he wouldn't be J. W. McAllister, would he?"

"No, *she* would be Mrs. J. W. McAllister."

"A woman owns this property?"

"Don't tell me you're a reverse chauvinist?"

"No...I'm surprised, that's all. What happened to J. W.?"

"He passed away a few years ago. Now Mrs. McAllister owns this and several thousand other acres. Why do you ask?"

"I need to talk to her about getting permission to drive through the meadow...."

"Pasture," he corrected.

"Whatever. The gate is padlocked, so I had to leave my car and walk. If I'm going to be staying here, I'll need a key."

"You're planning on staying here?" He sounded incredulous.

"I do own it. And I need a place to live. At least for a while."

"You have noticed a certain...lack of the amenities?"

"I assume I can have the electricity turned on within the next day or so."

"What about plumbing? You know there is none?"

Her expression of dawning horror amused him greatly. "Oh, my God!" she groaned. "There isn't a bathroom, is there?"

"Oh, there's a bathroom, all right. It just may not be the type you're used to. Come on, I'll show you."

He leaned the shotgun against the outside wall of the cottage and waited for her to follow him. He led the way around the corner, into an overgrown backyard. There, modestly shielded by evergreens, was a prim white building.

"As far as outhouses go, it's nothing fancy—only a one-holer." With a definite smirk he opened the door and stood aside. "However, it should be sufficient for your...uh, needs."

"It will have to be, won't it?" Hannah was staring so intently at the stark interior of the privy that she nearly missed his next disclosure.

"Over there's the well where you can pump any water you need."

"There's no running water, either?"

"Nary a faucet."

"Well, you needn't look so pleased about it," she said. "The fact is, I still have to stay here, even if it won't exactly be the vacation I was planning."

"Couldn't you find a motel somewhere?" he asked, more seriously.

"Finding one and being able to afford to stay there are two different things. Since this is more or less a roof over my head, and since it's free, I'm pretty much forced to take advantage of it."

"In that case, let me point out where Mrs. McAllister lives. You'll want to get over to see her before dark, so you can get settled in."

He laid a hand on her shoulder, turning her slightly. "See that big place on the hill? That's hers."

Hannah's eyes followed his pointing finger, coming to rest on the distant house, a blur of beige elegance against the green.

"Wow, it looks huge!" She looked up at Rook. "I suppose she's a rich old dragon, living in a place like that."

"All I know is, when she speaks, I jump!"

"Damn, I knew it. Oh well, if she won't be civil to me, maybe the lawyer will speak to her."

"There shouldn't be any problem getting access to your place," Rook assured her. "McAllister is tough, but she's in a partnership with her son, and he's a very reasonable man. Anyway, to get to her house, just follow the road from the main gate and turn left at every corner. You can't miss it.''

Hannah followed him back to the front of the cottage, for the first time seeing the beat-up truck parked in the middle of the sea of grass.

"That's mine," he said. "It's how I got here. I drove in the back way, but I wouldn't advise it with a car."

"I'll remember that. Uh, by the way..." Hannah stared down at her grubby tennis shoes as if trying to gather her courage. Finally, she tilted her head to look up at him.

"Could I ask you one favor before you leave?"

"Sure."

"Would you mind coming into the kitchen and telling me what has built a nest in the refrigerator? I'd feel better knowing...if I'm spending the night here."

He laughed, ducking his head to reenter the cabin. When she caught up with him, he was standing in front of the occupied appliance. "Pack rat," he said succinctly.

"Rat?" she echoed faintly.

"*Pack* rat. They're harmless."

"Great."

"Just sweep out the nest with a broom. There's nothing to worry about. They're hardly more than overgrown mice."

He brushed past her, on his way to the front door. In the middle of the room, he paused and looked back. "You aren't afraid of mice, are you?"

"Contrary to popular belief, not all women are afraid of rodents," she said firmly. "There is only one thing that really scares me...and that is a sna..."

As she spoke, her unsuspecting eyes had been sweeping the room. Drawn by a slight movement, they fell to the wooden rocker beside her and there, to her utter horror, was a slim, dark snake, curling sinuously about one of the spindles on the chair back.

"SNAKE!" she screamed, then screamed again. "SNAKE!"

With no notion of what she was doing, she leaped onto the couch and ran its entire length, sending up a smoke screen of dust.

"Oh, my God! My God!"

Unexpectedly, she hurled herself at the watching man.

"Oomph!" Rook muttered, arms going about her almost as much in self-defense as in chivalry. He put one arm beneath her knees, lifting her against his chest.

She was overcome with a feeling of security, as he cradled her to him. His strength was apparent in the easy way he held her. She felt his lips gently graze her hair. Her cheek brushed the rough tweed of his jacket and, with a sigh, she let herself be soothed by the comforting, familiar scent of him—the aroma of spicy after-shave, the tang of tobacco, the hint of leather.

Hannah's fingers burned. Opening her eyes, she saw them curled into the thick hair on Rook's naked chest. Her other arm was around his neck, her cheek butted up against his hard shoulder. He smelled of sun-warmed cotton...but there was also the definite odor of sweat and...yes, stale cow patties!

"Put me down!" she gasped.

"Don't say that like I attacked you or something. Remember, you jumped me."

"I did not jump you!" she exclaimed, wriggling within his grip. "At least, not intentionally."

He let her slide down his body until she stood on her own feet again, amused by the way she clung to his arm, sidling around behind him.

"Can you see it?" Hannah asked fearfully.

"If you mean that harmless, little snake, yes...it's still on the rocker."

"Can't you kill it or something?"

"Kill it? What for? It's just a garter snake, for God's sake. It isn't poisonous."

"Maybe not, but I don't want it in my house!"

"Since he's undoubtedly lived here all winter, he probably thinks he has a prior claim."

"Could you please dispense with the humor and get rid of that horrid creature?"

Disengaging his arm from her stranglehold, he crossed the room to pick up the snake, holding it carefully between thumb and forefinger. Hannah, finding she could not watch, turned her back on the proceeding, not looking up until she heard Rook say, "There! All taken care of. I put it on a sunny rock in the yard."

She whirled around. "You put it in my yard? In my *yard*?"

"I'm sorry—I suppose I should have driven into town and put it on the bus to Wichita...."

"You're a sarcastic son-of-a—"

"Whoa. Don't use your three-dollar swear words on me, lady! And don't ever ask me to do you another favor."

"That should be easy enough. With any luck at all, I won't ever see you again."

With that, she slammed the door in his face, sliding home the bolt on the inside with as much noise as she could manage. In a moment, she heard the roar of an engine and the clashing of gears as he careened off across the meadow...pasture.

As Hannah drove through the stone gateway marking the entrance to McAllisters' Acres, she began to regret she hadn't taken the time to change clothes and put on fresh makeup.

At least, she thought viciously, I combed my hair and wiped away the smudge on my nose. It wouldn't have hurt that miserable cowboy to have told me about it.

J. W. McAllister's home was beautiful—a three-storied Victorian farmhouse, painted a pale wheat color with lacy, white gingerbread trim and a fieldstone foundation. The house sprawled against a rounded hill, facing a landscaped lawn that sloped down to a reedy pond.

Hannah couldn't help but admire the fancifully curved steps as she climbed them to the covered porch running the length of the house. After ringing the doorbell, she turned and looked out across the fields. The porch was high, giving her an unobstructed view of the misted green prairies rolling on for miles in every direction. Toward the southeast, she could make out the peaked roof of her own cottage, the distance reducing it to dollhouse size.

The antique doors with panels of stained glass opened to reveal a small, gray-haired woman who smiled sweetly.

"I'd like to speak with Mrs. McAllister, please. My name is Hannah Grant."

"Of course! The granddaughter. Come in."

Rook certainly hadn't wasted time spreading word of her arrival, if even the maid knew who she was.

Hannah was ushered into an old-fashioned parlour and offered a seat on a Victorian sofa upholstered in toffee velvet. She let her appreciative gaze touch every corner of the lovely room and was admiring a bay window filled with baskets of ferns when she suddenly realized the gray-haired woman had seated herself and was waiting patiently for the perusal to end.

"Is Mrs. McAllister busy?" Hannah inquired.

"Why, my dear, I'm Mrs. McAllister," the lady said gently, as though informing her of tragic news. "Perhaps I should have introduced myself."

This is the old dragon? Hannah thought. The boss whose merest word makes Rook leap! Damn him—he has a criminal sense of humor.

"I understand you have made an offer to buy the cottage in the middle of your property," she said, somewhat abruptly.

Mrs. McAllister nodded, as unconcerned as if they were discussing the trading of recipes.

"Well, I own the cottage, and I've come out here to consider the sale. I'm going to be staying there while I do..."

"Then you'll need a key for the padlock on the gate, won't you?"

Hannah found herself clenching her teeth. Why was the woman being so nice, so reasonable? She had been prepared to fervently dislike J. W. McAllister. Of course, that was when she thought *he* was an obnoxious, pot-bellied, land-grabbing tyrant! Longtime resentment against the man to whom her grandmother had been forced to sell her land seemed rather unfounded at this moment.

"You'll need to talk to my son Winston about the key," Mrs. McAllister was saying. "He handles all the ranch business. In fact, he's the one who wants to buy your property. I can call..."

Just then they heard the faint creak of footsteps on the stairway. Looking up, Hannah caught her breath.

The man she knew as Rook entered the room and stood staring at her with what could only be described as an insolent grin.

He had obviously just come from the shower, for he was barefoot and his damp hair still glistened with drops of water. He wore nothing but a pair of overalls, one shoulder strap left unfastened to display a great deal of flesh lightly hazed with dark hair. The overalls hugged his hips and thighs, leaving Hannah amazed at the sudden indecency of her thoughts.

He walked up to Mrs. McAllister and put a casual arm about her shoulders.

The woman beamed. "Miss Grant, this is my son, Winston."

Winston! Son? Hannah felt her face contorting, but she didn't know if she was about to laugh or cry.

"We met earlier, though we were never formally introduced," Rook announced. "Winston Rookmeyer McAllister, at your service." He stepped forward to shake her hand. In a lower tone, he whispered, "How do you like my overalls?"

"How do you do." Hannah responded politely. "They might have fit when you were twelve years old," she hissed back.

His smile widened, and so did her eyes as she discovered the metal buttons on either side of the waist had been left undone. The overalls flopped open, allowing her a significant glimpse of bare hip and smooth, surprisingly tanned-looking flesh. Her cheeks flamed as she realized he could not possibly be wearing underwear. She wrenched her eyes away, but not before she heard his chuckle.

"Winston," his mother was saying, blithely unaware of her son's brazen behavior, "get the extra key for Hannah, will you?"

"Sure thing, Boss-lady."

Hannah was just refusing Mrs. McAllister's offer of iced tea when Rook returned. Explaining that she needed to get back to the cottage before dark, she seized the key and would have fled had not the woman continued talking in her vague, rambling way.

"I really don't see how you can stay in the old cottage, Miss Grant. It's in such deplorable condition. Perhaps you'd accept an invitation to spend the night here with us?"

"Oh, no," Hannah hastily replied. "That won't be necessary. I'm...I'm looking forward to being in my own place—really."

"Won't you be afraid?" Rook asked with curiosity. "No electricity...mice...who knows what else?"

Hannah raised her chin and glared at him. He realized that, if looks could kill, he'd already be pushing up sunflowers.

"Why should I be afraid? I've lived all my life in New York City. I ought to be able to survive one night on the Kansas prairie."

He simply grinned that infuriating grin.

"Well, if you change your mind, you can always come back," Mrs. McAllister said. "Winston, why don't you accompany Miss Grant to her car?"

"It's not..."

Ignoring her protest, Rook had already taken Hannah's arm and was walking her toward the door.

"I'll be over to visit when you are settled," Mrs. McAllister called after them. "I want to bring you some cuttings from my rose bushes. A cottage just can't have too many roses, can it?"

Rook held the car door for her as she slipped into the driver's seat.

Suddenly, all the resentment and dislike she had always felt for J. W. McAllister transferred itself to his son.

"Why did you let me think you were a hired hand?" she snapped, starting the engine. "I suppose you get your kicks by pretending to be a poor working man!"

He closed the door, leaning in her open window to give her a wicked smile. "No, I get my kicks by wearing bib overalls in front of prim, little girls who don't want to stare, but can't seem to help themselves."

"Oh!" she fumed. "You are despicable! Hateful! Twisted!"

He laughed heartily. "Don't forget slow-witted."

"That, too!"

She slammed the gearshift into drive, causing the car to lurch forward down the winding lane. Rook jumped back just in time to avoid treadmarks on his bare toes.

He stood watching the dark blue Mustang disappear in a cloud of dust, his face stretched into a fatuous smile. God, but she was bitchy. And he could hardly wait to see her again!

The pasture was shadowed by dusk before Hannah parked her car at the sagging front gate. Gathering up only those things she thought she would need for the night, she reentered the cottage.

From a grocery sack she took a box of matches and four thick candles, which she lighted and placed about the living room. She unrolled her sleeping bag on the couch, deciding she would sleep in the main room until the rest of the place was cleaned up. She glanced uneasily at the rocking chair, shuddering as she recalled the snake coiled there. If another one appeared during the night, she reflected, she wouldn't have to worry about housecleaning—she'd simply solve all her problems by dying.

Supper was scanty: a chunk of cheese, an apple and a can of cola. The atmosphere wasn't exactly conducive to a hearty appetite. She tried to read while she ate, but for some reason she couldn't keep her mind on the paperback romance.

Carrying the flashlight she kept in the car, she made a hurried trip to the outhouse before total darkness fell. When she returned, she bolted the cottage door and settled down for the night.

Yawning with fatigue, she crawled into the sleeping bag without undressing, placing the flashlight within reach. The candles were left burning, their feeble, flickering light staving off the terrors of the night.

For a time, Hannah stared at the ceiling, unable to go to sleep despite her exhaustion. It was so quiet! Accustomed as she was to the noises of the city traffic, it was unnerving to hear nothing at all beyond the prairie wind. She had never known absolute silence could be so . . . *loud*.

Her mind turned to the events of the day, and she experienced a hopeless feeling of confusion. There was nothing about this cottage to warrant keeping it, and yet how could she sell the complacent McAllisters something that had meant so much to her grandmother? It would be worth thwarting their scheme just because it had probably never been done before.

Suddenly, beneath the sound of the wind, she became aware of a faint noise—a distant, bloodcurdling howling.

Wolves! she thought wildly. My God, I didn't know they had wolves in Kansas.

The horrible hair-raising yowls went on so long, thankfully never getting any closer to the cottage, that she finally fell asleep despite her unease.

Her final thought of the day had nothing to do with the darkness or wolves or the terrible condition of the cottage. She was determinedly plotting her next assault on Rook McAllister's incorrigible arrogance.

Chapter Two

Hannah awoke early from habit, but for the first time in years she had no pressing reason to get out of bed. There was no subway to catch, no job waiting, no deadlines to meet. Her life was in limbo.

She was uncertain of her mood this morning. The anticipation she had felt all week was gone—one look at the cottage had banished that—but she didn't quite know what attitude remained.

She had intended to stay in Kansas long enough to put the memories of her grandmother into perspective, and yet a deserted cabin overrun with vermin certainly held no charms. But where else could she go? The simple truth was, she didn't have enough money to finance any more wild goose chases. The trip out had been more expensive than she'd estimated, and without a job she would have to be extremely conservative until she decided what to do with herself.

That seems to be the crux of the problem, she thought with a sigh. What am I going to do with me? Where do I belong?

Hannah knew that had she asked that of any of the handful of people who had ever known her well, they would have been as much at a loss for an answer as she.

She had often been called a dreamer. She drifted through life spending more time in her fantasies than in the real world. She dealt with harsh reality by ignoring it whenever possible. Some of the happiest moments of her life had been spent at her desk in a dingy office high above the streets of New York, where she worked as an editor of historical romances. When Hannah was engrossed in a well-written manuscript, the city could have crumbled around her and she would never have known. Or cared.

The unexpected closing down of her particular line of romances came as a devastating blow, stunning her as nothing had since the death of her grandmother. Oh, she still had a job with Royal Publishing, but she despised the glitz-and-glamour novels to which she had been assigned. Winter had been intolerable, for without her usual means of escape, she became aware of the crowded streets and sidewalks, the traffic, the ever-present threat of crime. With early spring came the certainty that she needed a change. Then, one afternoon shortly after she had received the call from her grandmother's lawyer, she realized she was staring out the window, but instead of the grimy, rain-slick streets below she was seeing a cottage covered with greenery.

That night she had unearthed the deed to her grandmother's property and on impulse called a typist she knew who had been looking for a place to live. A week later, having subleased her apartment and taken a leave of absence from her job, she left the city, fully intending not to return until autumn.

She had not once thought logically about what she would find at the end of her journey. Every time she tried being sensible, an image of a fairy-tale cottage intruded. Logic had never been her strong point.

Hannah struggled out of the sleeping bag and stood shivering in the damp morning air. But how could she have been prepared for this? She looked about, fearing she had neither the strength nor the ambition to undo the damage inflicted by fifteen years of neglect.

On her way to the outdoor toilet she went over her options once again, but they were few and far between. Given her current financial situation, the choices seemed to boil down to staying in Kansas for the summer or going back to New York. A temporary replacement had already been hired to do her job, and she would have to find another apartment. Wherever she went, while she was without a salary, she would have to live in the cheapest place she could find. Right now, that was undoubtedly this dusty pile of rock.

A prairie bird rose from the grass, wings beating noisily, and Hannah was startled out of her momentary funk. As she sniffed the freshness of the morning air, the frown on her face eased. The pasture behind the cottage ran on forever, broken only by misted hedgerows. She had never seen so much empty space! It was like viewing an unfinished landscape painting that quietly awaited the addition of its main subject.

And then that subject appeared. As she watched, a doe stepped forth from a thicket, pausing for a last nibble of tender leaves. On either side of her were fawns, their backs dappled with white, their oversized ears straining upward. Hannah caught her breath—she had never seen deer outside the zoo, although she remembered so well the stories her grandmother used to tell about the animals she had seen often when living on the prairie.

The doe's head went up and it seemed she looked directly at Hannah. Then, with a curious warning snort, she turned and bounded away, her tail a white flag. The fawns wasted no time in following, their tails upraised in miniature duplication.

Hannah was disappointed to see them go, but told herself she'd see them again. After all, hadn't she more or less made up her mind to stay? She would spend the summer, and that should allow her plenty of time to deal with the past and make plans for the future.

And, she decided with renewed enthusiasm, the first order of business would be to give the cottage a thorough cleaning....

* * *

Hannah began with an inventory of her new home. Starting in the kitchen, she looked through cupboards and drawers, putting aside the few useful things she found and making a pile of trash to be hauled away later. There were a broom and dustpan, both in good shape, but a sponge mop had been riddled by mice and the cans of cleaner and insect spray on the shelves were badly rusted. Silverware and utensils left in the drawers were so tarnished and stained she elected to throw them away and use what she had brought with her. She also disposed of the towels and dishcloths she found, for they had provided nests for a multitude of rodents.

Discovering a tiny stirring of domesticity, she happily began a shopping list: dish soap, scouring powder, Windex, ammonia.

She eyed the refrigerator with misgiving. Rook had said the pack rat's nest could be easily dismantled with a broom, hadn't he? Anxious to be rid of it, Hannah prodded the untidy mess once, then twice. Nothing happened, so she dislodged it with a hearty swipe. As the nest disintegrated, a shadowy gray form darted out, running between her feet. Her uninhibited scream tore through the cottage. The ratlike animal, frantic in his own fear, ran along the wall, seeking the way to freedom.

Hannah judged the distance to the front door and decided her chances of getting there unharmed were fairly good. If she could get the door open, maybe the pack rat would take advantage of the opportunity to escape. If not, she would!

Broom in hand, she dashed across the floor, dismayed to see the animal whirl and run her way. My God, was it rabid? She flung open the door and screamed a second time. Rook McAllister was standing there, hand raised to knock.

At the sight of the scurrying pack rat and the panic-stricken woman, he leaned against the door frame and laughed.

"Why, you...!" She raised the broom and swung it at him, knocking off his hat and grazing his shoulder. He laughed harder, and she swung the broom again. The pack rat, sensing he was no longer the most important quarry, scuttled through the door and away into the grass.

"Whoa, lady!" Rook cried, between guffaws. "Why are you hitting me?"

"Because you lied!" she raged. "You said a pack rat was only an overgrown mouse! Did you see that animal? He was at least a foot long!"

Dodging blows, Rook backed into the yard, still chuckling. "That's some imagination you have, New York."

"Just sweep out the nest with a broom," she mimicked, following him. "There's no need to worry. Just like there wasn't any need to worry about the wolves. The least you could have done was warn me!"

"Wolves?" He laughed again. "You probably heard coyotes."

"It doesn't matter. You could have . . . oh!"

All at once, she became aware of the four men standing just inside the gate. Face flaming, she saw them watching the scene with open amusement.

"Never saw anyone take a broom to Rook before," one of them drawled, "though I always did think it'd be good for him."

Hannah raised questioning eyes to Rook's.

"These are some of my hired hands," he informed her, still grinning. "This is Arlo, that's Dusty, and those two are Tracy and Jay. Guys, meet Hannah."

Flustered, she nevertheless spoke to each of them in turn.

"I told you she'd be glad to see us, didn't I?" Rook said.

"Yeah, that's what you said, all right," commented Dusty, "but I'm staying out here until she puts down the broom."

The others laughed easily and Hannah relaxed.

"There wasn't much to do on the farm today," Rook was explaining, "so the fellows and I came over to lend you a hand. That is, if you haven't decided to pack up and go right back home."

"No, I'm staying—at least for the summer. I ought to be able to stick it out that long."

"And then?"

"And then I'm going back to New York where I belong."

"And you'll sell this place?"

"I'm considering it."

"Good." He turned to yell over his shoulder. "Okay, boys, let's go to work."

"But..."

"Don't argue, Hannah. You'll be surprised at what we can accomplish in one day. Now," he paused for a sudden dazzling smile, "why don't you go back to what you were doing and let us get busy?"

She watched as the men began unloading a lawn mower from the ancient pickup truck. Next they lifted out a ladder and wheelbarrow.

"Rook, I want to talk to you," she said firmly. "Inside."

"All right, sure."

As they entered the cottage, someone started the mower and she could hear the men yelling back and forth to each other. She turned to face Rook. "How much is this going to cost me?" The anxiety in her voice softened the stark question.

"Having the guys help clean up the place? It won't cost you anything. I pay them a salary, and they don't care if they earn it here or over at Mom's."

"But I care."

"I know you can use the extra help."

"Why should you feel it's necessary?"

"We like to be neighborly out here."

"There's more to it than that, surely."

He shrugged. "Look, you know I want to buy this property. You just said you're only staying for the summer and then you'll probably sell. If we help get the cottage fixed up, it will give you a decent place to stay and save me having to do the work later."

"How practical," she said dryly.

"At least you have to admit it's to everyone's advantage for us to help you."

"Be that as it may, I insist on paying these men wages. As for you, I'd just as soon you didn't get involved."

"And why not?"

"My grandmother had very little use for J. W. McAllister. I don't think she would want to see me being friendly with his son and heir."

"Exactly what did your grandmother have against my dad?"

"She always maintained he took advantage of her when she was forced to sell the farm. In other words, I believe he cheated her out of a great deal of money."

"That's a lot of crap. My father was a tough businessman, it's true. But he certainly didn't have to resort to bilking widows to make money."

"Are you certain of that?"

"I am."

"Well, I'm not, so please, just keep your distance. And I will expect to pay these men a wage for whatever time they spend working for me."

"Oh, hell, have it your own way."

"Thank you."

He shifted his weight to the other foot. "Another thing, Hannah—I'm sorry about the pack rat. I guess I should have warned you he might still be around."

"You can make up for it by sweeping out the rest of the nest for me. I have a feeling there may be a wife and children."

When the yard was mowed and the weeds pulled away from the fence, it was apparent someone had once spent a good deal of time planting shrubs and flowers. A few straggling tulips came to light, as did a bed of jonquils. There were several lilac bushes, a forsythia already beginning to bud, and four bushes that Arlo assured her were flowering quince.

Two of the men checked the roof for needed repairs, while a third cleaned bird nests out of the chimney. They dumped lime in the outhouse and oiled the water pump, showing Hannah how to draw water.

Her list grew: a galvanized pail, new screen wire for the porch and windows, a hoe, rustproof paint for the gate.

Rook returned to take his men to McAllisters' for lunch, issuing an invitation to Hannah, which she promptly refused, preferring to wander about the yard eating cheese and a handful of crackers, marveling at the difference the morning's labor had made.

The hired men returned and she was relieved to see they were alone in the old pickup, with Rook McAllister nowhere to be seen. One of the men, she thought it was Arlo, came into the cabin, a cat tucked under each elbow.

"Here," he said, dumping them into her arms. "This is Tom and Jerry...well, Geraldine, actually. Rook sent them. They're barn cats and very experienced mousers. Besides, he thought they could keep you company."

"They're lovely," she exclaimed, admiring the yellow-striped tom and the calico female. Her eyes fairly glowed. "I've never had pets before. I suppose I should take mousetraps off my shopping list and add cat food instead."

Tom and Jerry seemed to nod their approval, then wriggled out of her hold for an exploratory patrol around the cottage.

In the afternoon, everyone worked inside. Load after load of trash was put into the wheelbarrow, trundled out and dumped into the bed of the pickup. They swept down walls and ceilings. They filled the buckets they'd brought with well water, sluicing down the walls and floors, sweeping the dirty water out the door, and repeating the process until the water ran clear.

Hannah found a large cardboard box in a trunk in the bedroom closet. It had been taped shut and addressed to her grandmother in New York though obviously never mailed. Inside she discovered treasure in the form of a hand-crocheted bedspread, aged to pale ivory. There were a few embroidered sheets, some curtains, and an assortment of lacy doilies, all of which had very probably belonged to her grandmother. For a few moments she was overwhelmed by memories of the plain, gentle woman who had raised her. Though the linens were yellowed and musty-smelling, thankfully, the metal trunk had protected them from the mice.

There were further additions to the growing shopping list: laundry soap, bleach, spray starch, clothespins.

The couch and mattresses were carried into the yard, where they were left to air after Tracy and Jay used the broom to rid them of dust. The broken chair was tossed onto the heap of rubbish in the pickup and the wooden rocker was put in to be taken away and repaired.

Hannah decided paint stripper was necessary for the table and chairs, as well as the shelved cupboard in the living room. She'd need ceiling paint and new fixtures for the two overhead lights.

A trapdoor in the living room opened into the attic. Stored up there was a card table and wooden folding chairs, some gardening tools and, to Hannah's delight, an old brass fire screen.

By late afternoon the worst jobs were done. Before leaving, Rook's men even helped unload the suitcases and boxes from the trunk and back seat of Hannah's car.

When they had gone, Hannah, feeling grubbier than she ever had before, rummaged through one of the boxes for a towel, washcloth and soap. Out back, she awkwardly pumped a bucket of water, telling herself it would be easier next time, and began what her grandmother would have called a sponge bath. The water was cold, but it felt so good to be rid of the grime that she didn't care. She saw a certain advantage to bathing in the open—she could be as sloppy as she wanted, and then simply toss the dirty water into the bushes. Later, when the weather warmed up, perhaps she could even bathe in the lake.

She stripped off her filthy sweatshirt and jeans and, clad in her underwear, pumped fresh water. She sat down on the raised circle of cement around the base of the pump, leaning forward to lather her feet and legs.

She could never imagine doing anything like this in New York! There would never be the privacy....

Was that the sound of an engine coming to a halt alongside her back fence?

As she scrambled for the towel, she heard a long, low whistle, followed by Rook McAllister's familiar voice.

"Well, how-dy, ma'am!"

Shielding herself as best she could with a hand towel, she glared at him.

"What are you doing here?"

"I just thought I'd drop by and see if you'd like a ride into town tomorrow. Thought it might be nice if you could get the electricity turned on."

"Yes, it would be, but I can manage on my own, thanks. I need a few other things, anyway."

"Dusty told me about your list. I figure you'll just about need a truck to haul it all back here. I'll pick you up about ten, okay?"

"Don't you ever have to work?" Aware of his appraising stare, she shifted the towel nervously.

"Once in a while. Not tomorrow, though."

"Do you realize you are staring?" she snapped.

"No, ma'am. I just thought I was grinning." He pushed his hat back and grinned even more broadly. "I didn't know you city gals were used to public bathing."

"It wouldn't be public if you would go away!"

He laughed. "Oh, all right! But, Hannah, my girl, you're in civilization now. You'll have to learn to take your baths indoors. We country folk are easily shocked."

"Get out of here!" she ordered, her exasperation giving way to the desire to smile.

"Yes, ma'am!"

He waved as the old truck rattled away, bumping across the pasture.

"And don't call me ma'am!" she muttered, cringing as she poured the bucket of water over her legs. It would be a miracle if she didn't catch pneumonia from this.

When Rook arrived the next morning, he brought her another gift—an antique copper bathtub.

"Oh, it's beautiful!" Hannah exclaimed, "but I can't accept anything so valuable."

"How valuable can it be if it's stuck away in the attic? Judging by last night, I'd say you could put it to good use."

The tub looked something like a big coal bucket, with fluted sides, a high back and ornate handles on either side.

Hannah thought wistfully of the warm baths she could have in front of the fire.

"I can see you're weakening." Rook read her mind. "Just think, you could heat a kettle or two of water on the kitchen range and presto—a hot bath! It'd sure beat freezing your extremely attractive buns off, running out to the pump."

Choosing to ignore his statement, Hannah asked, "Is it for sale?"

"Hannah, Hannah, Hannah. The way you talk about money all the time, I'm beginning to think you're a mercenary little wench. I'd rather talk about your buns."

"Rook, be serious. I'd like to have the tub, but I think I should buy it."

"Sorry, that's not possible. When I mentioned your bathing facilities to the Boss this morning, she remembered Granny's copper bathtub and insisted I bring it to you...as a gift."

"As a loan, maybe?"

"Oh, all right, we'll compromise. It's a long-term loan." He heaved a huge sigh. "Now, can we talk about your—?"

"I think we should get started to town—that is, if you're still willing. I have a lot of errands to do."

That morning Rook was driving a slate gray pickup, a much later model than the beat-up four-wheel-drive he used for work. It hummed smoothly across the pasture and through the deserted farmyard, where Rook, solemnly avowing his dedication to women's rights, allowed Hannah to unlock and open the gate. They drove down a short stretch of gravel road before turning onto the blacktopped county road.

As they crossed a bridge over the Whitewater River, Hannah asked, "Where are we going?"

"El Dorado. It's about fifteen miles from here. It has a good hardware shop and an old-time general store where I think you might be able to find some things you'll like."

"El Dorado, huh? City of gold ... ?"

He nodded. "Only, in this case, black gold. El Dorado became a boomtown when it was discovered to be in the middle of one of the largest oil fields in the country. Of course, the boom is long since over, though there is still plenty of oil."

As she had driven across the state, Hannah noticed the peaceable coexistence of oil wells, farm ground and cattle ranges, thinking it somewhat incongruous. "And I suppose you own more than your share of oil wells?"

His white teeth flashed in a broad smile. "Yep. We're doing all right in that area."

"I thought cattlemen hated oilmen, and vice versa."

"They've learned to get along better these days. Each has a healthy respect for the other."

"I see. Tell me, was there a great deal of oil on the property your family...bought from mine?"

He threw her a sharp look, but she gazed out the side window. "Hannah, I don't know what your grandmother told you about the McAllisters, but my father was no villain who cheated a helpless widow out of her property. I was only about thirteen at the time, but I seem to recall him saying he was doing her a favor by buying the land. And there was no oil...not then. All the wells on the west side of the property were drilled later. When Dad bought the place, there wasn't even much farm ground, just a lot of good pasture."

"I suppose he didn't really cheat her," Hannah admitted quietly. "You'll have to excuse me if I get a little bitter sometimes. It never seemed fair that Gran had to give up a place she loved so much. I guess it wasn't your father's fault."

"Tell me about your grandmother," Rook suggested, as they made a turn onto the state highway that led into town.

"She was a wonderful woman who never complained or felt sorry for herself. I always thought she'd had an interesting life. She was born in Missouri, but came to Kansas in a covered wagon about 1915."

"They still had covered wagons then?"

"They sure did. But you wouldn't think a city girl would have to tell a country boy something like that, would you? Anyway, Gran's father was a mule teamster at sawmills, so she spent her childhood moving from place to place. When she met Grandpa, she was ready to put down roots. They bought their farm and raised a family... and had a lot of happy years before Grandpa got sick. After he died, Gran was left with so many medical bills she was forced to sell the farm and move to New York to live with us."

"I've often wondered why she kept the cottage. It seemed an odd sort of thing to do."

"More sentimental than odd. You see, the cottage was the homestead where my great-grandfather lived until he could build a house closer to the main road. Then, when my grandparents were first married, they lived there. Later, after they moved, they'd go back to stay sometimes so the children could fish and swim in the lake. It became a refuge, a place to get away from things... especially while Grandpa was ill. He hated hospitals, so Gran hired a nurse and kept him at home. But I guess it got pretty bad toward the end, and sometimes she simply had to get out from under.... Later, even though she couldn't keep the land, she refused to part with that ten acres."

"It used to irritate the hell out of me when my father wouldn't let me and my friends use the cabin," Rook said, as they drove past the city limits and into the town. "It wasn't ours to use, he'd tell me, but all I knew was, it was smack-dab in the middle of our land! Who would ever know? Lots of times, when we'd be camping out down at the lake, we'd sneak over and spend the night there."

"How did you get in?"

"Crawled in one of the bedroom windows that had a broken lock."

"Did you ever get caught?"

"Nope. Believe me, my butt would have been kicked all over the north forty if I had've."

Hannah grew serious. "Rook, I know you said I talk too much about money, but I'd like to explain something. After paying off her debts and living thirteen years in the city, my grandmother only had about five thousand dollars left. She willed that and the deed to the cottage to her last surviving relative... me. I used what little money I had in savings to buy my car and get to Kansas. Now, without a job, Gran's five thousand is all I have to live on until I go back.

I don't think it will go very far, so that is why I sometimes seem to be too money-conscious.''

"Oh, well, it's an unusual trait in a female,'' he teased.

"I guess the condition of Gran's bank account is what makes me think she couldn't have received what the farm was worth. It just seems she would have had something more left. After all, she sold over three hundred acres.''

"Of course, medical expenses can be devastating,'' Rook said.

"I know. Still, I can't help but wonder...''

"Look, Hannah, I don't think for one minute that my father swindled your grandmother, but if it will make you feel any better, I'll be glad to check into it. If you're going to be here for the summer, I can't see any reason to let old resentments keep us from being...friends.''

"Would you? Check into it, I mean.''

"Yes, if you're willing to call a truce for the time being.''

"I suppose I am.''

"Great! I'll handle it, then.''

In town, the first stop was the rural electric cooperative where Hannah paid a deposit to have services resumed. The man they talked to obviously knew Rook, and it was due to his influence that a serviceman was sent out immediately.

"You should have electricity by the time you get home,'' Rook said.

The hardware store was next and the purchases boringly utilitarian—paints, brushes, paint remover and screen wire. But two blocks down the street Rook pulled up in front of a store with a high false front straight out of the Old West, and Hannah's attention was captured.

The General Store had everything. Rook leaned against the old-fashioned counter and watched with amusement while Hannah darted from one display to the next, as excited as a child in a candy store.

"Isn't this pretty?'' she asked, carefully setting a globed lamp on the counter with her other purchases.

"Yes, but it might be a good idea to buy some lamp oil to put into it,'' Rook informed her. "We get some pretty bad storms and you could be left without electricity for a while.''

"I really love this place," Hannah exclaimed, examining the bottle of cinnamon-scented oil he handed her. "They have everything under the sun, and I can't believe how inexpensive things are. Sorry, I didn't mean to dredge up money again...but, oh, Rook! Thank you for bringing me here."

On impulse, she put a hand on his arm and stood on tiptoe to give him an exuberant kiss on the cheek. He turned his head slightly so their lips brushed, and she tried to back away, startled. His hands came up to clasp her shoulders, and for an instant, he held her closer to him.

"Please don't," she said in a whisper. Then, brightly, "I apologize for getting so carried away."

At the warning note in her voice, he followed her gaze and saw the shopkeeper, elbows on the counter, watching them with interest. With a rueful grimace, Rook let his hands drop and Hannah moved away, her face rosy as she knelt to sort through a stack of ladies' magazines, some of which were more than 70 years old.

Hannah pretended to be engrossed in her shopping, but she couldn't help worrying about what Rook thought of her impromptu embrace. She heard the clerk make a low, unintelligible comment to which Rook replied with a chuckle.

Later, after the wicker chair and oak chest on which she'd splurged had been loaded onto the truck, buttressed by boxes filled with the various treasures she'd found, Rook announced he was taking her to his favorite place for lunch.

"I hope you like veals with chili," he said, pulling into Fred's Drive-in.

"I don't know—I've never had one."

"My, but you city children are underprivileged," Rook observed, ordering veals, onion rings and Pepsis, as if he'd done it a hundred times.

While they waited for their food, Hannah gave in to her curiosity. "What did the man at the general store say to you?"

"He said, and I quote, 'B'God, Rook, that was the shortest kiss on record...you must be losing your touch!'"

His touch? That sounded as if the young Mr. McAllister had a reputation with the ladies. For the first time, Hannah wondered about his personal life.

She supposed it would be reasonable to assume he had been involved with more than a few females in his time. Why not? He was obviously well-to-do, intelligent and personable. And she admitted as she watched him pay the carhop, he was undeniably good-looking, even if it wasn't in the subtly sophisticated way she herself preferred. Most women would find Rook McAllister irresistible.

She analyzed that idea as she studied him. All right, it probably had something to do with him being so careless and offhand about his appeal. Certainly he knew he was not Quasimodo, but on the other hand, he did not give the impression he considered himself Rhett Butler—or whoever was in vogue these days—either. His clothing was low-key, to say the least. Today he wore a plaid cotton shirt, sleeves rolled up, and the usual western jeans.

As she was taking inventory, he shifted his hips, raising them off the seat to return his billfold to the back pocket. No one else she knew wore their jeans so tight, but . . . well, there was a certain fascination about the custom, she decided.

Rook's smile, as he handed her a tissue-wrapped sandwich, was innocent, but the look in his eyes was not. It was definitely wicked, as if he could read her mind.

Unwrapping the veal, she took a bite and chewed thoughtfully. That disturbing contradiction must be the key to Rook's charisma. He was wholesomely sexual. Yes, that was it. She took another bite, casting a surreptitious glance in his direction. His innocent smile gave him the charm of a little boy, and the thick black hair tumbling across his forehead induced some sort of motherly feeling. Even now, Hannah's fingers itched with the need to smooth back the stray locks. On the other hand, the lean set of his jaw and the boldness of his gaze were blatantly and sensually challenging. Suddenly she noticed he was staring directly into her eyes.

"Do you like it?" he asked.

She swallowed with difficulty. "What?"

"The veal ... do you like it?"

"Oh! I ... uh, yes, it's delicious." She took another bite and discovered that it truly was.

Rook didn't quite understand his reaction to Hannah. Whenever he was around her, he felt as if he were smiling inside—as if his entire body were lighted inwardly by a huge, face-splitting grin. He couldn't figure it out. What was there about her?

He watched her over the rim of a Styrofoam cup. She was wearing another pair of those awful jeans, but the lightweight apricot sweater was rather nice. It proved things to him her baggy sweatshirt hadn't. With a slight smile, he reminded himself that the secret to a lady's charm had nothing to do with her sweater size, and let his eyes drift upward, past the ecru lace of the crocheted collar, along the delicate hollows of her neck to the obstinately pointed chin and sweet, wide mouth. He remembered their brief encounter in the general store with a surge of pleasure, and sensed the time was growing ripe for a second, more satisfying kiss. Oh, not now—maybe not even later tonight, but soon. Very soon, he vowed, watching those pale rose lips close about the straw in her Pepsi. His slow survey moved to her eyes, and he was jolted anew. God, she has terrific eyes, he mused. All that silver green, shadowed by those incredible lashes....

"Do I have chili on my face?" she asked bluntly.

He couldn't help but laugh, again experiencing that inner warming. His response had to stem from the contrast between her angelic looks and satanic wit. Well, there might be hell to pay, but he was convinced he wanted to get to know Hannah Grant much more intimately.

Hannah was tired but happy. The cottage was a mess, but it was a clean mess, and it would just have to wait until tomorrow for her attention. Boxes and sacks were piled all about the living room, on and around the new chest and wicker chair, overflowing onto the floor. She was sitting on the couch drinking a cup of hot tea and reveling in the luxury of having electricity. Not until the newly installed bulbs provided light that probed into every corner did Hannah allow herself to reflect on how nervous the shadows had made her. Too many creatures had, at one time or another, inhabited her living quarters for her to fully relax until now, when she was once again secure in civilized comfort.

That afternoon, before Rook brought her home, they had stopped at a supermarket for groceries. It was an up-to-date store with a bakery, a delicatessen and, to Hannah's delight, a flower shop. She made a final splurge there, buying baskets of ivy, potted flowers and plants and a graceful ficus tree in a brass tub. Having lived among concrete and steel all her life she craved the sight of growing things, and it was worth enduring Rook's good-natured teasing about her sudden tumble from financial conservatism.

"This truck looks like a hearse," he grumbled, trying to keep his mouth from twitching as he peered around the ficus tree on the seat between them. "I wouldn't be surprised if we don't pick up a funeral procession before we get out of town."

Hannah made a face at him. "It won't look like so many plants when I get them scattered around the cottage."

But, for tonight, the greenery was lined up on the mantel and along the windowsills, until proper places could be found. They filled the air with earthy freshness, overpowering the faint mustiness that remained.

Hannah was well pleased. She almost felt she could purr as loudly as the two cats lounging along the back of the sofa. For the first time, she was beginning to think she could turn this place into a home. A home where she could live and be content for the next few months.

A fire blazed in the fireplace, while outside the silent snow fell, shutting the cottage away in cozy seclusion. A Queen Anne table had been placed in front of the window, and on its shining surface was Hannah's electric typewriter and a stack of blank paper. Hannah herself was seated at the table, chin in hand, thinking. For some years she had been toying with the idea of writing a book of her own, and now seemed an auspicious time to start. Maybe she could turn out a best-selling novel that would make her fortune. Where should it be set? Scotland? The moors of England... ?

Hannah fell asleep, sitting upright on the ugly brown couch.

Chapter Three

Despite spending the night on the couch, Hannah was refreshed when morning came, waking with renewed energy. Dressed in old jeans, a bandanna covering her hair, she started work in the kitchen, washing down the appliances and cupboards with ammonia water. She had scrubbed out the refrigerator the day before when putting away the groceries, and though she had to admit it was something of an eyesore, it worked like a charm. Seeing the well-stocked freezer gave her a feeling of having settled in, and she smiled contentedly as she shut the freezer door.

Using the stepladder Rook had loaned her, Hannah began painting the walls and ceiling cream colored, a job that did not take long since the room was so small. She spent the rest of the day painting the wooden cupboards slate blue inside and out, and was pleased with the effect of the blue-gray color against the ivory.

The next morning she lined the shelves with paper, then unloaded the sacks of boxed and canned goods from the supermarket. Unwilling to leave her grandmother's china behind, she had brought it with her, and now it went onto

the top shelf. For every day, she had bought a partial set of
secondhand ironstone at the general store. The pots and
pans and electric skillet from her old apartment went into
the bottom cupboards, along with a small supply of bake-
ware.

The few towels and dishcloths she had purchased were
placed in a paper-lined drawer, and into the other drawers
went her grandmother's silverware and a handful of cooking utensils. Her small collection of cookbooks found a
home on the countertop, between two quart-sized crocks
with wooden lids, containing flour and sugar.

Hannah had found inexpensive print curtains she liked,
buying all the general store had to offer, as well as a matching slipcover for the couch. The majority of the curtains
would go in the living room, but she hung a ruffled tieback
at the kitchen window. The fabric had a slate-blue background, liberally sprinkled with tiny dusty-pink roses and
cream-colored daisies.

She lined the windowsill with green plants and put down
a woven rug of blue and rose that nearly covered the entire
floor, then stepped back to survey her handiwork.

Not bad, she decided. Not bad, at all.

As she took up a teakettle and started to the well for water, she recalled the incident with the pack rat and had to
smile. She wondered if Rook would be surprised at what she
had already accomplished.

She set the copper bathtub in the living room and after
filling it with a kettle of boiling water and two buckets of
cold, luxuriated in the closest thing to a real bath she'd had
since her last motel shower on the way to Kansas.

She spent the next day stripping the shelved cupboard and
the table and chairs, finding pretty pine surfaces beneath the
layers of grimy paint and varnish.

In the evening, she strolled down to the lake and sat on
the swing, soothed by its rusty squeak as she watched dusk
settle over the countryside. It was so quiet and peaceful, the
only sounds those of water lapping gently against the shore
and a faint wind rustling the new leaves on the trees.

At this moment, she was bone tired, but it was a satisfying sort of tiredness and she felt no regret at having left the city. Indeed, the only regret she had at all was that her grandmother could not be there to share the excitement of refurbishing the cottage.

Hannah had just finished scrubbing down the stones of the fireplace when she heard an approaching vehicle and looked out to see Rook and two of his hired men.

When she opened the door, Rook stood with hands on his hips, grinning down at her.

"We've got a free day. Put us to work," he said.

Hannah regarded him with a bemused frown. "Where are the other four?"

He looked puzzled. "Other four?"

"I thought there were *seven* dwarfs."

He threw back his head and gave a shout of laughter. "You witch," he drawled, "can it be I've missed your sassy tongue?"

Aware the others were watching with interest, she merely grimaced and did not admit she might have missed him, too. But neither did she send him away, saying nothing as he rolled up his sleeves and set to work.

The morning passed rapidly. Arlo and Dusty spent their time replacing the rusted screens while Rook painted the outside window frames and eaves. Inside, through the open windows, Hannah could hear the men teasing each other and she had to smile as she realized Rook took his share of good-natured jibes, boss or not.

She herself was using a long-handled roller to paint the living room ceiling. Trying to delay climbing down to move her stepladder, she leaned slightly forward, raising her arms to extend the roller as far as possible. Rook, coming through the front door, saw her precarious position and crossed the room in four long strides. He had intended to chastise her for being so careless, but as her arms strained outward, the thin cotton shirt she wore rose with the motion and he stood transfixed by the sight of smooth flesh right at his eye level. Without thinking further, he hooked his fingers into the belt loops of her jeans at either side of her waist and pulled her toward him, resting his cheek against her cool skin for an instant before turning his head and placing an audacious kiss on her bare stomach.

Hannah uttered a small scream and dropped the roller, which landed on the floor with a dull, paint-splattering *glop*. Her hands clutched at Rook's shoulders and he released the belt loops to slide his fingers upward to her rib cage, lifting her from the ladder to hold her against his chest.

"What . . . what are you doing?" she gasped, still recalling the warmth of his unexpected kiss.

"What's the matter?" he taunted, letting her slide downward along his body until she stood within the circle of his arms. "Hasn't anyone ever told you what a sexy navel you have?"

"You are crazy!" she snapped, hoping to conceal the confusion his actions inspired within her. "No sane person would sneak up on someone else like that!"

His ebony eyes sparkled. "Maybe not in New York...but, lady, you're in Kansas now."

"Which goes to prove that not all weirdos live in the city," she retorted, all too aware of his hands splayed against her back, beneath the cotton shirt. As she gazed up at him, it suddenly seemed his mouth with its absurdly attractive smile was coming closer and closer to her own. Her throat went dry and she swallowed painfully. "Now what are you doing?"

"Oh, let *me* guess!" came a droll feminine voice from across the room. "She has something in her eye and Doctor Rook is going to remove it. Isn't that what you think, Bev?"

"Either that or she fell off the ladder and he is about to attempt mouth-to-mouth resuscitation," came the reply.

"Of course, Rook does tend to apply mouth-to-mouth rather indiscriminately. Maybe she didn't fall off the ladder, at all!"

Rook groaned, releasing Hannah, he turned to face the two women who stood just inside the doorway. "All right, you've effectively managed to spoil the moment—you might as well come on in."

The curly haired blonde flashed a wide smile. "A gracious invitation, if I've ever heard one...."

"And to think...we even brought lunch," pointed out her companion, a woman with short, Indian-dark hair that matched her laughing eyes. She was carrying a large cardboard bucket, whose bright red stripes indicated it was filled with a well-known brand of chicken. "Extra crispy..."

"With all the trimmings." The blonde began setting the paper bags she held on the table.

"Well, I don't know who you are, but I'm glad to meet you," Hannah declared. "That chicken smells great!"

"So! Just when I thought I had your undivided attention, I find myself upstaged by a drumstick," scolded Rook indignantly.

The blonde stuck out a friendly hand. "Hi, I'm Janice," she said. "Dusty's wife. And this is Bev—she's married to Arlo."

"It's nice to know you," Hannah responded. "I'm Han—"

"Oh, we know who you are," Bev assured her. "In fact, we've heard all about you."

"Oh?"

"Yes, Arlo was so impressed by the way you chased Rook with a broom that he hasn't stopped talking about you!"

"I'm not usually so aggressive," Hannah said gravely, "but that was a very unusual situation."

"I'd love to hear about it over lunch," Janice told her. "Why don't you call the guys, Rook, while we set things out?"

Muttering something about bossy women, Rook gave Hannah a furtive wink and left the room. She understood the significance of the gesture perfectly—he intended to take up that little matter of the unfinished kiss at the first opportunity.

The six of them sat at the wooden table and ate enormous amounts of chicken, baked beans, potato salad and hot biscuits. Hannah was amazed to find herself included in the lighthearted banter as if the others had known her for years. Even more surprising, she was responding with a casual friendliness she had never been able to achieve in the city. There, she, like other people, seemed to have existed within protective barriers—here, she had not had time to erect those barriers before being immersed in the easy cordiality of the Midwest.

After lunch, the men went back to their work outdoors, and Hannah gave Bev and Janice a quick tour of the interior of the cottage.

"What plans do you have for in here?" Janice asked, when they entered the bedroom.

"Nothing too definite. I thought I'd paint the walls off-white." Hannah opened the trunk and drew out the crocheted bedspread to show them. "And I thought I might use this on the bed."

"Oh, it's beautiful," Bev breathed, examining the delicate openwork. "But you'll need something to go beneath it . . . you know, to show through."

"I have an idea," Janice spoke up. "I've got a set of king-size sheets that would work perfectly. They're sage green. And I have a spare dust ruffle in a pale blue-and-green floral print."

"I couldn't use your things," Hannah protested, somewhat embarrassed. "I mean, surely you need them yourself."

"Actually not. You see, they were wedding gifts last year, but since Dusty and I have a waterbed, nothing fits. The sheets are simply lying in the linen closet, honestly. At least take a look at them. . . ."

Eyes shining, Bev was making an intense study of the room. "I have another idea. Hannah, would you let the two of us decorate this room? We could be responsible for the painting and everything."

"I think it'd be fun," agreed Janice. "It'll be our official welcome-to-the-neighborhood gesture."

Hannah was helpless in the face of their growing excitement. Finally, she gave in.

"If we have to buy anything, we'll present you with the bill," Janice assured her, "but I think we'll be able to scrounge up everything we need without resorting to money."

"Hannah, you go back to your painting. Janice and I have things to do. First we need to measure your bed and the window, and get that bedspread soaking in bleach."

"Then we'll get started painting...."

Their voices trailed away as Hannah returned to the living room to clear away the debris from lunch.

Three days later, Rook drove Bev and Janice back to the cottage, where they shooed Hannah out of their way.

"Come on," Rook told her, "I'll take you shopping while these two put the bedroom together."

"What are we going shopping for?" she asked, as Rook turned onto the highway to El Dorado.

"Books. There's a used-book shop where I like to go."

"You read?" She eyed him with new interest.

"Your surprise is hardly flattering." He grinned. "Of course I read. A guy has to have some hobby to fall back on when he gets tired of carousing and womanizing."

"Hmm, I suppose so. What kind of books do you read?"

"You name it. I like history and westerns...even a good thriller, now and again. I must confess, however, I've never read any romances." He pulled into a parking space in front of the Bookworm. "But that is something I am about to rectify."

Hannah paused with her hand on the door handle. "You're going to start reading romances?"

"I want to read some of the books you've edited. Do you have a problem with that?"

She laughed. "Not at all. In fact, I can't wait to see this!"

The next hour sped by, leaving Hannah wondering when she had last had so much fun. Rook was astonishingly knowledgeable about books, and his opinions were both irreverent and entertaining. She pointed out various novels on which she had worked and, impressed, he bought them all. Hannah purchased a few hardbacks for the newly varnished shelves in the cottage living room, and a book of Kansas photographs for the coffee table.

After loading the sacks of books into his truck, Rook drove down the street to a western-wear shop. Hannah raised her eyebrows in question.

"Now, don't give me that snooty look," he warned, his mouth twisting up into a one-sided smile. "We're going to buy you a pair of real western jeans. I'm tired of looking at those things you wear all the time."

Hannah's chin shot up. "What's wrong with them?"

"They're too damned baggy. When I look at a woman in jeans, I want to know things are where they should be."

"Your opinion of women in jeans doesn't concern me in the least."

"Besides, I thought you might like to go horseback riding—you'll need a proper pair of jeans for that."

Without waiting for her reply, he hooked a casual arm about her waist and all but dragged her into the store, informing the salesgirl they wanted to look at Wranglers.

Asking Hannah's size, the girl sorted through a stack of denims, handing her a pair. "Here, why don't you step into the dressing room and try these on?"

Her green eyes casting daggers at Rook, Hannah disappeared into the cubicle and slammed the door. A few moments later, she reopened it and stuck her head around the edge.

"Sorry to disappoint you, but these are too small."

"Come on out and let me see," Rook demanded, crossing his arms over his chest and leaning against a display counter.

"Perhaps if you looked at them in the full-length mirror," suggested the salesgirl helpfully.

With an impatient sniff, Hannah stepped in front of the mirror. Her eyes widened in horror. "Oh, my lord!"

"What's wrong?" asked Rook. "They're a perfect fit."

"Perfect?" Hannah cried in a low voice. "They are indecently tight."

"Matter of opinion. What do you think, Miss?"

The salesgirl, flattered by Rook's attention, assured Hannah, "That is exactly how they're supposed to fit. Most of my customers would be thrilled if theirs looked half as good."

"But..." Hannah turned, managing an over-the-shoulder view of herself. "I don't think I can even walk in them."

Rook chuckled. "It's an acquired art—you'll catch on."

She met his gaze in the mirror and was suddenly breathless. Beneath the tilted-back cowboy hat he wore, his eyes fairly smoldered. When he unfolded his lean frame and came toward her, she feared he might have chosen this rather public place to resume the romantic interlude Bev and Janice had interrupted days before. Not knowing how to react, she simply stood her ground and prayed he would do nothing rash.

He towered over her for an instant, then placed a hand on her shoulder. She gulped audibly and closed her eyes. But instead of the touch of his mouth she expected, she felt his other hand boldly caress her bottom.

"Nice rivets," he commented, laughter in his voice. Her eyes flew open to stare at him. "You know... rivets. Those metal things on the back pocket. The workmanship is excellent."

Hannah let her mind fill with the choicest swear words this side of Brooklyn, but didn't dare speak them aloud. Later, she promised herself... when they were alone...

"We'll take the jeans," Rook was telling the clerk. "And she'd better have a pair of boots, too."

"Boots?" she cried, stunned. "Rook, you don't understand. I can't afford to spend a lot of money on boots!"

"I'll buy them for you."

"Not a chance," she muttered. "I refuse to be under that sort of obligation to you. I don't need boots, and that's that."

"What about all those prairie rattlers?" he asked dryly. "Boots could prevent a snakebite. Want me to tell you what happens when a snake bites you on the foot?"

"Oh, for heaven's sake! I'll take the damned boots—but I'm paying for them!"

He grinned. "Why not let me? After all, we rich cattle barons have to spend our petty cash some way."

"Save it for the medical bills you'll have if you don't learn to keep your hands to yourself!"

His grin widened.

* * *

As they drove back to the cottage along the narrow prairie track, the changes that had taken place were very obvious to Hannah.

The little stone cabin no longer looked derelict, but sat proudly in its small yard, shaded by newly trimmed trees and shrubs, enclosed by a fence shining with aluminum paint. A few bright spring flowers blew in the balmy wind, and along the screened porch, six recently planted rosebushes were showing tentative buds.

The forest-green eaves and window frames gleamed against the gray stone, and the green door sported a brass lion's-head door knocker rescued from a box of junk found in the attic.

Inside, the living room was as yet unfinished, but its ceiling was now spanking white, its floor slate-blue and its windows shiny clean, all awaiting the final touches Hannah had planned. The wooden surfaces on the screened porch had been painted white, and the addition of potted and hanging plants gave it the summery look of a greenhouse.

"Hi! We're all finished in here," Janice said, walking out of the bedroom, followed by Bev.

"Can I see it now?" Hannah asked eagerly.

"Sure."

The bedroom was beautifully old-fashioned and romantic. Like the kitchen, three of the walls had been Sheetrocked, with the fourth left in original stone. The smooth walls were cream white, as was the ceiling; the floor was covered with a thick green carpet. Both windows had long, ruffled curtains of sage-green fabric with crocheted curtain panels covering the bottom half of the glass. Against one wall was the old-fashioned oak commode that had been left on the porch. It had been refinished and now held a pitcher and bowl, with soft towels and a crystal dish of scented soap arranged close by. Behind it, an oval mirror in an oak frame hung on the wall.

In the opposite corner next to the closet door was the copper bathtub Rook had loaned her, fresh towels folded over the side.

But the focal point of the entire room was the bed. Hannah could hardly believe it had ever been merely an ordinary mattress wrapped in plastic. The two energetic decorators had transformed it into a romantic canopy bed by attaching a carved wood curtain rod to the ceiling, and from this suspending a long curtain of pale blue-and-green floral print. Edged with crocheted lace, the drape fell gracefully to the floor, pulled back at each of the front corners of the bed, which was itself covered with the crocheted bedspread whose openwork revealed more of the silvery green fabric used for the curtains. It was heaped with inviting pillows and skirted by a print dust ruffle.

Hannah was absolutely enchanted with the room, especially the bed which seemed to be highlighted by the late-afternoon sunlight filtering in through the windows. It struck her that it had been transformed into a place for lovers... a place for whispers and shared confidences, for soft laughter that lingered into the wee morning hours.

The single candle flickered and glowed, casting a golden net of light over the rumpled bed and the man who reclined there. The strong planes of his naked chest gleamed in the pale light, as did the mysteriously shadowed eyes drawing her from across the room. She let her gaze travel lovingly along the breadth of his shoulders and down the finely sculpted torso to the sheet lying so casually over his lap. On the table next to the bed was a forgotten book and his pipe, cooling in a flat glass dish. As she watched, his beautiful mouth curved into a smile and he held out one lean hand, beckoning her back into his arms.

"What's the matter, Hannah? Don't you like it?" Janice's expression was more than a bit perplexed.

"What? Oh! No... I love it! Really, I do. I was just lost in thought, I guess."

Hannah realized all three of them were staring at her as if she had suddenly become an alien being. She laughed nervously and tried to dispel their curiosity.

"It's the loveliest room I've ever seen—how can I thank you enough? You've gone to so much trouble...."

But, later, as the three of them were leaving, Bev stepped back into the cottage a moment to pose one last question.

"Confess, Hannah—you were thinking of a man back there in the bedroom, weren't you?"

"A . . . a man?"

"You should have seen the look on your face! It was so intimate that I, for one, felt like an intruder. Not that that bothers me, of course. Who is he?"

Knowing denial would serve no purpose, Hannah shrugged. "Just someone called Matthew," she finally answered. "No one important."

"Oh, sure!" Bev laughed. "Only important enough to make your eyes glow like stars and your knees turn to butter. Barely important at all."

When they had gone, Hannah leaned against the door and heaved a huge sigh. The man in her fantasy actually was important to her—important enough that she had long ago given him a name. Important enough that she knew every detail there was to know about him, despite the fact he was only a figment of her romantic imagination. He was the quintessential hero, his character distilled from all the lesser heroes in the hundreds of romance novels she had read. He was, to her, the perfect man.

Rook had badgered her unmercifully until she agreed to take an afternoon away from work at the cottage to go horseback riding. Nearly everything had been done by now, he reasoned, and it would do her good to get some fresh air and sunshine.

Glancing about at the hazy colors of the prairie, Hannah had to agree with him. She had thrown herself so wholeheartedly into renovating the cottage she had taken precious little time to enjoy the subtle beauty of the countryside. Rook warned her there was only about a month of idyllic weather left before the heat of summer began, and that argument won her over.

She felt very self-conscious as she went down the flagstone path to her gate, where Rook waited on horseback. "I know what you're thinking," she muttered. "I look a lot like Hoot Gibson."

Rook studied her from his vantage point on the back of a massive chestnut gelding, his black eyes taking their time with the inventory.

From the gleaming tips of her new boots to the brim of the western hat his mother had loaned her, there was, as far as Rook could tell, no resemblance whatsoever to Hoot Gibson. No, he was sure that illustrious citizen of the Old West had never filled out his jeans in quite the same way Hannah did. He admired the hug of blue denim over the curve of hip and leg a moment longer before his gaze traveled upward to the flowered shirt she wore. As manly as Hoot's chest had been, it definitely suffered in comparison to Hannah's, he decided, intrigued by the faint jiggle he could detect beneath the thin cotton.

"Naw... I think Hoot might have been a little taller," he said dryly.

She peered up at him, her face shadowed by the hat. "I thought we were going horseback riding. Where's my horse?"

"Over in the north pasture. Dusty's using it to move some cattle, but he should be done by now. We'll ride over and get it."

"Don't tell me a rich cattle rancher like yourself only owns two horses?"

"As a matter of fact, I own about a dozen. It's just that Dusty's old mare is the most docile of the lot, and let's face it, New York, riding around on the open prairie is different than riding Shetland ponies in Central Park."

"Who rode ponies?" she snapped. "The horses I've ridden were all full-grown."

"And older than Methuselah, I'll bet."

"I'm sure I wouldn't know about that. But you needn't worry, I do know a little something about riding a horse."

"Good. Well, come on up and we'll ride over and find Old Nellie."

"I'm supposed to get up there? With you?"

"Would you rather walk? Remember the rattlesnakes."

"Ah, but I'm wearing boots, so I should be adequately protected."

"Okay, then. It won't be more than a mile or so."

Hannah frowned. "Oh, all right, I'll ride. But, I know you for the lecher you are, so promise me one thing—no funny business."

"A promise easily made," he declared, grasping her arm and hauling her up onto the saddle in front of him. "I always take lechery very seriously." His mouth brushed her ear, his words echoing with sensual threat.

His arm slid around her waist and she immediately stiffened her back. "What are you doing?" she hissed.

"You don't want to fall off, do you?"

"No..."

"Then relax and sit still." His arm tightened again, and this time she made no further protest.

As they cantered across the open prairie, Hannah tried to ignore the feel of her body in such close contact with his, but found she was able to concentrate on little else. The warm breezes and the softly scented wildflowers dotting the endless grassland might as well have been nonexistent.

It was not long before, with a sense of relief, she saw several men on horseback surrounded by milling cattle. As they drew nearer, Dusty waved.

Rook reined in beside the hired man and, releasing Hannah, gripped the saddle horn with his hand. "How'd it go?"

"No problem. We got all the cows and calves moved into the east pasture—except for that black white-face. She still hasn't had her calf yet, but it should come any time now. Thought we'd better leave her where we could keep an eye on her, in case there's trouble."

"Good idea. We may have to get the vet out to look at her."

"Yeah. Well, I guess you came for Old Nellie here," Dusty said, "so I'll hand her over and let you get on with your riding."

"Won't you need her anymore?" asked Hannah.

"No, we're about done. I'd just as soon rassle that old pickup around, anyway."

One of the animals being herded raised its head and bellowed angrily. Startled, Hannah looked up. "What about these cows?" she asked. "Do they have babies?"

Rook and Dusty exchanged an amused look. "These are steers, Hannah," Rook explained.

"What's the difference?"

"What? A big-city editor like you doesn't know the difference between a cow and a steer?"

Hannah's chin rose defensively. "We don't have many cattle in New York, you know."

"A steer is a has-been bull," Dusty spoke up, as he dismounted. "If you know what I mean."

"I'm not sure..."

Rook chuckled. "Out here we say a steer is a bull who still has the inclination but not the equipment. Now do you understand?"

Hannah could feel a fiery blush creeping over her face. "That was crudely put, but yes, I think I understand. These poor animals are in a state that would benefit a great many human males I could name."

With a toss of her head, she threw her right leg over the horse's neck, intending to slide quickly to the ground before Rook could help. Instead, as she flung her leg around, she succeeded only in trapping his hand, still grasping the saddle horn, between her thighs. Even Dusty could hear her shocked gasp. Rook leaned forward for a closer look at her now-flaming face, unable to control the laugh that burst from his throat.

"Let me go!" she ground out through clenched teeth.

"Honey, you're the one who's got hold of me." He bent a significant look at his hairy forearm wedged tightly between her two jean-clad legs. "Not that I mind, you understand."

Hannah was furious, not only with Rook but with herself. She bent her knee, fairly slapping his hand away, then slid to the ground, where she would have stumbled had it not been for Dusty's hasty intervention. His smile was less noticeable than Rook's, and she was grateful for his polite self-control. She could imagine the story that would make the rounds of the old bunkhouse tonight—hell, she didn't even know if they had such a thing as a bunkhouse, but she knew the story would make the rounds, nonetheless.

Again with Dusty's assistance, she managed to struggle into the saddle, and with a nudge of her knees started the implacable mare ambling away. Not sparing Rook a backward glance, she told Dusty goodbye and fixed her eyes on a distant hedgerow.

With an admiring grin, Rook followed.

For the first few moments, phrases like "arrogant, chauvinistic lothario" raged through her head, but after a while, she began to calm down and became aware of her surroundings.

It was a beautiful day, in spite of everything. If only she could share it with someone worthwhile . . . someone like Matthew. A man who would treat her with deference, as a lady deserved to be treated. A man who would cherish and protect her . . .

Hannah always felt so regal, like an ancient queen, when she was riding through the peaceful countryside like this. Dressed in a flowing velvet riding habit that matched her eyes exactly, she sat sidesaddle on her favorite mount, a sleek bay stallion. Behind her, his proud, possessive gaze warming her, was Matthew, resplendent in tan riding breeches and a dark brown jacket that emphasized the muscularity of his shoulders and arms.

Suddenly, a long-legged hare darted from the underbrush, frightening the stallion and sending him into a wild and furious gallop. Hannah heard the terror in her own voice as she called out to the man she loved.

"Matthew! Save me!"

Hoofbeats thundered, echoing the loud thudding of her heart. Sky and earth became a confused blur rushing rapidly past. Ahead loomed a high stone wall—could the horse clear it? Would she be killed?

Then the hoofbeats grew louder, obscuring every other sound. Unexpectedly, a steely arm slid about her waist and she was being swept from the saddle and cradled against a broad chest heaving in fearful agitation.

"Hannah, my darling! I feared for your life." Sunlight glinted off the deep chestnut hair as he bowed his head in humility.

Nestled in his strong embrace, Hannah gazed into his adoring eyes and trembled. "Oh, Matthew," she breathed, raising her face for his worshipping kiss.

Hannah was abruptly roused from her fantasy by Rook's voice. "You'd better watch where you let that horse walk," he warned. "If you just give her her head like that, she might wander into a—"

At that moment, Old Nellie plodded straight through a thick clump of grass, sending a covey of quails into instantaneous flight, their wings whirring noisily.

"—nest of birds," Rook finished.

The mare gave a dramatic snort, shook her head and lunged forward, pulling the reins out of Hannah's hands. As the animal galloped headlong across the pasture, Hannah clutched its mane and surrendered to panic.

"Help! Rook...damn it! Help me!"

"Grab the reins," Rook yelled, curbing his own horse. "Get control of her." He was nearly standing in the stirrups in his anxiety.

Hannah moaned in utter terror. If she looked down, all she could see was the ground racing by—if she looked up, the sky was a whirling blur. Her heartbeats boomed like thunder, blotting out the sound of the horse's hoofs pounding the earth. With each jouncing step the mare took, Hannah's body was flung upward, slamming back into the saddle with a painful thud. Every time she bounced, the air was squeezed from her lungs in an embarrassing *whoof*.

"Roo...*whoof*...ook!"

Then she saw the fence looming ahead!

A deadly looking affair consisting of three tight strands of barbed wire, it was directly in Nellie's path. Hannah had a momentary vision of the mare trying to clear the fence, and knew the two of them would end up entangled with the sharp metal barbs. She waited in vain for a strong, masculine arm to rescue her from the runaway horse—she prayed for the sound of her name on her savior's lips. Nothing happened.

Nellie continued her headlong flight and the fence rearing up before them might as well have been nine feet high. Hannah closed her eyes.

Seconds before Nellie's heaving chest struck the barbed wire, she veered to one side, coming to a complete and absolute halt. The motion was so unexpected that Hannah's body did not stop, but slid sideways out of the saddle and plummeted to the ground in a graceless heap.

"Hannah, are you hurt?"

More stunned than injured, Hannah looked up to see Rook spur his horse and ride toward her. A cold, unrelenting fury seized her as she realized he hadn't even been in pursuit of the runaway. Stiffly, she got to her feet and brushed off the seat of her jeans.

"Are you all right?" he asked again, his face tight with worry.

"I may survive... no thanks to you!"

His face broke into a wide grin. "Yeah, I guess you're okay."

"Why didn't you come after me?" she demanded, hands on hips. "You didn't even make an effort to stop that horse."

"I couldn't have stopped her," Rook stated firmly. "If I'd have ridden after you, it would only have spooked her more. She might have gone straight through that fence."

"I hope you don't expect me to believe that!"

"Believe it or not, it's the truth. I suppose you thought I should have been right there to save you... like in some damned romance novel."

She glared at him, nose high in the air.

With his fist, he pushed his cowboy hat to the back of his head. "My God, you did! I can't believe it."

"I thought you would be gentleman enough to try and rescue me. I should have known you'd prefer to sit back and enjoy the show. Well, I'm sorry to disappoint you. I should have broken a leg, at least!"

"Don't be an ass!"

"Don't call me names, you... you mangy prairie dog!"

Rook wanted to laugh, but it was definitely against his better judgment.

"Hannah, calm down..."

"Don't you dare tell me to calm down," she snapped. "In fact, don't even bother to speak to me again. I'm tired of your stupid jokes."

"This was no joke. I couldn't know Nellie would bolt like that. I tried to tell you to watch where you were riding, but your mind was a million miles away. It was your own fault, sweetheart."

"My fault?" she fairly shrieked. "You told me you had picked the most docile horse you had, and now you're trying to make it my fault that she turned out to be wild and uncontrollable?"

"You never tried to control her. But if you'll get back on, I'll give you a few riding lessons."

"You're a lunatic if you think I'd ever get back on that old nag."

Hannah bent to retrieve her hat, clapping it on her head. She then turned her back and started walking away.

"Where are you going?" Rook demanded.

"Home."

"What about Nellie? You can't just leave her here."

"That's what you think."

"Hannah." A warning note sounded in his voice, but she squared her shoulders and resolutely kept walking. "Hannah Grant, you come back here."

"Fat chance."

"You get back on that horse right now."

"When hell freezes over." She kept walking.

"Very funny. Are you going to ride Nellie back or not?"

"Not."

"Damn, but I'd like to smack your butt...."

"Try it and die," she taunted, pausing to regale him with a Bronx cheer.

Jaws clenched, Rook rode over to the mare, now peacefully grazing, and taking her reins began leading her behind his own horse. He slowly followed Hannah's retreating figure.

"Go away and leave me alone, McAllister."

Suddenly, he urged the gelding forward, maneuvering him in front of Hannah, blocking her way. Leaning toward her, Rook fixed her with a steely gaze.

"Who the hell is Matthew?" he asked quietly.

Hannah looked up, eyes wide. "Who told you about Matthew?"

"Bev warned me about him—I guess she thought someone should be honest enough to tell me there was another man in the picture."

"For your information, Matthew is the only man in the picture." Hannah stepped around the horse and continued walking.

"All right, I admit I was an imbecile for not recognizing that a woman like you would probably be involved in a relationship with some man. Guess I just couldn't imagine any guy worth his salt letting you travel clear across the country."

"Unlike you, Matthew doesn't try to tell me what to do."

"So what happens now? I suppose you expect him to show up here, lusting after you?"

"Matthew doesn't lust."

A sudden twinkle appeared in Rook's eyes. "Oh, I see. That explains a lot. No wonder you get so testy—they say sexual frustration can do that to a person."

"I've never been frustrated ... at least, not until I met you!"

"Really? How interesting."

"I'm not talking about *sexual* frustration, and you know it," she cried. "Just plain ordinary, everyday frustration— the kind that gets on your nerves and makes you crazy."

"So I make you crazy, do I?"

She spun around. "Yes, you do! And I don't like it. I want you to leave me alone!"

"After all that I've done for you?"

"Let's not go into that," she stormed.

"Hasn't this little tirade gone on long enough?"

"You ain't seen nothin' yet!"

"You know, I can be just as stubborn as you can."

"Good."

"Hannah, will you stand still and listen to me?"

"I wouldn't waste my time."

Scowling, he stopped the horse and sat looking after her. Distracted, he watched the angry sway of her derriere for a few moments before calling out, "Hannah, a real horsewoman wouldn't let an animal scare her. She'd get right back on and show it who's boss."

"Let the horse be the boss, I don't care," she flung over her shoulder.

"For the last time, come back here and ride this horse."

Hannah stopped, turned to face him, and in short, terse syllables told him exactly what he could do with his horse.

Rook looked somewhat shocked, then grinned sheepishly. "Maybe I'm not her type."

"Oh, I'm sure you'll do. Horses and jackasses are closely related." She flashed him a nasty smile. "I read that in a book somewhere."

With that, she whirled about and trudged off. Rook watched her go, experiencing alternating anger and admiration.

"They sure grow 'em tough in New York," he muttered, pulling his hat low over his brow. He sat staring after her until she was only a dot of color against the landscape. Then, when he was certain she had reached the cottage with no further mishap, he began the ride toward home, the meekly docile mare following slowly behind.

Chapter Four

Hannah shifted restlessly on the newly slipcovered couch, a book lying forgotten on her lap. Behind her, draped over the back of the sofa, the two cats, Tom and Jerry, had abandoned themselves to contented sleep. In front of her, a small fire leaped and danced on the grate. The flames seemed to keep time to the music coming from the portable radio on the oak chest she used as a coffee table.

Overhead, rain drummed on the roof in a different rhythm, a more somber cadence accented with an occasional cymbal crash of thunder.

Hannah tossed the book aside and got to her feet, wandering to the window. Flashes of lightning turned the night into a rain-washed underwater world of pale green, the wind-tossed trees waving like seaweed. It was a genuine spring storm on the prairie, but to her surprise she wasn't frightened in the least.

In fact, she thought, if I had someone to share it with it would be positively cozy.

Briefly her thoughts flicked to Rook, but because she hadn't seen him since the day they'd gone horseback riding she could only assume he was still angry with her. Of course she couldn't really say she had gotten over her own anger, but it seemed to have faded from wrath into something more like disillusionment.

Oh well, his absence had allowed her the past few days to turn her energies to the completion of the cottage and now, as she looked around the room, she experienced a feeling of pride.

At the far end, in front of the long windows with their frilly print curtains, were the table and chairs, the wooden surfaces rubbed with oil instead of revarnished. The same treatment had brought a natural sheen to the wood of the cupboard between the bedroom and kitchen doors, and now its shelves were filled with books, family photos and plants.

She had formed a small conversation area by placing the couch so it faced the fireplace, with the white wicker chair just to the left. On the other side, by the window, was the repaired rocking chair, a piecrust table and a wildly luxuriant ivy plant in a hanging basket.

A sudden, sharp flash of lightning zigzagged across the black sky, followed by a shattering explosion of thunder. Hannah's hand jerked upward toward her throat as the lights in the room flickered, dimmed and went out, leaving her standing in the eerie firelight, trying to catch her breath. Maybe spring storms on the prairie were a bit more lethal than she'd first thought!

She groped her way into the kitchen, fumbling for matches and the oil lamp. She felt a moment of gratitude to Rook for taking the time to fill the lamp, then show her how to turn up the wick and light it.

She set the lamp on the shelved cupboard, liking the way its wavering flame cast an ebb and flow of mystery over the room. She switched the radio onto battery power, but instead of the severe weather forecast she expected to hear, one of her favorite Lionel Richie songs was playing. It added an aura of romance that made her long, more than ever, for someone with whom to share the night....

Hannah let the sensual music wash over her as she danced across the room, long skirts swirling around her legs. She paused before a mirror framed in carved oak, not quite able to believe the beautiful woman reflected therein was actually her. Backlighted by the fire, a riot of shimmering brunette hair fell to her waist. Its darkness was repeated in the winged brows and thick lashes that defined wide silver eyes—eyes glowing with suppressed excitement and the ancient knowledge of a female who, loving and loved in return, becomes a seductive enchantress. Her lips curved upward in a tremulous smile . . . she was growing impatient for her lover.

Matthew would be here soon, she knew. Matthew—the one man who could touch her heart with his sweet tenderness. She longed to lie in his arms all night and listen to the rain. Her pulse began to hammer at the thought.

Suddenly, the door flew open and Matthew was there, his arms filled with roses. . . .

Someone was kicking the front door, Hannah realized, and without thinking she hurried to throw it open. There stood Rook, his arms filled with a wriggling black-and-white calf.

"Damn it, didn't you hear me yelling?" he growled, glaring at her. "This calf is heavy."

The animal looked at her with huge, brown eyes, its pitiful bleat managing to echo Rook's reproach.

Hannah simply stared, her mouth dropping open. Rook strode into the room, bringing the scent of the rainy night with him. He was wearing a mud-smeared yellow poncho over his shirt and jeans, and his hat was soaked with moisture. A strand of dark hair was plastered carelessly across his forehead. He deposited the wet calf on the floor in front of the fire and looked back at her.

"Got any old towels?" he asked abruptly.

"What?"

"Old towels—do you have any? I need to get this calf dried off."

Hannah shook herself slightly and took a closer look at the scene.

"Am I dreaming or have you actually brought a cow into my house?"

"You're not dreaming, except that it's a bull, okay?"

"Please! Spare me another lecture on bovine sex, will you?"

"Sweetheart, when you and I discuss sex, it won't be bovine and it won't be with a newborn calf between us, I promise you that."

Her eyes flashed. "No, if we ever have such a discussion, there'd better be something a heck of a lot more substantial between us—say, the Great Wall of China!"

"Hannah, will you just get the damned towels?"

His growing impatience motivated her, at last. She made her way into the bedroom, locating the stack of towels on the closet shelf. She grabbed half a dozen and carried them back to the living room, tossing them to him.

Rook seized a couple and immediately began rubbing the calf's bedraggled black coat.

"What's wrong with him?" asked Hannah, watching intently.

"Nothing yet, but I've got to get him warmed up. Calves born during bad weather are easy prey to pneumonia if they're not taken care of. This little guy happened to have a mother who had twins but decided to claim only one of them. Throw some more wood on the fire, will you?"

On their last workday at the cottage, Dusty and Arlo had left a tidy woodpile and Hannah, envisioning a fire on a cool night, had brought some of the smaller logs inside, standing them upright in a crock beside the fireplace. Now she blessed her foresight and taking two chunks of dry wood consigned them to the flames.

"Have any trouble getting the fire started?" Rook casually inquired, working briskly.

"None at all. It may surprise you to learn I was once a Girl Scout."

"Nothing about you surprises me." He grinned and nodded toward the can of charcoal starter on the mantel. "Is that how New York Girl Scouts learn to do it?"

Hannah stuck out her tongue at him. "Well, I couldn't find two sticks to rub together," she retorted.

The calf stirred, turning his white face toward her. Despite herself, Hannah began to think it was rather sweet-looking. She dropped to her knees and picked up a towel.

"He seems to be showing a little interest in his surroundings," Rook said. "That's a good sign. Look, I've got to drive over to the house and get some colostrum for him. Can you keep him warm?"

"Rook! You're leaving me alone with him?"

"He won't bite. All he cares about is being dry and getting something to eat."

Her eyes widened, causing him to grin wryly. "Fortunately, you don't have anything to worry about on that score, either."

Before she garnered the courage to ask precisely what he meant by that remark, he was gone, slamming the door behind him. She could hear the roar of the truck engine, and then it was lost in the thunder. She shuddered and looked back at the calf. He was observing her with big, soft eyes that, she noticed with amazement, were surrounded by thick, straight lashes a Broadway actress would kill for. The flat, pale pink nose twitched with curiosity, and then she felt the damp swipe of the calf's tongue on her hand.

Oh, Lord, he thinks I'm his mother, she thought, with some alarm. Nervously, she laughed at herself and renewed her efforts with the towel.

She judged Rook to have been gone about twenty minutes when the calf began to experiment with straightening, then kicking his thin legs. Hannah's active imagination shifted into overdrive as she worried that something was seriously wrong. Was the animal truly sick? Could he be preparing to go into convulsions? He weakly rocked his body, lurching forward and Hannah, still on her knees, leaned back, hands over her mouth in horror.

How could Rook leave her alone with a dying animal? My God, she could barely take her own temperature...how was she supposed to know what to do in this situation?

She heaved a sigh of relief when the door banged open again, admitting Rook and a rainy gust of wind.

"Thank God, you're back," she cried. "Something is wrong with him!"

"Damn."

Rook dropped the blanket-wrapped object he held onto the couch and, flinging his hat aside, shrugged out of the poncho. He knelt beside the calf, running assessing hands over its body. Then, mouth tilted in a smile, he reared back on his haunches, folding his arms across his chest.

"What is it?" she breathed. "What's happening?"

"There's a technical term for it," he said. "Those of us who know cattle . . . call it 'walking.' "

The calf lurched again, this time getting his spindly legs beneath him. They wobbled, nearly buckling, but, as Rook steadied him with strong hands, he stood, clearly pleased by his own cleverness.

"You mean he was only trying to stand up?"

"That's right. Remember, he's less than an hour old, and just like everything else the first time is always the most difficult."

Hannah gave him a sharp glance, but he appeared to be engrossed in unwrapping the parcel he'd carried into the room. Was it her, or did he continually make suggestive remarks?

Her disbelief at seeing what had been in the blanket caused the conjecture to be forgotten almost immediately. Rook was holding a giant plastic baby bottle, fitted with an enormous pink nipple and filled with yellowish milk. As she looked on, he squirted a little of the liquid on his forefinger and stuck it into the calf's mouth. The animal sucked tentatively, then with more vigor. The withdrawal of Rook's finger was followed by a swift intrusion of the nipple, bringing such a human look of surprise to the calf's face that Hannah had to laugh. Surprise faded, to be replaced by greed and Rook's arm jerked as the calf took a long pull of milk.

"He likes it," she commented in delight.

"Not only does he like it, it's necessary for his survival."

"Milk?"

"Not just any milk, but mother's milk—colostrum, the milk secreted before and after giving birth." Rook tightened his grip on the bottle, as the room filled with the noisy sounds of the calf enjoying his first meal. "Newborn calves need it right away, so we always buy extra from a dairy and keep it frozen for emergencies. All I had to do was rush home and heat some—we still have electricity over there, by the way."

He turned his attention back to the animal. "Hey, slow down, fellow. I'm not going to take it away." A froth of milky slobbers ringed the calf's mouth, satisfaction gleamed in its eyes.

Impressed by the gentle strength Rook used in handling the animal, Hannah covertly studied the man.

Light flared from the fireplace, casting his lean face in bronze and emphasizing all the angles and hollows. Black lashes threw tangled shadows on his high cheekbones; in his concentration, his lower lip was caught and held by straight, white teeth. Water dripped from his hair, and as she watched, an errant drop traced its way along one slashing eyebrow, curving downward past a slightly curling side-burn to tremble momentarily on a square jaw before plunging to the floor.

She decided that maybe she had been too hard on Rook over the riding incident—after all, a man who was innately kind to animals couldn't be all bad, even if he didn't seem to have much notion of how to handle women. No, she corrected herself, sneaking another quick glance at him, he would know how to treat most women. He just didn't know how to deal with her.

Somewhere, hadn't someone done a survey that proved the majority of females preferred men who employed typical caveman tactics? Assuredly, if a girl was impressed by that outdated "Me Tarzan, you Jane," routine, Rook should have very little trouble bowling her right over. Very little trouble, indeed, she suspected.

"Want to try it?" he asked suddenly, grasping one of her hands and placing it on the bottle. "It's fun."

"Fun? If I didn't know better, I'd say you suffer from maternal instincts, Mr. McAllister."

"I'd prefer to think of them as *paternal*, but yes, I guess all farmers have them. That's what causes us to do things like go out in the middle of a rainstorm to check on a cow who's about to calve. It's fortunate I did, too, because this little guy was pretty cold and weak."

As he released the milk bottle, Hannah clasped it with both hands, stunned by the strength of the animal on the other end.

"Weak?" she groaned, as the calf tugged and pulled, causing her to bounce about like a cork on water. Trying to reestablish her balance, Hannah yanked back and pulled the nipple free. She reeled sideways and the calf followed, butting at the bottle with hungry insistence.

Rook's hands caught her around the waist, and he settled her against him, using his body to brace her for the calf's onslaught. Although the calf calmed down once the nipple was in his mouth again, Rook did not move away from her. Hannah could feel his thighs against her lower back, and the thump of his heart where his chest rested against her spine. Stiffly, she tried to inch away, but his hands were firm, sliding lower to rest on her hips. Feeling too embarrassed to create a scene, she stayed where she was, consoling herself with the theory that the poor hayseed probably thought he was being gentlemanly.

When the last of the milk gurgled from the bottle, she slowly started to breathe again. Rook got to his feet, pulling her up with him, and while she fidgeted with the bottle she held, he settled the sleepy calf on the blanket he'd brought.

"Hannah."

She looked up and instantly wished she hadn't. The intent expression on his face set off all her alarm systems—it was going to be one of those moments that change everything, she could feel it.

She managed a feeble laugh and held out the milk bottle. "This...ah...this looks like something a circus clown would use in his act. It's hard to believe it serves such a useful purpose."

Rook smiled faintly, taking the bottle and setting it carefully on the mantel. His eyes were no less intent.

"I...I think I'll fix some hot tea," she murmured, taking a step backward. "Want some?"

"You don't have any electricity, Hannah," he reminded her.

"Oh." She nervously rubbed her hands together. "Well, how about a Pepsi? I'll get them...."

She started off, nearly at a run, but he calmly reached out and grasped an elbow, drawing her back to him.

"Hannah, quit trying to run away from this."

"From what?" Her mouth was so dry she could hardly speak. "Oh, Lord, I really do need that Pepsi."

Quickly, before he could stop her, she pulled away and fled into the kitchen.

Breathing heavily, she leaned on the counter, thinking, When exactly did I lose control of the situation?

One minute they were playing nursemaid to a calf and the next... dear heavens. Now she knew how the poor fox felt when he heard the baying of the hounds! Rook had been transformed into a predator practically before her very eyes, and that left the role of prey to her.

Prey, she thought with something akin to hysteria. It's time for the prey to pray.

But what should she pray for? She didn't actually know what Rook had in mind...oh, crud, she did, too! She knew exactly what he wanted, and it scared the hell out of her!

"Did you get that Pepsi?" His voice came quietly from the doorway, causing her to jump guiltily. She spun around and saw him standing there, looking about ten feet tall in the shadowy light.

"I'm just getting it now. Want one?"

"No, thanks. I'll have a drink of yours."

With the electricity off, the interior of the refrigerator remained dark when she opened the door, but she was glad because it gave her an excuse to take her time searching for the can of cola. All too soon, it seemed, her fingers closed around it.

She opened the can and took a long drink, finding it helped to steady her. As a little natural wiliness returned, she handed the can to Rook and neatly escaped into the living room when he tipped his head back to drink. She was trying to decide whether to sit down in the rocker or stay on her feet when he came up behind her.

"Thanks for the drink."

"You're welcome." She looked toward the calf, willing it to wake up and demand attention. Instead, it snored softly and snuggled deeper into the blanket. Her fingers trembled slightly as she took the can of Pepsi from Rook.

"Hannah, I don't believe you."

She heard the amusement in his voice and was irritated by it. "What do you mean?"

"Here you are, a scrappy little girl who thought nothing of disrupting her entire life on a whim...a girl brave enough to drive clear across the country by herself and take up residence in a ruined cottage full of varmints...."

"What is the point you are trying to make?" she asked sharply.

"I don't understand why that feisty little hellion has turned into a scared rabbit just because I intend to kiss her."

"I am not a scared rabbit," she flared, taking a few steps away from him. That's right, Hannah, old girl, she counseled herself—keep moving. It's always harder for a guy to get amorous when his victim is on the move. Get the couch between the two of you, if at all possible.

She sauntered oh, so casually toward the oil lamp, ostensibly checking the wick before turning to face him over the back of the couch.

"I repeat, I am not a scared rabbit."

"Then come here and let me kiss you."

"No!"

"Why not?" he taunted. "I say you're afraid."

"I'm not! Why should I be?"

Her brave words were immediately followed by a weak scream as he suddenly vaulted over the couch and grasped her upper arms.

Her free hand came up to press against his chest. "Wait...we've got to talk."

"What's there to talk about? You've known this was coming ever since the first day we met. I've been remarkably patient, I think."

"But I need to...we need to discuss—"

"We've had a number of discussions before now, and not one of them has ever done more than frustrate the hell out of me."

"Well, I'm sorry about that, but the fact remains there are certain things we need to get straight between us."

His face broke into a perfectly charming smile, as he rolled his eyes heavenward. "Out of the mouths of babes..." he murmured.

There he went again, with his maddening innuendos!

She used both hands to push him away, sloshing Pepsi onto his already damp shirt in the process.

"Hannah," he groaned, "what is the big deal about a simple kiss? A *first* kiss, I might add—a humiliating admission for a generally fast worker like myself."

Hannah nodded her head violently, taking advantage of her freedom to put some distance between them. "Precisely my point! You are a fast worker... your own friends implied that you were indiscriminate in your... well, your affairs of the heart."

"Is this going to be an affair of the heart, then?" He came close enough she caught the gleam of white teeth.

Run, Red Riding Hood, she thought wildly, there are wolves in Kansas, after all!

"Rook, we are two very different kinds of people."

"God, I hope so!"

"Be serious for a minute, can't you? What I'm saying is, well, you apparently have a reputation where women are concerned... On the other hand, I don't...."

"I should hope not."

She could have sobbed in frustration. "I'm not just looking for a good time, the way you are! If I'm going to get involved with a man, I want it to amount to something. Do you know what I mean?"

He began walking toward her again. "No, what do you mean?"

"It should be something...well, special. Not simply a way to pass a rainy evening."

"All I want to do is kiss you, for God's sake. Do I have to sign a contract for that, lady editor?"

"Of course not. It's only that I think a first kiss should be meaningful... perfect. The perfect setting, the perfect embrace. That kind of thing."

"Hannah, you're awful damned pretty, but, honey, you're so full of bull your eyes are brown."

"I knew you couldn't possibly understand!" she stormed. She whirled away, but he spun her back to face him. Just as he attempted to encircle her with his arms, she scampered off to the other side of the table. She warded him off with an imperious hand. "Don't come near me, McAllister! I want you to take your damned cow and go home!"

"Come out from behind that table and act like a grown woman."

"Not a chance!"

A split second before he made his move Hannah sensed it and ducked away, racing to the door of the screened porch. She had it open several inches before his hand slammed down beside hers, pushing the door shut, his body holding her captive against it. She twisted around and in that moment, looking into his fierce eyes, she had a vision of what she wanted their kiss to be.

She was lost in the aquamarine depths of Matthew's eyes, his strong arms the only thing that kept her from drowning completely. With a sweet half smile, he raised a hand to brush back a strand of her hair, trailing his fingers down one cheek to cup her chin. Gently, he touched her mouth with his own and then, gathering her closer within his embrace, deepened the kiss. She could hear the strains of violin music, could smell the scent of lilacs....

Gradually, the scent of flowers gave way to the less romantic smell of wet calf, the violins were replaced by the noise of static from the radio. And Rook's eyes still gazed into her own, mysterious and compelling, causing her knees to quiver.

As his mouth lowered to hers, she tried to turn her face away and only succeeded in bumping his nose, necessitating a change of direction on his part. This time their teeth clanked together and with an impatient sigh, Rook growled, "Hold still!"

"That wasn't exactly the perfect kiss," she said, almost triumphant at having been proven correct.

"How could it be, with you struggling like that? What's the matter, Hannah—afraid to give me a chance?"

He stepped away from her, then unexpectedly raised his hands to either side of her face, fingers slipping beneath her hair to cradle the back of her head as his thumbs lightly forced her chin upward. This time his aim was right on target, the kiss solid, devastating in its effect. His mouth was a fascinating combination of firm, unyielding arrogance and soft, coaxing tenderness. He opened his lips slightly, rubbing them with erotic thoroughness against hers, sparking tiny threads of fire that trailed downward and outward, making her incapable of standing on her own. The strength of his hands, so easily holding her prisoner, won her over. He wasn't bending her to his will so much as making her forget his will hadn't been hers from the start.

Of their own volition, her arms lifted to drape themselves around his neck and she shamelessly strained against him.

"Hannah . . ." His voice was a husky whisper close to her ear.

"Hmm?"

"Sweetheart, you're pouring Pepsi down my back."

"Oh!" Hannah's senses returned with a vengeance, and she let her arms drop. Sure enough, loosely clenched in her limp fingers was the bright aluminum can. "Oh, God, Rook, I'm sorry," she stammered, upset with herself.

With a short, joyful chuckle, he took the can from her and set it on the floor. "I knew it would be like that," he claimed. "I knew you'd be a great kisser. Was that perfect or what?"

His fingers curled around her wrists as he led her toward the couch. He dropped onto it, not relinquishing his hold.

"Where were the violins?" she murmured. "The lilacs?"

He looked puzzled. "What are you talking about?" He tugged on her arms, lying back on the sofa and pulling her down on top of him. "Come here and explain, Hannah."

Somehow, the words just wouldn't come. With his heart thudding loudly in her ear and his long legs entangled with hers, she had lost the thread of her thoughts. In all honesty, she had to admit it felt good to be lying there with him. Maybe violins weren't so essential, after all.

They stared into each other's eyes for a long moment, and just as Hannah began to think she was going to have to initiate the next kiss Rook's hand curved around the back of her neck, bringing her face down to his. But his lips had barely touched hers when, with jarring impact, the electricity came on and the room was flooded with light.

Hannah reacted with a startled jump, toppling them both off the couch to land in a crumpled heap on the floor.

"Blast the efficiency of these modern power-and-light companies," Rook swore. "Why couldn't the crews have waited until after the storm? There's no damned sense in such dedication to duty!"

"I know," she softly agreed, trying to get up from where she was wedged against the oak chest without doing Rook any serious damage.

Awakened by their voices, the calf wobbled to his feet and greeted them with an expectant look.

"I think your little friend is hungry again," Hannah said, her laugh only a bit shaky.

"Yeah, well, I suppose the worst of the storm's over and I better take him back to the farm and pour some more milk down him."

"I suppose so."

"I don't want to go. You'll just have to promise we'll finish this conversation later, all right?"

"All right."

He grinned. "I don't trust you when you're so agreeable."

"Does that mean you prefer me to be disagreeable?"

He considered the idea. "I'm not sure. Let me think about it, okay?"

"Okay."

He glanced about the room. "You've done a good job with the cottage, Hannah. You ought to show it off."

"How do you mean?"

"Maybe you should have some people over or something."

"That's a good idea."

"Don't sound so surprised. I do have them occasionally, you know."

"Why don't I fix dinner for Dusty and Arlo and their wives? Do you think they'd come?"

"Only if I can assure them I'm invited, too."

"Well, in that case, I guess you can tag along. How about Friday night?"

"Perfect." He winced. "There's that word again. I'm beginning to detest the sound of it."

She laughed. "I've got a question—what's your favorite meal?"

"Steak and potatoes," he answered without hesitation.

"All right. Now I have a second question—is your calf housebroken?"

"I take it that's a hint for me to get out of here?"

He donned the poncho once again, placing the damp hat on his head. Then, with a grunt, he lifted the calf into his arms. Hannah hurried to open the door. Outside the rain had slowed to a mere drizzle, and the sound of thunder was distant.

In the doorway, Rook leaned forward over the calf to give her a gentle good-night kiss. "See you Friday," he promised with a wink.

Hannah quietly shut the door and leaned back against it. She'd been right to be afraid of Rook McAllister. How had she known he would elicit such a response from her?

Dear God, she couldn't help but wonder what she might have offered him had he shown up at her door with an armload of roses!

Chapter Five

Hannah drove into town on Thursday to do some laundry and shop for groceries. She was excited by the prospect of entertaining guests for the first time in the cottage and had spent hours on the menu. Steak and potatoes seemed a little ordinary to her, so she had labored over ways to dress them up, finally deciding on Steak Diane and a cheese-and-whipped-potato soufflé. That, along with salad and hot rolls, should be adequate. But dessert, she vowed, would be something special.

On Friday she spent the morning cleaning the house. Later, as she mixed the dough for hot rolls, she mentally admitted she was glad the other couples would be present that evening. If there was one thing she didn't need, it was to be alone with Rook. His actions the night of the rainstorm made it obvious he was interested in starting a relationship—how she disliked that word—and she knew she was not.

It isn't Rook, she told herself, turning out the dough onto the floured countertop. It really has nothing to do with him.

It was simply that she had had it with the whole man/ woman thing. Oh, she still believed there was someone—the perfect someone—out there for her, but experience had taught her patience. At this point, she was willing to wait until he showed up, even if it meant she didn't find Mr. Right until she was a frail old lady in a convalescent home. *Dating*, that wistful 1950's word for today's frantic "race to mate," took far too much time and energy for what it was worth. She'd been there and she knew.

While she kneaded the dough, she let her mind slide back over the men she had known and dated in the past. With a shudder, she realized she hadn't thought of most of them in years...and for good reason. She seemed to attract nice-looking men with good jobs, only to discover by the third date there was something completely and irrevocably wrong with each of them.

Her first big disappointment had been Justin, who eventually proved as weird as the science-fiction novels he wrote. Then there had been Ted, who lived and breathed computers—driving her crazy with jokes about his "most significant byte" or his "specialized functions" in what were supposed to be romantic moments. He was succeeded by Chad, a dyed-in-the-wool sex maniac who refused to let romance get in the way of his libido. As a parting gift, Hannah had presented him with the addresses of female quintuplets she'd met in college. She had abandoned the search for true love after Stephen, a bright young executive with a sinus problem which seemed to give him a headache whenever things got the least bit serious. Those ill-fated relationships had, in turn, made her feel dull, old-fashioned, prudish and insensitive.

After a while, she had begun to doubt her own worth as a human being. Each time well-meaning friends set her up with a blind date, she later found herself apologizing and getting out of it.

She wasn't a snob—she wasn't!—she simply had a staggering list of qualifications for the man with whom she hoped to spend the rest of her life. It had nothing to do with looks or money or ethnic background. It had everything to do with romance, with idealism, with emotional compatibility...things she had yet to discover in any of the males she had met. For that reason, she had given up on dating. She hadn't gone out with anyone for the last six months and, frankly, she hadn't missed it. Then along came Rook....

Not that there wasn't plenty wrong with him—and it hadn't taken more than one meeting to find it out. He was too sure of himself, too cocky, and too determined to have his own way. She had a feeling that, if she ever let him into her life, he wouldn't be so easy to get rid of—at least, not until he'd gotten all he'd come for. She turned the blob of dough over and began to knead it with additional vigor.

Rook was too rich. Too idle. And she couldn't ignore the matter of his looks. No man who looked as good as that could be trusted, she was certain. She could almost bet it would take a fire hose to rid him of the women who undoubtedly hung around on a regular basis. Handsome men were nothing but trouble, especially handsome men with doting mamas and lots of money.

And I definitely don't need that, she thought, pummeling the bread dough viciously.

Suddenly she realized the dough she had been attacking had quietly given up. It lay on the counter in total surrender, pale, listless, flat.

Damn you, Rook McAllister, she swore silently, scraping the floury mass into the wastebasket and reaching for a new package of yeast, preparing to start the process all over again.

Hannah lighted the pale green candles set in clear glass holders and invited her guests to seat themselves. She was pleased by the compliments the simple elegance of her table elicited, but couldn't prevent herself from checking it once again with a highly critical eye. There was a clear bowl of lilies of the valley in the center of the white damask cloth, the vivid green of their leaves repeated in the rolled napkins at each place. Delicate strands of ivy decorated her grandmother's china, which gleamed pearly gray, the silver rims of the plates sparkling.

Hannah glanced up to find Rook watching her. He looked different tonight, more dressed up than she had ever seen him. He was wearing a light gray western shirt with pearl snaps down the front and on the cuffs, and instead of the usual denims, sharply creased charcoal slacks. His dusty boots had been replaced by a pair of dark-gray snakeskin, so obviously new that Hannah almost expected to see a price tag dangling. Despite the western cut of his clothing, there was a sophistication about his appearance. Gone was the casual, rough-edged cowboy; in his place was a much more worldly man, one who would turn heads anywhere he went. His hair seemed blacker, his skin more tanned, his dark eyes more devastatingly wicked.

Hannah gave herself a mental shake, glad she had placed Dusty and Janice on one side of the table, Bev and Arlo on the other. It seemed safer with Rook at the far end, opposite her. It would be easier to ignore him that way. Ignore him until later when, at an appropriate and private moment, she could firmly dispel any thoughts of a romantic entanglement he might be entertaining.

However, Rook refused to be ignored. When she returned from the kitchen carrying the salads on a serving tray, he held her chair for her, dropping a casual hand onto her shoulder before returning to his own seat.

She was still mesmerized by the smooth pull of gray fabric over his buttocks when she realized he was asking a question. "Shall I pour the wine?"

Hannah struggled for composure, acutely aware of the ill-concealed smirks that passed among the other four. Apparently they were enjoying Rook's natural assumption of the role of host, and no doubt thought there was some significance in it. She hoped to heaven no one had noticed her ogling him.

As pleasantly as she could manage, she nodded in agreement and began to serve the salad.

"I hope you don't mind if I put these little fish things to one side and don't eat them," Janice said, scraping the anchovies from her salad.

Hannah glanced around the table and saw that no one was eating the anchovies she'd used as a garnish. No one, that is, except Rook. As her gaze fell upon him, he lifted a big forkful of salad to his mouth and chewed enthusiastically, anchovies and all.

"You didn't get these critters out of the horse tank, did you?" Arlo asked with suspicion.

"What?"

"We put goldfish in the tanks to keep the water clean," Dusty explained, sorting through his salad with his fork. "What are these weird things?"

"Those are alfalfa sprouts," Hannah replied, somewhat miffed. "Don't tell me you've never seen them before?"

"Not in a salad. We let alfalfa grow, then bale it to feed the livestock." Dusty winked broadly, but Hannah, looking down at her own plate in consternation, failed to see the gesture.

"Dusty," admonished Bev, picking up her wineglass. "Behave yourself."

The dark-haired woman took a small sip of the dark wine, then choked. "Oh!" she gasped. "What kind of wine is this?"

"It's an Italian wine my family sometimes drank at holidays," Hannah began, lifting her own glass.

With the exception of Bev, everyone around the table took tentative swallows.

"Hmm, delicious!" proclaimed Rook, though his mouth twisted slightly as he spoke the words.

Arlo looked about wildly, as if searching for a place to spit the offensive liquid. Finally his Adam's apple bobbed deeply. "Gawd!" he bellowed.

"Oh, honey," Janice cried sympathetically, "I think your Italian wine has gone to vinegar."

Unhappily, Hannah had to agree. "I brought the bottle from home with me. Maybe it got too hot in the car or something." She shrugged, fighting the urge to cry. So far, absolutely nothing had gone right. "I'll get the steak and a pitcher of ice water."

"I'll help," Bev offered, jumping up to follow Hannah. She gave Arlo a jab with her elbow as she passed, hissing, "Quit acting like a jerk!"

"He *is* a jerk," Dusty commented. "How else is he supposed to act? Right, Rook?"

Rook merely nodded, leaning back in his chair to watch Hannah as she scurried to the kitchen.

There was something different about her tonight, he decided, studying her flushed face—something very appealing, very stirring.

She was wearing evening pajamas made of slinky material in a mauve color that made her eyes fairly smoke. The tunic top clung to graceful curves, then fell in a straight line until gathering to one side at the hips and tied in a loose knot. Her legs were encased in trim pants of the same color, ending at the ankle to show off the plain black spike heels she wore. Around her neck was a long scarf that matched her pantsuit, and as she moved about, the ends of the slithery material slipped forward over her shoulder, causing Hannah to continually fling them back. Each time she did so, the sensuous grace of her movements caught and held Rook's admiring eye. There was an unconscious eroticism in the way she arched her neck, lifting an impatient hand to fling the errant scarf back into place. The dangling gold and amethyst earrings she wore shimmered in the light, exotic against her dark hair.

The clothes and jewelry gave her a classy image and yet, as sophisticated as she looked, there was a definite fragility about her. A vulnerability that showed in her face as she hovered over the table, so anxious for everything to go right.

Rook scowled at Dusty and Arlo, silently damning them for their harassment of Hannah. It was meant as a joke, he knew, but after all, she wasn't some homegrown prairie flower who would understand their brand of humor and answer in kind.

Lord, he thought with a ghostly smile, it is definitely something new for me to be feeling both horny and protective!

And all because Hannah Grant looked like a little girl dressed up in her mother's clothing. Then, as he watched her walk across the room again, all such thoughts disappeared. No, there was absolutely nothing even remotely adolescent about her. He found himself getting to his feet.

"You go ahead and pour the ice water, Bev, and I'll help Hannah in the kitchen."

Ignoring Dusty and Arlo's comments, he strode from the room to find Hannah bending over the open oven door.

"Everything's going great, Hannah," he glibly lied. "I can't wait to get to the main course."

"Don't be nice to me," she warned. "Right now I can't handle sympathy."

"Then how about some help with that dish?"

"Be my guest," she answered, holding out the steaming casserole. "At least the potato soufflé turned out all right."

A delicate cheesy crust rose in golden-brown perfection over the top of the dish, filling the kitchen with a savory smell.

Rook grasped the pot holders and took the casserole from her. "Hmm, that sure smells good!"

Hannah, bearing the meat platter, followed him back to the table, almost daring to hope the rest of the meal would pass without incident.

"Observe what we have here," Rook said proudly, plunking the casserole down onto the table. "Doesn't this look terrific...?"

His words died as, before his horrified eyes, the perfect soufflé heaved a gusty sigh and settled tiredly back into its dish.

"Seems like you had a blowout," Arlo said dryly.

"What happened?" choked Rook.

"You set the dish down too hard," Janice informed him. "Soufflés are very touchy."

"Oh, God, Hannah, I'm sorry," Rook said, a comical expression on his face.

Hannah carefully placed the platter containing the Steak Diane on the table, fighting the urge to throw it against the nearest wall. Something told her it was going to be a long time before she forgot this dinner party.

"It doesn't matter, Rook," she managed to say. "You were only trying to help. I should have warned you."

"Never mind," soothed Bev. "I'll bet it will still taste good."

Moments later, all the plates were filled with generous servings of steak and potato and, to Hannah's relief, everyone was eating with good appetite. Arlo was the only one who seemed to have a problem with the fluted mushrooms that accompanied the steak, and even he complimented the yeasty hot rolls.

"My grandmother taught me to make them when I was about twelve years old," she explained. "At least that's one thing I couldn't mess up!" She colored guiltily as she recalled how exasperating thoughts of Rook had caused her to ruin the first batch of dough. She was glad they need not know about that.

"Hey, I saw old man Dickson in town yesterday," Arlo said, "and he told me he bought twenty head of Santa Gertrudis cattle straight off the range in west Texas."

"The hell you say! He'll have to build fences ten feet high to keep them in," Rook laughed. "Or it'll be roundup time all year long."

"Saw the price of cattle is up again," Dusty interjected. "Think we ought to...?"

As the masculine conversation concerned itself with farm business, Hannah turned her attention to the women.

"Next week is our home extension meeting, Hannah," Janice was saying. "Would you like to go as our guest?"

"Home extension? What is that?"

"It's a club for homemakers," Bev told her. "We study cooking or interior decoration. There's going to be a demonstration of wheat weaving at this particular meeting."

"Well, I don't know..."

"You think about it, hon," advised Janice. "If you decide you'd like to go, we'd be glad to have you. I guess it's not everyone's cup of tea, though."

"Oh, really, it might be fun," Hannah said faintly. "I'll let you know."

"In June I'll be doing a lesson on making goat's milk cheese," Bev said, making a face. "You wouldn't want to miss that!"

"Oh, that reminds me," Janice broke in. "Speaking of goats... old ones, that is... did you hear the Epsons are getting a divorce?"

"No! Heavens, after all these years . . ."

"We better get started working that ground up north," Arlo was commenting on the other side of the table. "While it's relatively dry."

"You're right about that," Rook replied. "We can run all the tractors, but something tells me the old International is due for a long haul in the repair shop. . . ."

Hannah sighed. This stupid dinner party was not going at all as she had envisioned it. The meal itself had been close to disaster, and the conversation had never once approached the sparklingly witty level she had hoped for. With determination, she cut through the barnyard chatter with a question of her own, designed to lead the others away from the farm and a bit closer to civilization.

"By the way, has anyone seen any good plays lately?"

The query was met with total silence—total, *surprised* silence. She was aware of the two women exchanging odd looks, and of Arlo scratching his head. Dusty grinned, as usual. She saw Rook open his mouth and knew she couldn't bear to sit there while he tried to gloss over her ignorant remark. They probably didn't even have theaters in this backward place! But, hell, how was she to know?

"I'll get the dessert," she muttered, fleeing to the kitchen.

Viciously, she scooped ice cream into dessert dishes, slamming them onto a tray. She would struggle through this last course, then herd her guests out the front door and commence her new life as a hermit.

Never again, she vowed; never, never again. I will squelch any social inclination that may arise until I get back to New York.

With a little more caution, she placed the chafing dish of hot cherries onto the tray and carried it to the table. Dashing back to the kitchen, she seized the small saucepan of heated brandy and a book of matches.

"I'll just ignite this brandy," she said breathlessly, "and voilà! We'll have Cherries Jubilee."

Everyone seemed properly impressed as she struck the match with a flourish and held it to the brandy, which immediately flared into blue flame.

"Oh!" squealed Janice and Bev at the same time. Hannah experienced a tiny thrill of accomplishment. No doubt they would soon be asking her to demonstrate this skill at their extension meeting!

"Hannah!" Rook yelled, jumping up so quickly his chair tipped over backward. "Look out!"

The end of her scarf had fluttered forward, falling into the blazing brandy. A curl of flame surged up the shiny material, reaching for her hair. Hannah let out a frightened shriek as her hands flew up to bat ineffectually at the fire. Suddenly a wave of ice water hit her directly in the chest and the danger was past.

Rook, the empty pitcher in one hand, grabbed her arm with the other. "Are you all right?"

"Yes, I think so," she answered in a shaky voice. She pulled the scarf from around her neck and stared down at it. The synthetic material had melted into a hard, blackened twist.

Slowly, she let her shocked gaze move from the burnt scarf to the dishes of ice cream puddled with water, then past the smoking cherries, to the pale, concerned faces of the four other people at the table. Despite the entire fiasco, or maybe because of it, she began to feel amusement bubbling up inside her. It felt good to relax for a change and let it out.

As peals of laughter rippled forth, Rook eyed her intently. Finally, deciding she was not hysterical, he joined in, and then—one by one—the others started laughing, too.

"Whew! A good laugh can really clear the air," Hannah observed. "I guess things can only get so terrible. Look, everyone, I'm sorry tonight has been such a bust!"

"Bust?" Arlo exclaimed. "Hell, it looks to me like the party's just started!"

More laughter, very relieved laughter, accompanied his remark, and then everyone was pitching in to help clear the table.

Rook leaned forward to touch the ruined scarf in Hannah's hands. "Damn, I sure am sorry to see this scarf go. I thought it was real sexy the way you kept tossing it back over your shoulder." He grinned, but there was a look of something suspiciously like pride in his eyes as he regarded her. Puzzled, and a little embarrassed under the interested gazes of the others, she merely smiled and took the scarf to deposit in the wastebasket.

In short order, the dirty dishes were stacked on the counter and Hannah's guests were seated around the fireplace, eagerly starting a game of Trivial Pursuit.

"Put on some music, will you?" Dusty suggested.

Hannah paused by the small stereo in the corner, selecting several Broadway musical albums. As she crossed the room, a tune from *Porgy and Bess* began playing.

"*I loves yo', Porgy...,*" the low, sultry female voice intoned.

"What the...?" Arlo began.

"Ah, one of my favorites," Rook cut in smoothly.

Bev and Janice exchanged a quick, eye-rolling look, and Arlo subsided into silence.

Rook was sitting on the floor, his back resting against the couch. He reached out to take one of Hannah's hands, tugging gently. "Sit here by me. The fire will dry your clothes."

Hannah had nearly forgotten the soaking she'd gotten, but now as she glanced down, she was mortified to see how the thin damp fabric clung to her breasts. Without further ado, she dropped down onto the rug beside Rook, leaning forward to hug her knees, thus shielding her anatomy.

"Spoilsport," he whispered into her ear.

The game got under way with the decision that each couple would form a team. Hannah had played often with her friends in New York, but she couldn't quite imagine these cowboys and their wives tackling it with the same energy, skill or enthusiasm. She was rapidly proven wrong. Surprisingly, they all turned out to be more than adequate players—even Bev, whose answers were sometimes endearingly scatterbrained.

Halfway through the hard-fought game, Rook dropped a firm arm around Hannah's shoulders, pulling her close beside him. She was reminded of the talk she planned to have with him later, and ruefully imagined the ruination of his good mood. Dreading that moment, she made no protest when he took one of her hands and laid it on his thigh, his fingers absently stroking hers.

"Your question, Janice," Arlo was saying, pulling a card from the box. "How many times a year does a penguin have sex?"

Janice groaned. "Where do they get these questions, anyway?"

She and Dusty conferred in low tones for a moment, and then she said, "Not knowing any penguins personally we're going to have to make a guess. We say it's once a year."

"Hey, that's right. Good guess."

"Wow, those poor penguins," said Bev, causing herself to blush as the others laughed heartily.

"Your turn again," said Arlo, waiting while Janice tossed the dice. "Okay, what's the hardest substance in the body?"

"Why not ask the penguin?" Rook suggested dryly.

A series of even more hilarious responses followed before Janice came up with the correct answer—tooth enamel.

When it grew late, Arlo, Dusty and their wives left, thanking Hannah for a very entertaining evening and promising to resume the Trivial Pursuit challenge at a later time.

Rook stood close behind her as she saw them out, and when they had driven away he leaned forward to push the door shut.

Before she knew what was happening, Hannah found he'd slipped his arms around her waist, backing her against the closed door.

His first kiss landed somewhere along the side of her neck, sending an unwanted warmth spreading throughout her body. She stiffened as his lips traveled upward, touching her earlobe, her temple. She put her hands against his chest thinking to push him away, but relentlessly, his mouth sought hers, rendering her action useless.

"It was a great evening, Hannah," he said after a long moment. "I was proud of you."

She leaned back to look up at him. "Oh, sure," she countered. "Especially when I practically became a human torch."

He nuzzled her neck, breathing in the fragrance of her hair. "You weren't the only one about to go up in flames tonight. I got pretty warm a time or two myself."

She looked at him in surprise.

"I knew I was in trouble the minute I saw you in this slinky getup." He ran his hands up her back to her shoulders, then let his fingers wander back down her arms to her waist, then lower to her hips. "I love the way this ties in that big knot," he murmured. "It makes you look like some lucky man's birthday present—a present I know I'd enjoy unwrapping."

His lips were descending again, but Hannah, taking a deep breath, quickly sidestepped him. "Rook, we've got to talk."

"That's the same thing you said last time."

She nodded solemnly, forcing him to take note of the seriousness of her expression. "I know."

"All right, whatever you say. Want to walk down by the lake?"

"Let me get a sweater."

They followed the winding path through the trees, coming out at the edge of the moon-silvered water. Arms wrapped about herself, Hannah stared up at the night sky without speaking. Finally, Rook broke the silence.

"What did you want to talk about?"

Reluctantly, she met his eyes. "Look, I think this is something we need to discuss before it goes any further. I think...well, your actions lead me to believe that you might be interested in... in starting a relationship."

"I was under the impression we had already started one," he quietly replied. "You know, I don't throw ice water on just anyone. I have to be pretty serious about a woman."

"Serious is something you can't ever seem to be," she snapped.

"Okay, Hannah, I apologize. Go ahead and have your say."

She began to walk along the sand beach, and he fell into step beside her. "The problem is, I think you are interested in some kind of... for lack of a better word, I'll use relationship. I suspect you are looking for an affair...."

"Ah, there's a better word."

". . . and I'm not."

He threw her a sharp look, but didn't say anything more. The heels of her shoes sank into the soft sand and she tottered, causing him to reach out and take her arm to steady her.

"I've really had it with the whole dating scene," she went on with determination. "Most men only want one thing, and it's something I'm not willing to give."

"I'm sorry, but I can't resist interjecting a question at this point. Just what is this 'one thing' all men are after?"

"Don't be dense! You know as well as I do that a physical . . . that *sex* is all you really want from me."

"Let me get this straight," he said, stopping and turning her to face him. "Is that how you see me? As some panting, drooling, sex-crazed fiend lusting after your chaste little body?"

"No . . . yes! Yes, I guess I do."

"And you'd be exactly right!" he said, laughing lewdly and contorting his face into a leer. Panting heavily, he groped at her with fumbling hands as she uttered a small scream and backed away. "Damn, I've got to practice my drooling," he muttered. "At least I've mastered the lusting part—as a matter of fact, *all* my parts are lusting."

"Rook! Stop it! It's impossible to have a reasonable, mature conversation with you."

He abandoned his sex-maniac routine abruptly. "Sorry. I'm through fooling around." His eyes brightened as he considered the possibilities of that statement, but suddenly, seeing the strained look on Hannah's face, he sobered. "I'm ready to listen, honey. I won't say another word until we get back to the cottage."

"It isn't that I don't like you, Rook. I do . . . you're fun to be with, and you've been a big help to me. But I'm just not ready to start anything with anyone. So you see, there is really no sense in leading you on."

Forgetting his promise not to speak, Rook asked, "Does this have anything to do with Matthew?"

"In a way."

"What way?"

"Well, this may sound funny to you, but I'm determined to wait for the right man and that man is someone like Matthew. I've had it with hot-blooded Romeos who aren't interested in anything more permanent than a one-night stand."

"You're holding out for marriage?"

"Not just marriage," she stated. "But a marriage like my mother and father had. The happiest, most romantic marriage I've ever seen."

Rook took her arm and they began walking again. Hannah was quiet for a long time before she spoke.

"It was a case of good old-fashioned love at first sight. At least that's what Gran always used to say. My father was working as a photographer for a news magazine, and one day he saw my mother in the foreground of a picture he'd shot of an apartment fire. He was so fascinated by her photo that he went back to the scene of the fire, going from door to door until he found someone who could identify her. They were married two months later, and in all their years of marriage they never fell out of love with each other."

"Where are they now?"

"They were killed in a terrorist bombing while my dad was on a photographic assignment in the Middle East. Mother always went with him when they traveled."

"Where were you?"

"At home in New York, going to school. My grandmother was living with us, by then. She always said they would have wanted things to turn out the way they did— neither of them could have survived without the other. That's how strong their love was, how committed they were to each other."

As the night wind stirred around them, Hannah raised a hand to brush back a strand of hair from her face. "Even when jobs were scarce and times rough, my father managed to scrape together enough cash to bring her flowers or gifts. And every Saturday night they had a ritual I'll never forget. They always had dinner by candlelight, just the two of them. Champagne if they could afford it, beer if they couldn't. I used to sneak out of bed to sit at the top of the stairs and peek down at them. I was so proud because they were such beautiful people and so obviously crazy about each other.''

"Hannah..." Rook's hand curved around the back of her neck, almost as if he thought she needed comforting. She moved away from his touch.

"Don't you see? That's how I want it to be for me, too. I want that kind of love or none at all." She shivered slightly. "Have I made myself clear? Do you understand anything of what I am trying to say?"

"Yes, I think I do."

"I don't want just fun and games and nothing else."

Rook nodded. "You're cold," he said abruptly. "Let's go back to the house."

They didn't talk on the way back to the cottage and Hannah sensed she had finally gotten through to Rook. She fully expected him to say a polite goodnight at the door, then get into his truck and drive out of her life forever. She tried to tell herself that would be for the best.

Rook held the door for her, and she turned to face him, steeling herself for the farewell she knew was coming. Instead, he plucked the sweater from her shoulders and gave it a careless toss, before pulling her into a fierce embrace.

"Rook?"

"Hannah, you've had your say. Now just shut up and let me have mine."

His mouth closed over hers with swift deliberation, his hands roving restlessly up and down her back. He pressed into her, his mouth demanding a response from her. She struggled halfheartedly.

"Rook... please. Didn't you hear what I said?"

"I did, and now I'm expressing myself," he said. "I'd appreciate a little cooperation."

"But..."

As his lips claimed hers again, he bent to put an arm beneath her knees, lifting her high against his chest. Feeling dizzy and slightly disoriented, Hannah's arms went about his neck, to cling weakly.

What was wrong with her? She wanted to summon righteous indignation, even burning anger, but all at once she felt as if she were on a wild roller-coaster ride, capable only of hanging on. At that moment, she knew Rook was in complete control of the situation. As frightening as that thought was, she realized there was little she could do about it.

Rook walked the few steps to the couch, then dropped onto it, cradling her on his lap. His mouth never left hers, just increased its demand, making her lips open softly in submission. One of his hands cupped her jaw, the tips of his fingers easily capturing the back of her neck, keeping her face close to his as he traced the outline of her mouth with his tongue, tasting and teasing.

Then his hand fell away from her face, dropping onto her shoulder, sliding back and forth, enjoying the feel of the slick material beneath his touch. Searching fingers moved lower, to cup and fondle her breast. A boldly questing thumb drew circles that disconcerted Hannah, causing her to catch her breath and press closer to him.

Rook gently forced her back against the pillows piled in the corner of the sofa, using his free hand to lift her unresisting legs onto the couch. He let his hand trail along their silken length, stopping to fumble with the straps of the frivolous spike heels she still wore. When the first shoe had been discarded, he took her foot in his hand, rubbing and soothing the tired arch, before turning his attention to the other foot.

"Hmm, that feels so good," Hannah whispered, eyes closed.

He chuckled softly. "If you think that feels good . . ."

In a few seconds, she could feel him untying the knot at her hips. Funny, no matter how she tried to bring a protest to her lips, no sound came—no sound but her unsteady breathing.

"I knew this would be like opening a birthday present," he said, freeing the knot and sliding his hand upward, unfastening the hidden buttons that closed the garment to the shoulder. When the last button was undone, he pushed the front of the mauve tunic aside. Hannah's eyes flew open at the sound of his sharply indrawn breath.

She was wearing a delicate lilac lace bra, one whose scalloped cups barely covered her rounded breasts. Rook honestly couldn't remember ever seeing anything he thought more beautiful . . . unless it was the incredibly dreamy look in her silvery eyes as he allowed his hand to sweep over her skin, lightly skimming the smooth ivory flesh.

"My God, you're beautiful," he rasped, bending his dark head to place a kiss just above the front fastening of the daring scrap of lingerie. "Lord, I never meant for this to go so far. . . ." He moved over her to place a quick kiss on her lips. "I only wanted to punish you a little for the things you said by the lake."

"Punish me?" she murmured, raising her head just enough to return his kiss.

"Yeah—I don't take rejection well."

Rook groaned loudly, agonizingly aware of her soft, half-naked form beneath him, completely accepting, open to his every touch. Her eagerly submissive attitude following so closely on the heels of her adamant denial, was driving him right to the brink of insanity.

He moved his mouth over hers once more, the blazing need he had fought to keep in check until now suddenly threatening to overwhelm him.

"Hannah?" The one word, spoken in husky hesitation, expressed the dozens of questions he needed answered. Her reply, in the form of a sizzling kiss, told him everything he had to know.

Seemingly of their own accord, Hannah's fingers began pulling at his shirt, grasping the lapel to tear at the snap fastenings, baring a chest covered with swirls of black hair. She heard him catch his breath at the feel of her fingertips burrowing into the haze of hair, tightening in her sudden passionate frenzy.

"Oh, Rook, what are we doing?" she gasped, gripping his shoulders.

"Give me a second and we'll see if we can't figure it out." He smiled, his hand lowering to the waistband of his dress slacks.

Just then, without warning, cold reason asserted itself, and Rook's hand stilled. Dazed, he pulled away from her and brushed a hand over his eyes. "Damn, we really got carried away, didn't we? Almost forgot something very important...."

Hannah gazed at him with large, passion-drugged eyes. "Important?"

"*Very* important," he assured her. "I didn't come over here expecting anything like this to happen. I'm . . . I'm not prepared."

Hannah blinked. "Prepared?"

He smiled crookedly. "Birth control, sweetheart. These are modern times—the era of responsible sex." He heaved a long, gusty sigh. "I don't suppose you are any more prepared than me?" he asked, hopefully.

Hannah struggled into a sitting position. "You actually shattered a moment of spontaneous passion to conduct a lecture on birth control?"

"Believe me, love, there are several things I'd rather be doing at this moment. But it just wouldn't be smart. And you'll never know how sorry I am about it, either."

"I can't believe you! That is absolutely the most unromantic thing I've ever heard of!"

He ran an unsteady hand through his tousled black hair. "Hannah, there is nothing I want more than to make love to you. But I refuse to take a chance that might hurt you. We could make a mistake we'd end up paying for for the rest of our lives." His dark eyes were somber. "I love children, but I want to be sure I've picked out the right mother for them before I commit myself to fatherhood. Understand?"

Hannah fought down her frustration. He was right, she knew he was. It just seemed such a cold-blooded way to end what had promised to be a highly satisfying experience.

Lord, what's the matter with me? she thought, grumpily straightening her clothes. I'm the one who didn't want him starting anything . . . and now look at me, half furious because he stopped in the middle!

When had she ever been so confused?

Rook stood up, looking rumpled and unhappy. His hair fell forward over his forehead, his shirttail was half in, half out. He put his hands on her shoulders and pulled her up to stand before him.

"Next time, I promise, you won't get away so easily."

"Perhaps there won't be a next time."

"There will be, and you know it." He dropped a soft kiss on her mouth. "Now, come on—I'll help you with the dishes, and then I'd better get out of here and go home."

As Hannah heated dishwater, she realized how tired she was. Too tired to even appreciate the humor of seeing Rook McAllister, well-to-do young playboy, competently drying her grandmother's china with a terry-cloth dish towel. Too tired to even feel guilt about the small deception she was perpetrating. She wondered what Rook's reaction would be if she told him the truth—that she was on the Pill, and had been for several years due to a minor medical problem.

As she rinsed out the dishpans and hung the towel up to dry, she knew she probably wouldn't ever tell him willingly. She supposed a normal person would undoubtedly have blurted it out in the heat of the moment, and the fact that she had not done so convinced her more than ever her subconscious was safeguarding her best interests. But how long could this excuse to keep Rook at arm's length last?

At the door, he gave her a long, lingering kiss, then told her goodnight, his eyes filled with regret.

"Next time," he promised, brushing her cheek with the back of his hand.

Hannah shut the door and leaned against it. Even those two ordinary words from the man's lips made her giddy heart start to hammer within the confines of her lilac lace bra.

She sensed she was in real trouble this time.

Chapter Six

Hannah was sitting cross-legged on the floor of the screened porch, papers scattered all around her, when she heard the distant roar of an engine and looked up. Presently, an old red tractor pulling some sort of farm equipment appeared on the narrow road that led past the cottage.

She watched as the tractor drew close to her yard and then stopped; the driver swung down from the seat and began walking toward her. Even with a wide-brimmed straw hat shadowing his face, she knew it was Rook by the way he walked, long legs covering the ground in quick, energetic strides.

She went out to meet him, and when he saw her coming he paused, hand on the front gate.

"What happened to you?" she asked, realizing this was a different side of Rook than she had yet seen.

"Nothing. I've been working ground."

He was dressed in ancient jeans faded nearly white and a chambray work shirt, sleeves rolled up to reveal dirt-begrimed forearms above hands gloved in worn leather. Beneath the hat, his face was several shades darker than usual, due to the layers of dust clinging to it. Sweat-dampened earth beaded his forehead, darkened his brows and lashes, lining his eyes exotically and swathing his jaw with a premature five o'clock shadow.

"To say you are filthy would be an understatement," she said, a smile hovering about her mouth.

He pretended to scowl. "I'll be charitable and assume you are merely shocked to find that I really do work on occasion."

"You've shattered the image of indolent playboy forever," she concurred. "I'm certain they wallow in dirt of an entirely different sort."

"I'm sure of it. I've always been partial to good clean dirt, myself."

"What exactly have you been doing? What is that contraption hitched to your tractor?"

"It's a disk harrow. I've been disking the field north of the old farmhouse, getting it ready to plant. I was so close, I thought I'd stop by and see what you were doing."

"I'm going through a box filled with some of Gran's things. I should have done it sooner but somehow, back home, I just didn't have the heart." She ran a casual finger along the metal bars of the gate. "So I brought it with me. Today seemed like a good day to tackle it."

"Not an easy job, huh?"

"Actually, it's not as bad as I thought. I've found some fascinating things—the birth records of her children, the family Bible and a ton of letters she saved. It'll take me all summer to get them sorted out."

His teeth gleamed white in his dirty face. "Well, you know the old saying. All work and no play..."

She looked up at him, squinting against the late-afternoon sunshine. Over his shoulder, she could see the sparkle of the lake. "Meaning?"

"How would you like to take a little time off from your labors and come to a party next weekend?"

"What kind of party?"

"It's the McAllister barbecue we have every May. It's a chance to get all our friends and neighbors together for a good time. It promises to be quite a wingding this year."

"Well, that settles it. I've never been to a wingding before."

"I might have guessed."

"Tell me, what does one wear to a wingding?"

"You'll need a whole wardrobe for this party," he answered. "Better start out pretty casual and bring something to change into later, for the dance. And don't forget a swimsuit and your pajamas."

"Pajamas? My, you do plan a variety of activities for your guests, don't you?"

"Did I forget to mention you'll be staying overnight?"

"I don't recall hearing that bit of information."

"The dance goes on 'til the wee hours, so it's just simpler to put everyone up for what's left of the night."

"However, I really don't see any reason I couldn't make it the short distance back to the cottage."

"Tradition, Hannah," he said seriously. "It's tradition to spend the night. But don't worry, my mama will be there, so I'll be on my best behavior."

"In that case, I'll come."

"Good. Why don't I drive over to get you about three Friday afternoon?"

"Whatever you say."

"Well, guess I'd better get the old tractor back to the farm. I'll see you in a couple of days, okay?"

"Okay."

He hesitated a moment. "If I wasn't so dirty, I'd come through this gate and kiss you goodbye."

Her hands gripped the top of the flimsy barrier, carefully keeping it between them. She couldn't seem to think of anything to say and after a few seconds he shrugged in disappointment. "All right, I can take a hint. But just remember, I'll probably have had a bath before the barbecue."

She had to laugh. "I'll keep it in mind."

The month of May in Kansas often started out cool and ended in sweltering heat, with a variety of weather in between. Yet, somewhere in the midst of all that barometric indecision, the state enjoyed some of its finest days. The McAllister barbecue took place on just such a day.

The afternoon was sunny, the temperature moderate. A light, balmy breeze blew over the prairie, ruffling the blue-stem grasses and the clusters of wildflowers with a teasing touch.

Hannah saw the old pickup hurtling down the lane and seizing her overnight bag called a last goodbye to the cats, who were already busy snooping around the extra food and water she had put out for them. Then securing the door behind her, she hurried down the flagstone path and through the gate.

She felt an undeniable twinge of regret when she saw that instead of Rook the truck contained Bev and Janice.

Bev pushed open the door and slid over to make room for Hannah. "Rook sent us to get you because he got tied up with some important guests who arrived a little early."

"I see." Hannah tossed her bag into the back before climbing in beside Bev. "Well, I don't mind."

"He wouldn't stand you up for just anyone," Janice said, blithely grinding the gears and backing the pickup around. "These guests are his special favorites."

"Redheads or brunettes?" she asked dryly.

"Some of each, I think," Bev said, grinning. "Maybe even a blonde or two."

"In all shapes and sizes, I might add." Janice threw her a quick look. "Rook isn't partial, you know—he likes all of them."

"I'll just bet." Hannah tried to ignore the tiny stab of jealousy she was experiencing. She had made it abundantly clear she was not having any sort of romance with the man. Could she blame him for seeking it elsewhere? Still, she didn't think it had been entirely necessary for him to invite her to the party just to show off his success with other females of his acquaintance. Parading his harem was a very petty gesture on his part.

Vehicles of every description were parked along the lane and in the drive at McAllisters' Acres. There was an assortment of pickup trucks and cars, a few vans, even a small bus. Hannah noticed an impressive black Lincoln that looked as if it were a block long, parked between a motor-cycle and a beer wagon. Obviously this was going to be a rather eclectic party. Somehow she would have expected nothing else of Rook.

Mrs. McAllister greeted her warmly. "Come along, dear, and I'll show you to your room. You must promise to just make yourself at home now."

Try as she might, Hannah could discern no trace of guilt or insincerity in the woman's manner. Could it be possible her grandmother had been mistaken about J. W. McAllister? Surely if the man had been a cheat, his own wife would have known it.

Of course, she reasoned, Rook's endearingly obtuse mother wasn't exactly the type of woman whose husband would consult her about business. As long as she had a nice home and ample money for her little charities, she would probably never have questioned the ethics of his management.

The room Mrs. McAllister had designated for Hannah was on the second floor and very lovely. Everything in it gave the impression of a bedroom in an English country house, from the thick beige carpet to the cabbage-rose pattern of the Laura Ashley wallpaper and curtains.

"What a pretty room," she exclaimed, admiring the sloping ceiling and long, narrow windows. "I may spend all my time in here."

"Oh, that would never do," Mrs. McAllister laughed. "Winston has already come up to the house twice to ask if you've arrived. I don't think he would allow you to hide out."

"But I thought he was busy with...with his special guests," Hannah ventured, putting her bag inside the closet and following Rook's mother down the stairs.

"Oh, he is," the gray-haired woman said airily. "But you know Winston—he has enough energy to entertain everyone."

Hannah bit her tongue, not quite trusting herself to make any comment.

Mrs. McAllister led her down a hallway to the back door, which opened onto a poolside patio, crowded with people.

She made a few quick introductions as she ushered Hannah through the crowd, but her primary interest was in locating her son. She paused at the edge of the lawn, pointing out a grassy field beyond a tennis court.

"You go on down there so Winston can quit worrying about you."

The field had been marked off for the softball game that was now under way. Several spectators were watching from the sidelines, either in lawn chairs or on blankets in the grass.

Hannah felt shy about approaching alone, but she knew she couldn't hover uncertainly for the rest of the afternoon. She had only taken half a dozen steps, however, when she heard her name being called and looked up to see Rook trotting toward her.

Each time she saw him he looked different. And damn him, no matter whether he was dressed in fancy western regalia or covered with dirt, he always managed to look wonderful.

Today he was wearing a bright yellow tank top that clung to his torso, and hanging casually from his lean hips were the briefest jean shorts it had ever been her privilege to observe. The legs had been torn away along the sit-down crease at the top of his thighs, leaving a ragged fringe. Hannah stared at the few raveling threads left hanging and wondered if they tickled his long, pleasantly furred legs.

Instead of the usual cowboy hat, he wore a yellow-and-white baseball cap, which he now thrust back on his head, as he took his turn studying her. His nearly black eyes started with the top of her wind-combed hair and traveled downward, past the sleeveless white cotton T-shirt she wore, to the pastel plaid shorts and then lower, all along the length of shapely leg to the ankle socks and white Nikes.

Despite the warm sun, Hannah shivered. The touch of his eyes was almost as physical as the caress of his hands would have been.

"You look sensational, New York," he said seriously. "You're going to make a heck of a center fielder."

"Huh?"

"Center fielder," he repeated. "We need one, and it isn't going to hurt a thing to have a decorative one."

"But I don't know how to play baseball," she protested, as he took her hand and started pulling her toward the group of people she now realized was watching them.

"Softball," he corrected. "And you don't have to worry about a thing. Dusty will be the rover, so he'll catch everything that comes your way. If you don't at least stand out there, my team is going to have to take an automatic out each time through the lineup."

"Oh, now I see why you were so glad to see me." She sniffed. "I should have known you had some ulterior motive."

As they joined the other members of Rook's team, Hannah quietly looked about to see if she could discover which ones were the special guests Bev and Janice had mentioned. Other than herself there were only two women on the team, and neither of them seemed Rook's type. One of them was close to twenty years older, and the other was standing arm-in-arm with a man wearing a T-shirt that matched hers. Besides the two women, the team seemed to be mostly young boys, ranging in age from seven or eight to about sixteen. Puzzled, Hannah sat down on the team bench and watched as Rook prepared to take his turn at bat. It was definitely a fascinating performance.

First he took a practice swing or two with the aluminum bat and then, leaning it casually against his groin, bent forward to scoop up dirt, which he rubbed on the bat handle as well as his hands. Stepping up to the plate, he planted his feet wide apart and wriggling his denim-clad rear end in a most eye-catching manner crouched into his batting stance. Just before the pitcher released the ball, Rook broke concentration long enough to direct a swift look over his shoulder at Hannah. Catching her eye, he grinned engagingly.

"Stree-i-i-ike!" yelled the umpire, a bearded giant of a man in a flowered western shirt.

"Strike?" Rook exploded. "Damn, Lefty, you'd better clean your glasses."

"Ain't wearin' glasses," Lefty informed him. "Batter up!"

Rook repeated his ritual, this time crouching even lower, while his teammates urged him on.

A couple of younger boys jammed their fingers into their mouths to produce ear-splitting whistles, while the older of the two women, waiting to bat next, heckled the pitcher good-naturedly.

Hannah watched the windup, amazed at the way the pitcher was able to loop the ball high into the air before it leveled off at the plate.

Whack!

A cheer went up as Rook's bat made contact with the white sphere, sending it hurtling through the air.

Hannah was on her feet cheering with the rest of the team as Rook gave a rebel yell and started off around the bases. The softball landed in the tall grass beyond the outfield, and hadn't even been retrieved yet when Rook crossed home plate.

"A homer!" screamed one of the boys, as they all surged forward to congratulate Rook. Palms slapped against palms amid enthusiastic grunts of "All riiight!" and "Way to go, Rooker!"

Rook came straight toward Hannah, seizing her elbows in his hands and pulling her against him for a quick, hard kiss. Before she could speak, his action prompted a flood of catcalls and teasing remarks from the others.

"Wow, Rook, is this your woman?" The question came from a long-haired boy, who watched them with interest.

"She sure is," Rook answered easily. "Hannah, this is Billy."

Their conversation was disrupted by the umpire's shout. "Batter up!"

The game was resumed, with Rook settling on the bench beside Hannah to point out the boys one by one, telling her their names. Suddenly his relaxed banter faded as he spied one of the younger boys sitting in the grass at the end of the bench, a glum expression on his freckled face.

"Excuse me a second," Rook muttered, getting up to make his way toward the boy. "Hey, Tim, what's up?"

Hannah watched as he knelt beside the boy. "The others said I couldn't bat 'cause I ain't no good."

"Shoot, they were just teasing you, Tim. You know the rules—everyone who plays gets to bat. Come on, looks like it's your turn next."

The boy looked at Rook in surprise. "But what if I make an out? We could lose the game."

"It's just a game, Tim—we can't win 'em all. Besides, I don't think you'll make an out."

"Will you show me how you hold the bat?" Tim asked uncertainly. "Brian says I hold it wrong..."

Rook rose and reached out for a bat, pausing a moment to send a word of encouragement to the boy now at the plate. Then he turned back to Tim, who stood gaping up at him, his eyes full of hero worship.

"First thing you've got to remember, Tim, is not to grip the bat too high. Put your hands here...and here. Yeah, like that. Now..."

Hannah sighed. Right before her eyes, the man she thought of as pampered and self-centered was turning out to be a kind, caring human being. Damn, he had no right! How much easier it would be to immure herself against him if he didn't keep providing these little insights into his real character. She recalled his concern over the cold, wet calf the night of the storm, and thought now of his unfeigned delight in showing an uncertain young boy how to hold a bat!

Thumbs hooked in the rear pockets of his shorts, Rook watched Tim approach the plate; he called out some last-minute advice and nodded encouragingly.

Moments later, Tim hit the ball past the third baseman and Rook leaped into the air, waving his arms and blaring, "Go! Go!"

Even when a runner going to third was thrown out to end the inning, Tim was received as a hero. He jogged back to the bench, his face wreathed in smiles.

"I did it!" he cried. "I hit the ball!"

"Way to go, buddy," Rook said. "Give me five."

Amazed at the camaraderie sports inspired in men, Hannah looked on serenely—until Rook tossed a worn baseball glove her way and motioned toward the outfield.

"Better get out there, Hannah."

"But..."

He had seized his own glove and was walking away, a hand on Tim's shoulder as they recounted the exact details of the boy's hit.

"They'll be doing instant replays all evening," laughed Dusty, falling into step with Hannah.

"Yes, I can imagine."

"Rook is damned good with these boys," the lanky hired hand stated, in an almost defensive tone. "They all think the world of him."

"Who are they?" Hannah looked up at him.

"They're from a boys' ranch up by Augusta. It's a home for wayward boys—you know, boys that have been in trouble with the law or the ones who don't fit into foster homes."

"What's the connection with Rook?"

"He's just made them his special project, I guess you could say. He likes to spend time with them, either at the ranch or out here. He has the whole bunch out several times a year."

Hannah smiled. "I must admit I'm amazed."

"Amazed?"

"It's difficult to get used to the idea of Rook McAllister as a benevolent big brother."

"It doesn't...upset you, does it?"

"Upset me? Why should it? Actually, I'm rather impressed."

"Most of the women Rook has dated have been a little jealous of the time and money he spends on the boys. Thought you might feel the same way."

Hannah gave him a severe look. "For one thing, I hope I'd never be petty enough to be jealous of whatever someone else is willing to do for underprivileged youngsters. That would take a pretty small human being. And another thing, I should tell you that Rook and I are not dating."

"Hmm, that's odd," Dusty commented. "I thought you were getting pretty friendly."

"Has Rook said something?"

"Hey, you two! Are you gonna stand there and chat all day or are we gonna play ball?"

Startled, Hannah looked up to see the umpire glaring at them. Hastily she fled to the section of the outfield to which Dusty directed her. From his position as shortstop, Rook grinned and waved, then turned his attention to the batter.

Hannah was on edge for the first two batters, but when one walked and the second hit a fly ball that Dusty easily caught, she began to relax. As Rook said, all she had to do was fill a spot in the lineup.

Not even in her wildest daydream had she ever pictured herself standing in the middle of a baseball diamond, a clumsy glove on her hand and a borrowed ball cap on her head. Strange, but when Rook had invited her to a barbecue she had had something entirely different in mind....

The scene was faintly reminiscent of the barbecue in Gone with the Wind. *Hannah, dressed in sprigged muslin with enormous hoop skirts, sat beneath an oak tree on a green velvet lawn that unrolled right to the front steps of a beautiful Southern mansion. Gathered around her was every eligible man in the county, each vying for her attention. A handsome blond was handing her a plate heaped with food, a dashing redhead was offering her a frosted mint julep. A tall man with dark hair obligingly held her parasol. And then, striding into their midst, dressed in the elegant gray uniform of the Confederate Army was Matthew. His sardonic glance, the casual way he removed the thin cheroot from his mouth, the enchanting smile with which he favored her—all made the other men around her seem nothing more than callow youths. Brushing them aside, she rose. He whispered her name....*

"Hannah! Hannah! For God's sake, look out!"

Dusty and Rook were both racing toward her, Rook shouting her name as he ran. She saw Dusty catch his foot in a clump of grass and be sent sprawling, and then suddenly she was only aware of the huge white spheroid looming before her. She screamed once, covered her head and ducked. There was a rush of noise—the thudding of feet, the rasp of denim, an agonized groan—and something hurtled into her.

Hannah lay still for a long moment, breathless beneath the heavy weight lying across her body. Cautiously she opened one eye . . . and met one of Rook's looking back.

"What do you think you are doing?" It sounded as if the words were squeezed out of her.

"I was trying to keep you from getting hurt," he snapped.

"I don't think your plan worked."

"Why didn't you move out of the way when we started yelling at you?"

"I . . . I guess I didn't hear you."

"You just stood there like a zombie. God, I thought you were going to get hit right in the head."

"Would that have been more painful than being crushed?" she ground out.

He raised himself onto his elbows and glared down at her. "You reacted just like a woman! Stood there staring at the damned ball and then at the last minute screamed and covered your head."

"What else was I supposed to do? I didn't see the stupid ball coming."

"Why not? You were looking right at it. It was like you'd fallen asleep or something."

"Well, it doesn't matter, does it? I mean, don't you think you should get off of me and put an end to the sideshow? It seems everyone is staring."

Rook glanced up. Indeed, not only his teammates, but the players from the other side had begun to gather around, some laughing, some still not certain that Hannah had not been seriously injured.

Rook got to his feet and held up his glove. Nestled deep within the webbing was the softball.

"Out three," he said dryly. "Game's over."

Hannah, wearing a two-piece swimsuit of flaming red, agreed to meet Rook at poolside.

She was almost sorry she had. The sight of him in abbreviated black swim trunks made it very difficult for her to retain a ladylike poise and not simply stand and stare. Why couldn't he have been one of those guys who liked to swim in baggy surfer shorts?

When she thought about it, however, her strong reaction to Rook's well-displayed masculinity made sense. Of course! She was merely having a physical response prompted by months and months of total abstinence. She hadn't realized she had gotten to this stage, but now she knew she would probably feel the same about any reasonably good-looking man who chose to appear in public half naked.

They were greeted with enthusiasm by the others, and Hannah glanced warily at the churning water. There seemed to be boys everywhere, swimming, splashing, diving, and battling over four fat inner tubes.

"Hannah," Rook said severely, "did you buy this swimsuit at the Smithsonian?"

"It's not that old-fashioned," she said with a laugh.

He walked around her in a circle, his eyes sliding up and down her body. "Well, basically, it's a fine suit, but it does seem to have a surplus of material. Come on in the water, maybe it will shrink."

Hannah tried to swim a few laps, but there were so many bodies that it became an obstacle course. Then, when the game of water volleyball Rook was trying to organize, turned into an impromptu game of "Shark," she made a hasty retreat. She found a seat at a table shaded by a striped umbrella, and from that vantage point watched the antics of Rook and his young friends.

"My son sometimes acts more like a ten-year-old now than when he was one."

Mrs. McAllister slipped into the seat next to Hannah and handed her a frosty glass of lemonade.

"I wanted to sit and rest a minute," she explained, taking a sip from her own glass. "And I thought you looked like you could use something to drink."

"Thanks."

"Are you having a good time?"

"Yes," Hannah replied, surprised to realize she actually was. Large crowds were ordinarily not her thing, but today she hadn't had much time to notice how many people were milling about the grounds. Since her arrival, every moment had been devoted to Rook and his craziness. "You have a beautiful home . . . really beautiful."

"How nice of you to say so. I'm quite proud of it." Mrs. McAllister smiled indulgently as three of Rook's young companions exerted all their strength to dunk him. "Of course, to Winston, it's just a house. A place to hang his hat—all three dozen of them—and entertain his friends."

"I understand he does a lot of that," Hannah remarked, absently. "Dusty tells me he manages to do a great deal for these boys. It's plain to see they love him."

"More importantly, he loves them. They've given him the opportunity to relive his own childhood . . . to make up for the things he missed."

"I don't mean to sound rude, but what on earth could Rook have possibly missed growing up surrounded by all this?"

"I'm ashamed to admit it, but my son grew up without one very essential thing—the love of a father."

"But he had a father," Hannah began.

"Oh, yes, he had a father, all right. But one who didn't have the time or patience for him."

For a moment, Mrs. McAllister's expression lost its usual sweet vagueness and Hannah got a glimpse of hidden strength. "Winston's father was concerned with one thing: making money. His ambition—greed, if you prefer—left little time for anything else in his life. Making deals on land or drilling for oil were more important to him than his own son." She sighed, her eyes following Rook as he gave a skinny redheaded lad a lesson in swimming. "Winston did everything he could to get his father's attention. He made good grades, excelled in sports, joined every club. In the end, none of it mattered, J.W. always found fault. An *A* in history was worthless, better be studying geology. Lettering in varsity sports was a waste of time, he should have devoted that energy to learning stocks and bonds. He never approved of Winston's friends, never liked his hobbies. But mainly he just never had time to notice how the boy nearly killed himself trying for approval . . . or even a kind word."

"And so Rook has adopted these kids," Hannah murmured, "in an attempt to show *them* that someone cares. That they have someone's interest and attention."

"I believe that's the reason. And of course most of these boys either do not have fathers or the relationship is less than ideal. My son likes to think he makes a difference."

"From what I've seen today, I think he does, too."

Mrs. McAllister smiled gently. "Winston doesn't like to talk about his struggle for J.W.'s affection, so I usually don't say anything. But I wanted to tell you because I believe you will be someone very important to him. I thought it might help you to understand him a little better."

"I'm glad you told me, Mrs. McAllister. In a way, it explains several things."

"Call me Helen, won't you? I think we are going to be great friends."

The two women exchanged a long, assessing look. "I hope we will be," Hannah said, meaning it.

"Now, tell me about your cottage. How are the rose-bushes doing?"

Wonderfully enticing aromas drifted through the open window from the barbecue pits below. Hannah laid aside the blow dryer, ran a brush through her hair and stepped in front of a full-length mirror to check her appearance.

After a refreshing shower, she had changed into the khaki-green sundress and loose, jungle-print jacket she intended to wear for supper and the dance to follow. Frowning, she saw that her nose and cheeks were slightly pink and knew a crop of dreaded freckles could not be far behind. Well, so much for glamour...

As she left the borrowed bedroom she was stricken with a sudden impulse to see what Rook's room looked like. Could it possibly reveal anything more of the man to her?

She glanced up and down the hall; no one was in sight. She had left Rook frolicking in the pool; he would probably be occupied for a while longer. If she dashed in and out surely she could make at least a cursory inspection.

The room was large and at first glance as tidy as a hotel suite. Dark wood, forest-green carpeting and bold blue-and-green tartan made it clearly masculine.

The only clue that the room was occupied at all was the trail of discarded clothing scattered from the bed to a closed door she assumed led to a bathroom. Hannah recognized the yellow shirt and jean shorts Rook had been wearing earlier. She rapidly averted her eyes from a pair of crumpled red jockey shorts and in so doing noticed a door leading into an adjoining room.

Curious, she walked into the room, which was barely more than an alcove. The only article of furniture was a scarred rolltop desk and chair; the walls were lined with shelves that contained books and photos and trophies of every sort imaginable. A framed board held a variety of ribbons from county and state fairs.

Her gaze traveled over the rows of books, noting the range of selections—from classics to current best-sellers. He had even held on to some boyhood favorites. The paperback novels he had purchased that day at the Bookworm were stacked on the desktop, one of them lying open. So he was reading them, after all.

Turning to leave the room, Hannah's attention was captured by a large, framed portrait of a man. She knew at once it had to be J. W. McAllister. The painting, done in oils, was of a large man standing beside a stone fence, gazing off into the distance at what was presumably his own private land. He was dressed in casual western attire, with a big Stetson hat and boots that sported his personal brand. There was no mistaking the aura of power about him, or his look of fierce, possessive pride.

It seemed significant that this painting should dominate the entire wall, when elsewhere in the room there was not a single photo of the man and his son.

"Miserable bastard," she muttered, as she swept out the door.

"I beg your pardon?"

Hannah found herself face to face with Rook, who was nude except for the bath towel draped loosely about his hips.

"Oh!" Words failed her.

"I was about to take a shower when I thought I heard a noise." He grinned. "But, honey, I explained about my mama being in the house. I'm real flattered if you've sneaked in here to attack me, but . . . well, the Boss frowns on that sort of thing. Especially when we have other guests."

"I guess I've been caught trespassing, huh? Sorry about that."

"No problem. Of course it does raise interesting questions. Like, what were you looking for?"

Hannah raised her chin. "If you must know, I was looking for some clue to the real Rook McAllister."

"Are you sure there is such an animal?" he asked.

"I'm beginning to wonder. Just when I think I've learned a few of your secrets . . ."

"And just what secrets are those?"

"Can't tell. They're secrets, after all."

"I could force you to tell me," he teased, stalking toward her, his face breaking into a wide grin. "In fact, it might provide a very pleasant interlude."

She backed away. "Don't you try anything funny," she warned. "And for God's sake, hang on to that towel!"

"Did you realize you are constantly running away from me?"

"I'm not."

"Are, too. But, Hannah, something tells me the time is coming when you won't always be able to make a successful escape."

Ignoring the gentle threat of his words, she said, "I promised your mother I'd help with the serving."

She reached the door to the hall and wrenched it open. Helen McAllister stood there, hand raised to knock on her son's door. When she saw Hannah she smiled pleasantly, not at all distressed to see her.

"Hello, Hannah dear," she beamed. "I was just coming to remind Winston he needs to pay the beer man."

Rook favored them both with his most entrancing smile. "Don't worry, Mama," he said sweetly, "I've already explained to Hannah how you feel about my being ravished under your roof. She has agreed to wait."

Hannah uttered an indignant squeak and fled down the stairs.

Supper was a spirited affair. The guests ate their way through mounds of grilled steaks, baked potatoes, green salad and sourdough bread. Apple and cherry pies were served for dessert, and when Rook presented Hannah with a piece of the cherry pie, he couldn't resist at least one wicked remark.

"Shall I put this to the torch? I nearly forgot that you prefer *fancy* desserts."

She tried not to smile. "You're treading on very thin ice, McAllister."

"I love living dangerously." The caressing look in his black eyes gave her a jolt. The events of this day had very effectively peeled away all the layers of self-protection she had struggled to build up. With a sigh, she knew she was going to have to start all over again. She really couldn't afford to get too caught up in the man and all he represented.

Throughout the meal, Rook had lavished attention on his guests from the boys' ranch, and the reason soon became apparent. Rules dictated that the boys obey a nine-o'clock curfew and as soon as supper ended they were loaded onto their bus by the two ranch officials who accompanied them. As he said goodbye, Rook reminded them of their next outing, a trip to the city, and then with a roar the bus was gone.

"I'm very impressed with your interest in those boys," Hannah said quietly as they walked toward the backyard.

"Somebody needs to give them a break," he said tersely.

Now she understood those few words much better than she would have earlier. With chagrin, she also realized she was not only beginning to like Rook McAllister a great deal, she was beginning to respect and admire him, as well. Soon—very soon, she feared—she might be in over her head.

The thought was more than a little frightening.

*   *   *

All day long Hannah had been expecting a barrage of females to bear down on Rook; it was at the dance that they
appeared.

"Ha, you should have known those bimbos wouldn't
show up until after the ball games and swimming were
over," Janice said. With distaste, she eyed the taffy-haired
blonde who had commandeered a dance with Rook. "They
might smudge their mascara or muss their hair."

Hannah laughed. "Rook doesn't seem too perturbed."

"He's a man—he doesn't know any better."

There was absolutely no doubt about Rook's being a
man, all right. He had looked positively virile all day. Now,
in jeans and a short-sleeved cowboy shirt, he looked dis-
turbingly attractive. Hannah's reverie was interrupted by a
hand laid lightly on her arm.

"Hello, Miss Grant. I'm Gerald Overton. Unfortunately, I haven't had a chance to speak to you before."

"How do you do."

"Would you care to dance?"

"I . . . all right."

Hannah soon learned that the stocky man in the impec-
cable gray suit was a local banker, the one, he told her
smugly, whose family had always handled the McAllister
accounts. He claimed a lifelong friendship with Rook, but
any sign of mutual admiration was lost in the brief exchange that took place when Rook disengaged himself from
a pretty brunette and cut in on them.

"Hi, Moneybags," he drawled, irreverently. "You don't
mind if I claim my girl, do you?"

"As a matter of fact . . ."

Rook whirled her away, leaving Overton speaking to
himself.

"That was rude," she scolded, resisting a smile. "I
thought the two of you were friends."

"Even friendship has its limits," he said enigmatically.

Hannah had never danced beneath the starry night sky
before; the effects of the pale moonlight and cool wind were
exhilarating. Despite the fact that Rook held her tightly
against him, he moved easily in time to the music provided

by a complicated stereo system. Before long, Hannah felt herself relax, her head resting on Rook's chest. Something urged her to give up her resistance to his charm.

Just for tonight, a tiny imp inside her head wheedled. Enjoy yourself now. You can be strong tomorrow.

"Hannah," came Rook's voice, low and intense. "You're slipping away from me again."

"Mmm?"

"Just when I think I'm making progress with you, you go away somewhere I can't follow."

"I'm sorry," she murmured, looking up at him. "Maybe you should give me a good reason to stay here."

He grinned broadly. "My pleasure."

His arms tightened around her waist as he bent his head to hers, the brim of the western hat he wore creating a small, intimate darkness for the kiss they shared.

After a moment, he raised his head. "One of these days, Hannah, we're going to have to watch the sun come up together."

From habit, her rebellious mind retreated from the warm, soft sound of his voice.

"Who's that singing?" she whispered.

"Hank Williams, Jr.," he replied, resuming his slow exploration of her mouth. "This song is one of my favorites—'Blues Man.'"

"Mmm . . . nice."

"*Hey, baby, I love you,*
Hey, baby, I need you . . . '

Locked in each other's arms, they forgot the song, forgot to dance. They stood in one spot, swaying together, lost in a kiss that seemed as mysterious and endless as the star-swept night above.

With morning came a certain amount of reason. The barbecue had only confirmed Hannah's notion that she was running scared and that Rook was in hot pursuit. At this moment, nothing seemed as vital to her as getting back to the safety of her cottage where she would have time to think, to plan her next move. Time to digest all that she had learned about Rook McAllister in the last day.

She hurried down the stairs, overnight bag in hand. She had a quick breakfast by the pool, and then Hannah thanked Rook's mother and told her goodbye, while he had gone to get the truck so he could drive her home. And suddenly she felt as if she couldn't get there fast enough. It was simply too dangerous to remain in Rook's world a minute longer.

She hurled herself through the kitchen toward the back door, just as Rook strode in. They collided with a jolt, and though he threw steadying arms about her, her purse and suitcase went flying. The suitcase burst open, scattering clothes over the kitchen floor.

Hannah dropped to her knees and began shoving articles of clothing back into the bag. Gradually, she became aware of Rook standing beside her, one hand extended.

Questioningly, she glanced up and was startled to see a teasing look in his eyes.

Lying upon his open palm was a round plastic compact containing a dated circle of pills.

"Oh, damn," she mumbled, snatching up the compact. She tossed it into the suitcase and snapped the lock.

Taking the case from her, Rook turned and walked out the door, whistling innocently.

Chapter Seven

Following the barbecue, Hannah felt like a mouse waiting for the cat to pounce. Now that Rook knew her little secret, she worried incessantly about what his reaction would be. Did he think there really was another man? Would he now feel he had every right to do his damnedest to seduce her? She wasn't sure she could trust herself to be impervious to his considerable charm any longer.

But, like a master tactician, Rook suddenly withdrew from the field, making no effort to confront her for the best part of a week, cleverly using the interval to regroup his forces. Then, just when Hannah had not only relaxed her guard, but had actually begun to wonder why he had not commenced the expected pursuit, he made his move.

It was nearly five o'clock in the morning when, in that vulnerable state between waking and sleeping, Hannah found herself drifting into one of the fantasies that had always sustained her. The face that appeared before her was Matthew's but the voice was Rook's. . . .

"One of these days, Hannah, we're going to have to watch the sun come up together."

They were dancing, whirling slowly down the length of a marble-floored ballroom, the lilting strains of a Strauss waltz filling her mind. Matthew's intensely blue eyes gazed down into hers. Long, narrow windows at one side of the room stood open to admit fresh, damp air, while outside, the stars were rapidly fading from a predawn sky. Overhead, hundreds of prisms shimmering from the crystal chandeliers replaced the stars....

They had danced the entire night away, Hannah realized, marveling because she didn't feel the least bit tired. Matthew's nearness provoked a thrilling vitality; she thought she could go on waltzing until the end of time.

But Matthew, with a sweetly sensual smile, whispered into her ear that he was weary of dancing, and swept her into his arms. The gown she wore, long and flowing, shot through with glittering silver threads, trailed on the floor behind them as he carried her up a long flight of stairs to a room dominated by a huge bed, its gauzy draperies floating in the flower-scented breeze.

Matthew settled her in a cushioned window seat, pointing out the faint sheen of sunrise in the eastern sky. Palest lavender shadowed the horizon, where delicate streaks of gold were beginning to etch their way upward.

Seemingly from nowhere, he produced two glasses of iced champagne and a porcelain basket of fresh sliced peaches.

"To you, love," Matthew intoned, raising his glass. "To...us."

The champagne was cool and tart against her tongue. When she bit into a slice of peach, Matthew leaned forward to kiss the sweet juiciness from her lips, the flavors of fruit and wine mingling deliciously.

With gentle, trembling fingers, Matthew brushed the gown from her shoulders and she shivered as the cool air caressed her skin, followed by the heated touch of his mouth. Over his shoulder she could see the sun as it began a languid ascent into morning.

With murmured endearments, Matthew rose and, taking her hand, led her away to the bed. As his impatient body bore her down onto the silken coverlet, she sighed deeply An errant shaft of sunlight stroked her closed eyelids....

Hannah groaned and turned her head on the pillow. Suddenly her eyes flew open.

Light! Someone was shining a light in her eyes!

She sat up in bed, struggling to hold back the scream that was rising in her throat. The beam of a flashlight coming through the bedroom window remained steady, though now that she was sitting upright, instead of shining in her eyes, it was focused on the gaping front of her nightshirt, which rose and fell with her terrified breathing.

"Hannah, it's me—Rook. Let me in!"

Rook? Lord, she might have known!

"What do you want?" she yelled crossly.

"Go unlock the door and I'll tell you."

"Is something wrong?"

Her question went unanswered, the ensuing darkness telling her he had already started toward the front door. With a surge of temper, she tossed aside the covers and leaped out of bed, switching on lights as she went.

"What do you think you are doing?" she raged, yanking the door open. "You almost scared me to death! I thought you were some kind of pervert."

Rook's calm smile was infuriating. "I knocked several times, Hannah. I guess you didn't hear me. I got worried about you."

"I was perfectly all right until you shined that fool light in my eyes. I almost had a heart attack!"

"I'm sorry," he apologized, with a laugh. "I didn't stop to think that I might scare you. In fact, I just supposed you would know it was me."

"Now, how on earth would I have known that?" Hannah put her hands on her hips and glared at him.

"I gave you fair warning the other night at the dance."

"Fair warning of what? That you might go completely over the hill and show up here in the middle of the night like . . . like some depraved maniac?"

"We'll just have to discuss my depravity another time. We've got to hurry now."

"Hurry?" She threw her hands into the air. "What are you talking about?"

"It's a little after five already. If we're going to make it, we've got to get a move on."

"Make it?"

He grinned. "To see the sun come up, Hannah. Remember? I suggested we do that some time."

"But I thought you meant stay up all night. You know, like normal people!"

"Honey, in Kansas normal people who want to see the sunrise get up early. I take it that that isn't how it's done in New York?"

"God, no! No one sane would get out of bed at this hour."

He kicked the door shut behind him. "You're right. Why should we waste time outside in the cold when we can be absolutely... *normal* staying right here in bed?"

"Stop where you are!" she warned, putting out a restraining hand. "All of a sudden, I have an uncontrollable urge to see the sun come up over the prairie!"

His smile tilted rakishly. "Ah, yes, those uncontrollable urges. Aren't they the damnedest things?"

"You wait here and I'll get dressed," she said, ignoring him.

"Only if you insist. You look mighty cute in that little striped nightshirt."

"Sit!" she commanded, pointing to a chair. "I'll be back in a minute."

Nervously aware of Rook's presence in the next room, Hannah hastily donned a pair of jeans and a sweatshirt, taking only enough time to brush her teeth and run a comb through her hair. She had just grabbed a pair of warm socks and her tennis shoes when a shadow loomed in the doorway and she looked up to see Rook standing there.

"About ready?" he asked casually, though there was nothing casual in the look he leveled at her rumpled bed.

Several tantalizing thoughts leaped into her own mind, causing her to croak, "Ready?"

"To go?" he said, wrenching his gaze away from the cozy temptation of pillows and blankets.

"I . . . I still have to put on my shoes and socks," she replied. "I'll do that in the living room."

"Good idea." He stood aside to let her leave the room, then switched off the light with a heavy sigh and one last quick glance at the bed.

Hannah sat down on the couch and started pulling on one of her socks. This outing was going to be a mistake, she just knew it, but good heavens, they couldn't stay here!

Rook dropped down beside her. "Here, I'll help," he offered, taking the sock from her hand. "It works better if you put it on from the open end."

"Oh!"

I've got to pull myself together, she thought. There is simply no need to become so darned rattled just because of this one bothersome man.

Her good intentions dissipated immediately as Rook's warm fingers closed about the arch of her foot.

"You feel like an ice cube," he exclaimed, briskly rubbing her foot in his hands.

"What do you expect?" she managed to ask. "Dragged out of bed at this ungodly hour!"

He leaned forward, gently bending her leg—the only barrier between them—until his face was just inches from hers. "Remember, sweetheart, I offered you the option of going back to bed. If you're ready to reconsider...?"

She found herself looking into his teasing eyes, thinking they weren't really black at all, but a deep, dark, *dark* brown. Suddenly she straightened her leg, pushing him away.

"I'd love to see the sunrise," she said pointedly. "And I'm capable of putting on my own shoes!"

Wrenching her foot from his grasp, she hurriedly demonstrated that fact beneath his amused gaze, then jumped to her feet to seize the jacket hanging on a coatrack near the door.

"I'm ready," she announced.

"So am I!" he agreed, heartily enough to make her face flame. She turned abruptly and slammed out the door.

It was just beginning to be light enough for her to see that Rook had driven the old pickup this morning. He opened the door and handed her in, then strode around to the driver's side. He had left the motor running, so the cab of the truck was comfortably warm.

"I know a place a couple of miles from here where we will have a marvelous view of the sunrise," he said, shifting gears and backing the pickup around. "We ought to get there with about thirty minutes to spare."

"Thirty minutes," Hannah groaned. "What will we do for thirty minutes?"

Oh, bite your tongue, she silently scolded herself.

Rook shot her a pleased look. "I've got something special in mind."

"I'll just bet you have," she retorted.

He frowned. "Hannah, as usual, you wrong me. What do you have against eating breakfast?"

"Breakfast? You brought breakfast?"

"Well, sure. What else did you think I meant?"

"No comment," she muttered, turning to look out her window at the darkly shadowed prairie.

After a short drive down the gravel road, Rook turned the truck into a rutted lane that wound across a pasture, then spiraled upward to the crest of a squat, flat-topped hill, sparsely covered with a thicket of cedars. He maneuvered the pickup into place, backing it expertly between two clumps of trees.

"Wait a minute, Rook. The sky is getting light behind us. How are we going to watch the sun come up facing this way?"

"We aren't, silly. When we get into the back, we're going to be facing the right direction. Come on."

He took her hand and pulled her across the seat with him, then scooped her up and dumped her into the bed of the truck. Just as she opened her mouth to register an indignant complaint, she realized she had landed on a soft surface. Sleeping bags! Rook had filled the truck bed with downy sleeping bags.

"Oh-oh," she said, scrambling to her feet.

Rook threw his long legs over the side of the truck and landed beside her. "Relax, Hannah. This isn't the 'grand seduction,' you know."

"No," she agreed wryly, "there certainly isn't anything grand about it!"

"It isn't a seduction, at all," he stated impatiently. "In case you haven't noticed, it's pretty damned chilly out here. I just thought you'd like to be warm while we're having breakfast and waiting for the sun to come up."

"Oh."

"If it makes you feel any better, you can have your own sleeping bag. Take that blue one." He turned away to unearth a picnic hamper from the mound of sleeping bags. "Why you women think men have only one thing on their minds, I'll never know. Lord, what makes you think I could possibly be thinking of sex at a time like this?"

Hannah unzipped the blue bag and crawled into it, resting her back against the cab wall. "I'm sorry, Rook. I guess it has become a habit to expect . . . well, to expect the worst of you."

His eyes were so shadowed by the perpetual cowboy hat that she couldn't read their expression, but she thought his voice held a touch of hurt. "I know, and I guess it's my own fault."

"Look, I'm sorry I was so accusing. Can't we just pretend this conversation never happened and start over again?"

There was no mistaking the smile behind his words this time. "You've got yourself a deal. Here, have some orange juice."

She accepted the Styrofoam cup he filled from a thermal carafe and couldn't prevent a tiny smile. Styrofoam—when only a short time before she had been dreaming of iced champagne in crystal. Why did reality have to be so mundane?

Rook set out paper plates, napkins and a Tupperware bowl of chilled melon balls. "Hey, I almost forgot something," he said, shoving the hamper out of his way and diving over the side of the truck. "Be right back."

Whistling, he disappeared and in a moment, Hannah heard the rusty protest of hinges as he raised the hood of the pickup. This was followed by a muttered "Ouch!" and a metallic crash as he closed the hood again. When he rejoined her, he was juggling an aluminum foil-wrapped package in his hands.

"What on earth . . . ?" Hannah began.

"Cinnamon rolls," he replied, dumping the package and settling himself beside her. "Our cook makes the best homemade rolls in four counties, so I begged some for our breakfast. Then I used an old trick Dusty taught me and heated 'em on the manifold."

"The manifold? What's that?"

He slid one of the huge, steaming rolls onto a paper plate and handed it to her. "It's the pipe between the carburetor and the engine. Dusty wired an old baking pan to it and we use it all the time when we're out. Did you know it's possible to cook a beef roast that way?"

Hannah had to laugh. "Either you are ingenious or you're the worst liar I've ever met."

"I'm not surprised you haven't heard of such a thing. I don't suppose you city people have much use for ideas like that."

"No, not ordinarily. Well, the rolls are delicious, no matter how you heated them."

Rook chewed thoughtfully. "You know, Hannah, someday you're going to learn something about me. I always say what I mean and I never lie."

"Very commendable," she said lightly, but instantly her mind was flooded with the recollection of the many audacious things he'd said to her since their first meeting. Uneasy, she directed his attention to the eastern sky. "Look, it must be getting close to sunrise."

All along the unbroken line of horizon, the sky was flushed with a shell-pink color, which deepened to rose at the point where the sun would soon appear. A faint wash of gold overlaid the pink, gilding the bottom edge of the few fragments of cloud drifting above, bouncing the color back to earth to spill across the empty prairieland.

"It's going to be pretty, all right. Of course, it can't compare to one of our winter sunsets—they're the prettiest thing you'd ever hope to see. Yessir, Colorado may have its Rockies and Arizona its Grand Canyon, but Kansas has the most beautiful winter sunsets anywhere."

With surprise, Hannah glanced over at Rook. With one thumb, he pushed his cowboy hat farther back on his head and looked a little defiant. "Yes, it's true—even insensitive clods like me can appreciate the beauties of nature."

"Did I say you were an insensitive clod?" she queried.

A dimple appeared in one cheek. "You must have. You've called me everything else."

She tossed her head. "Not quite. If challenged, I could probably come up with one or two new labels."

"I've no doubt." He put their empty plates back into the hamper, taking out a Thermos and two plastic cups. "Are you cold? How about some hot chocolate?"

"Sounds good." She watched as he poured out the chocolate, adding marshmallows from a bag inside the hamper. "Good heavens, you thought of everything, didn't you?"

"It probably comes from camping out so much when I was young," he said, capping the Thermos and putting it away. He moved the hamper to one side, then leaned back to sip his own hot chocolate. "Tell me, have you ever done anything like this before?"

"Not even remotely."

Rook's gaze took on an amused glint. "So? A whole new experience, huh?"

"Are you kidding?" She laughed. "Everything is a new experience with you."

A different sort of light kindled in his dark eyes, and she silently cursed herself for her ill-considered statement. Knowing his mind, he would put entirely the wrong interpretation on that remark!

Rook leaned forward to set his chocolate on the hamper. "Hannah..."

She tipped the cup she held and took a hasty drink. "Mmm, good hot chocolate," she assured him. He moved closer and she shrank away, taking another sip. Over the rim, her eyes were huge and wary.

When at last she lowered the cup, Rook reached out and took it, placing it out of the way beside his own.

"Uh, it must be almost sun-up," she stalled.

He studied her for a long moment. "You have a marshmallow mustache," he teased with a slow half smile.

"Oh, great!" Hannah fumbled for a paper napkin, feeling absurdly childish. She dabbed inefficiently at her mouth until he took the napkin from her.

"Here, let me."

Embarrassed but obedient, Hannah lifted her chin and closed her eyes. Her mind was busy with ways to handle the situation. She felt a certain tension between them, as well as an impending sense that something monumental was going to occur unless she could ward it off. A traitorous little voice in the back of her brain asked, Do you really want to ward it off? That same voice reminded her that a man who relished watching sunrises and sunsets was a cut above average....

One of Rook's hands crept up under her hair to close around the back of her neck and at the same time she felt his touch on her lips. Her eyes flew open in shock. Instead of the napkin, he was using a much more primitive means of removing the sticky marshmallow from her mouth, stroking his tongue along the edge of her upper lip.

"Mmm, good hot chocolate," he whispered, his other hand sliding up the front of her jacket to cup her chin and draw her face closer to his. His mouth descended again, delivering warm, moist, nibbling kisses.

Hannah found her own hands clutching the lapels of his denim jacket, then slipping inside, drawn by the warmth of the sheepskin lining. When she felt his hand move inside her own coat, she began to shiver uncontrollably.

"You're cold," Rook muttered, drawing back to look into her face. "Hannah ... sweetheart, let me warm you."

Her eyes fell before his compelling gaze, and she buried her face against his chest. Her throat felt so constricted she could barely breathe, and she knew beyond doubt her heart was hammering loudly enough for him to hear it.

She realized Rook had taken her lack of reply for acquiescence when she heard the rasp of a zipper. She couldn't resist a swift peek.

His laugh was low, throaty. "I'm only getting into this sleeping bag with you, love."

"I knew that," she choked, blushing. "What else would you be doing? I just wondered ... is there enough room?"

Tossing his hat aside, he kicked off his boots and climbed in beside her, deftly pulling the zipper upward again. "Luckily, it's a double sleeping bag."

"How convenient! No wonder you suggested I take it."

"Oh, no, you don't, Hannah. I'm not going to let you get sarcastic now, of all times."

With that warning, he hauled her back into his arms and resumed the pillage of her mouth. Deep within the sleeping bag, his long legs entangled with hers, one of his stocking-clad feet beginning a slow, sensual rub up and down her calf. Alarmed, she pressed the palms of her hands against his chest and pushed, but he only tightened his hold on her. She wriggled within his grip and heard his low moan as he ground his body even closer.

She wrenched her mouth from his, gasping, "What are you doing, Rook? I'm . . . I'm warm enough now."

His breath was hot against her ear as he gave a strained laugh. "You're telling me!" He kissed her again. "Let's get out of these coats."

Struggling upright, he straddled her body to shrug out of his jean jacket and toss it aside. His maneuvers within the confines of the sleeping bag rendered her totally incapable of further protest, and as his hips twisted against her own, she felt the first insistent flutterings of lust—desire, she corrected primly—spring into being. It had been a long time since she had been in such a position. . . .

Pardon the pun, the silent imp in her mind chortled.

In a daze, she realized Rook was removing her own coat; he hurled it to the end of the truck bed and leaned over her again with deadly intent in his eyes.

"Rook . . . do you think this is wise?" she asked faintly.

"Ask me again later," he murmured, bracing a hand on either side of her head and lowering his mouth to hers.

She was upset that her traitorous lips submitted so willingly to his kiss; they became soft and compliant, shaping themselves to his demands as if they had no other purpose in life. Her mind reeled with the stunning awareness that she was losing control. She had never meant for such a thing to happen, but undeniably her body was sending forth clamorous requests for more of what he was offering.

Feeling the heat of his hand as it slipped beneath her sweatshirt and stroked bare skin, she thought, Oh, God, what *is* he doing?

"Rook, did you . . . did you . . . ?"

"Ply you with melon balls?" His mouth had inched its way to her earlobe, which he now tortured with tiny, tickling kisses.

"Just so you . . . uh . . . so you could . . . ?"

"Have my evil way with you?"

His tongue trailed a scorching line from her ear to the base of her neck.

She swallowed deeply, able only to nod feebly.

"Yes, sweetheart, what did you think?"

Beneath the fleecy sweatshirt, his hand swept upward to stroke and fondle one of her breasts. Her skin was so sensitive, she could feel the lace of her bra pressing into its softness under the slight roughness of his touch.

"Your scheme will . . . never work!" she moaned softly, attempting to twist away from the sweet havoc he was wreaking.

Rook inadvertently chose the single best method of subduing her. He rested his face against the curve of her neck and brushed a kiss onto that most vulnerable spot. Hannah was lost. A slow, delicious shudder began somewhere in the area of her toes and worked its way upward, leaving her flesh tingling, yearning—literally *aching* for fulfillment.

"Oh, you wretch!" she whispered, turning her face to his. "I never could resist a kiss on the neck . . . in just that spot!"

"You mean, like this?" He repeated the caress with a mouth that refused to stop smiling, and she arched her body into his. Once again he felt the sensation only Hannah gave him, that of being illuminated from within. It was as if his solar plexus was luxuriating in beams from his own personal sun.

Sun? he thought. Oh, yeah . . . sun!

"How's the sunrise coming?" he asked, distracted by the satiny feel of her breast impertinently springing to life against his palm.

She opened her eyes to look over his shoulder. "Hmm, good! I mean ... it's doing just fine," she managed to reply, galvanized by his boldness as he unsnapped her jeans.

Hannah's intended protest died a painless death, to be replaced by eagerness generated by another well-placed kiss on the neck. Suddenly she was abetting Rook's cause by easing out of her jeans and underwear, gladly kicking free of them. At the same time, she reached upward to grip the front of his shirt, gently pulling to release the snaps, baring his chest for a series of swift, heated kisses.

The look of disbelief on Rook's face quickly changed to one of sheer delight, and with a low exclamation of pleasure he began to rid himself of the encumbrance of his own clothing. As he turned back to wrap Hannah in his arms again, the feel of his naked, hair-roughened legs enclosing hers gave her a sharp thrill of pleasure.

With deliberation Rook slowed the pace, capturing her mouth in a long, stirring kiss as his hands roved over her, teasing and massaging, causing her long-suppressed passions to flare dangerously.

Hungrily impatient, her arms encircled his neck, drawing him down as she pressed even closer. With satisfaction, she heard his breathing become rushed and ragged, and then his hands were grasping her hips, urgently guiding her into the embrace she desired.

Her small cry of pleasure merged with his shaken growl, their breaths mingling steamily in the frosty air. Hannah welcomed surrender to his superior strength, marveling in his ability to use his overwhelming masculinity to reduce her to a quivering, mindless mass of wild emotion.

She could hear the low drone of Rook's voice in her ear, panting, "Oh, God ... Hannah ... oh, damn! Damn!" and answered him with soft, joyful cries of her own. She had forgotten how wonderful making love could be ... no—no, she had never known anything like this! Torn between the desire for completion and the hope that the incredible sensations she was experiencing would never end, she felt herself hurtling upward and outward, seeking ... reaching for and finding ... total, blinding, soul-wrenching ecstasy. With a hoarse cry, Rook's arms tightened convulsively and then he, too, stepped out into space and soared with her.

And behind them, in an explosion of brilliant red-gold beauty, the sun burst into glorious morning.

The chilly fingers of a brisk morning wind tangled the hair at Hannah's temples, causing her to sigh and burrow deeper into the sleeping bag, snuggling close to the warm body beside her.

Hannah stirred reluctantly, not wanting to disturb the heavenly lassitude that had fallen over her. She could not remember ever feeling so content, so lazily, drowsily replete. So satisfied.

Too wonderfully weary to open her eyes, she envisioned her surroundings—the dark, safe security of her own bedroom and the romantic curtained bed which, even in its current rumpled state, provided blessed privacy for herself and her lover. Her lover...

She put out her hand and Matthew was there, just as she had known he would be. In the most rapturous moment of their lovemaking, he'd promised never to leave her, and she had believed him. He was the only man she'd ever known worthy of her complete, unquestioning trust. And, she thought with a sigh, how lucky she was that he was also the only man who had ever inspired her to such heights of delirious passion. What they had experienced together had been more than a mere physical joining of their bodies; it had transcended the earthly plane, allowing them to soar together, their flight through the heavens melding their souls. They had become two wind-borne doves who had mated for life.

Hannah could feel the peaceful rise and fall of his chest beneath her hand, and of their own volition her fingers became restless, stroking and caressing the firm, smooth skin. Magically, she felt the sudden tensing of his muscles, the sweet acceleration of his heartbeat. No longer relaxed in sleep, his own hands curved around her shoulders, drawing her close. As always, his overwhelming presence shattered her thoughts, made her his willing slave.

"Oh, Matthew," she whispered. "Matthew..."

Hannah forced her eyes to open, immediately losing herself in the depths of a gaze as devoid of light as a midnight sky. To her horror, she found she was enfolded in Rook McAllister's embrace, half lying on him, while one hand boldly fondled his chest. Even more horrifying was the fact that one of her bare legs was thrown over his hips, with the proof of his approval plainly evident against her thigh.

My God, she thought wildly. What have I done? Oh, my God!

Rook favored her with a half smile and a quick kiss on one corner of the mouth. "I told you our sunrises were really special, didn't I?"

"I...I've got to go home," she muttered, struggling out of his grip to sit up.

Rook frowned. "Is something wrong?"

She groaned inwardly. Wrong? Good lord, yes, everything was wrong! What had she been thinking of?

She glanced about, taking in her surroundings with a sinking heart. She and Rook had fallen upon each other in the back of a rusty old pickup like two libidinous teenagers at a drive-in movie! It was humiliating; worse than that, it was tawdry.

"I just want to go home," she repeated in a quiet voice.

"Hannah...?"

She avoided looking at him, fishing for her clothing at the foot of the sleeping bag.

Rook unzipped the bag and silently located her jeans. On his second try, he found his own as well as the scrap of blue lace that was her underwear. Refusing to meet his eyes, she snatched the panties from his grasp, ignoring the faint chuckle she thought she heard. She turned away as, still within the sleeping bag, he began to struggle back into his jeans, and when he crawled out, standing up to zip them, she kept her gaze fixed determinedly on a hawk freewheeling in the morning sky.

"I'll leave you alone to dress, Hannah," he said gently, seizing his jacket and slipping over the side of the truck bed.

After a rapid check to make sure he really had gone, Hannah hastened into her clothing, her cheeks burning hotly as she recalled in great detail how quickly she had gotten out of it earlier. As soon as she stood up to put on her coat Rook was there, his hands lifted to help her out of the back and into the cab.

Neither of them spoke on the short ride to the cottage. Hannah hugged the door on the passenger side, staring out at the passing hedgerows. Rook, after several puzzled looks in her direction, concentrated on driving, the muscles in his jaw setting tighter and tighter.

At the door of the cottage, when she would simply have slipped inside, he caught her arm and drew her to him. "Thank you for the most wonderful breakfast of my life," he murmured, his deeply brown eyes searching her face. Softly he let his mouth caress hers, as though testing her reaction. He seemed at a loss as to how to interpret her current mood. "Our time together doesn't have to end now, you know."

"I...I really have a lot to do today," she lied, wishing he would go away.

"Such as?"

"Lots of things. I may go into town."

"As a matter of fact, I have an appointment in town myself. I was sort of hoping you'd like to go along. I'd treat you to another veal with chili at Fred's."

She took a deep breath and steeled herself against his wheedling smile. "Sorry, Rook, but I really do need to get some important things done today."

"All right," he conceded. "How about tonight? Can I see you then?"

"Well, I . . . I suppose so."

She was willing to promise anything just so he would leave. She needed to be alone to sort out the complicated mess in which she now found herself.

He leaned down to brush a kiss on her forehead. "Good. I'll look forward to this evening." With a final kiss on her lips he was gone, whistling jauntily as he threw himself into the old pickup and roared away.

Hannah watched until he was out of sight, her mouth tight with self-disapproval. How could she have sold out like that? How, with all her dreams of perfect romance, could she have settled for something as common as a Kansas cowboy and his rattletrap truck?

She spent the day mentally exorcising whatever madness it was that had gripped her, and in the late afternoon got into her car and drove to town. After shopping a couple of hours, she went to a movie, deciding to stay for the second feature which lasted until midnight.

When Rook arrived at the cottage shortly after sundown he found it dark, empty and definitely unwelcoming.

Chapter Eight

Three days had gone by since the sunrise breakfast she'd shared with Rook.

If only that had been all they'd shared, she thought with irony. If only she had not let herself get so carried away by meaningless physical gratification. If only...

Over and over, she had recounted the reasons why she should never have gotten that close to Rook McAllister in the first place. The trouble was, they were all good, valid reasons and always had been; it was just so appalling how easily he had overcome them.

Well, she told herself firmly, there is only one solution. Don't go near the man again. If you aren't strong enough to keep your hands off him, then avoid him at all costs.

She concentrated on Matthew, on the love-filled marriage her parents had shared and on the dreams she had long nurtured for her own romantic future. And she reminded herself that Rook's family had very probably cheated her grandmother out of a good deal of money. In sudden, silent lectures she warned herself that there was no place in her life for someone like him. No place, at all.

On the day following the fiasco at sunrise, as she moodily referred to it, Rook came to the cottage. Having been expecting him, she'd taped a note to the front door saying she had gone for a long walk and didn't know when she'd be back. Then she had locked the door and crept about all morning, feeling like a criminal and a louse. It was childish to hide from him, she knew, but she had to strengthen her resolve before facing him again. If she didn't get herself psyched up to nip their relationship in the bud, he'd do something else underhanded such as engineering another passionate picnic; and she'd melt like a cream puff under a sunlamp.

When he'd driven up to the gate, Hannah watched from the front window as long as she dared, but a good look at his black hair glinting in the sunshine, his hard biceps revealed by rolled-up shirtsleeves, and his lean, denim-clad legs covering the short distance to the cottage, had sent her scurrying for shelter in the darkest corner of her closet. Though she realized the immaturity of her actions, she crouched there, fists over her ears, for what seemed like hours. Finally she heard the roar of the truck motor and knew he'd gone. When she checked the note she'd left, she found he'd added a line of his own:

Hannah,
I know you're trying to avoid me and I'm not going to let that happen. I'll be back tonight.

Rook

Even his handwriting is arrogant, she thought, wadding up the note and tossing it into the nearest wastebasket.

The rest of the day was spent in frantic thought. The only way to avert the evening's confrontation was to be gone, she decided at last, and promptly changed clothes and put on makeup. She'd go visit Bev and Dusty, and if they weren't home she'd throw herself on the mercy of Janice and Arlo. Even if she had to endure a demonstration of making goat's milk cheese, she was still buying time—time to build up immunities to his infectious charm.

As it turned out, the evening wasn't much of a success. Bev and Dusty welcomed her in a friendly manner, but it seemed all they wanted to talk about was Rook. Dusty kept insisting they call and invite him over, until Hannah eventually confessed he was what had driven her to seek their company in the first place. It was clear that neither of them understood her aversion to Rook, and by the time she left she was convinced they thought her an incurable mental case. They had chronicled the man's every asset, lauded his virtues and downplayed his vices. Hannah departed with a wan smile, recognizing her mistake in thinking Rook's friends would allow her to forget his existence.

When she arrived home, relieved to find he was not waiting for her, she read the note on the front door. She had written: "Gone to visit friends." Below it, he had written: "All right, you coward! This is war!"

The next evening she again abandoned ship. She'd thought of one or two additional things she needed from the grocery store, and then she would go somewhere for dinner, and perhaps take in another movie.

All the way to El Dorado, she was preoccupied with worries about Rook. How long would it be before his boiling libido slowed to a simmer so she could calmly discuss *friendship* with him? She heaved an exasperated sigh. How long would it be before her own did the same?

She parked in front of the Dillons supermarket and went inside, absentmindedly selecting a shopping cart. Near the checkout stands were the racks of paperback books, a display that never failed to get her attention. From habit, she paused to look for books she had edited and quickly found two. Pleased, she picked them up and was admiring the colorful covers when a deep voice purred in her ear.

"If you weren't such a scared little rabbit, you could have romance in your own life and not have to just read about it!"

The books slid from her nerveless fingers into the shopping cart as she spun about to face the speaker.

"Rook! What are you doing here?"

"Talking to you—something that seems to have become damned near impossible lately."

She tried to ignore how attractive he looked, as he towered over her. He was dressed in a white Kansas City Royals sweatshirt and jeans, his hair faintly damp from the shower, his eyes fairly smoldering. An angry tic marred the freshly shaven smoothness of his stubborn jaw.

Hannah really didn't know how to respond to his accusation. It was completely justified, and she knew it.

"Well?" he challenged. "Am I right?"

She swallowed hard. "Yes, you're right," she agreed. "Now, if you'll excuse me, I've got a lot of shopping to do."

His hand reached out to seize the cart. "Oh, no, you don't, sweetheart. I've been lurking around just so I could follow you when you left the cottage, and now we're going to have the conversation you've been avoiding all week."

"Not in the grocery store," she stated, sounding more firm than she would have believed possible. She turned and started walking away down the first aisle she came to. Rook, pushing the shopping cart, followed.

"Where then?"

"I don't know. Somewhere more private, I should think." She pretended to examine the displays of fresh fruit.

"Yes, I should think so, too. But the way you've been hiding out, I know damned good and well you have no intention of going anywhere private with me."

"Can you blame me?" she asked, carefully choosing four kiwi fruits.

His eyes narrowed. "I'm not sure what you mean by that...."

"I mean that I don't trust you."

Suddenly he grinned. "Are you sure that's it? Don't you really mean you don't trust yourself?"

Before Hannah could get past indignant stuttering, he leaned closer and added, "By the way, did you know that the kiwi fruit is considered a powerful aphrodisiac?"

Hannah dropped the fruit as if it had burst into flame.

"I agree," he drawled, putting out a hand to touch her cheek. "Who needs 'em?"

Hannah brushed away his hand and scurried down the aisle. Relentlessly he followed, catching up with her in the bakery department, positioning the cart to block her escape.

"I want to know why you're acting this way," he demanded.

She turned to face him. "You lecher! Did you ever stop to think that maybe some women don't enjoy being attacked by you?"

A dimple replaced the tic. "Come on, Hannah. *You* enjoyed it."

"I did not!"

"And, honey, I sure didn't have to attack you...."

Pride made her deny the obvious. "Are you insinuating that I was a willing participant?"

"I'm not insinuating anything. I'm saying it outright. Hell, if you'd enjoyed it any more, we'd probably both have ended up in the hospital."

"You are the most arrogant, the most conceited...the most egotistical man I've ever met."

"Rather trite expressions for an editor to use."

"You want originality? All right, you strutting...stag! You're like a marauding coyote in perpetual heat!"

"You missed me, huh?" He leaned toward her and she backed away, pressing up against the glass display case.

"If you dare come any closer, I'll shove these rhubarb tarts right up your nose!"

"Big talk for a scrawny kid like you," he taunted, putting a hand on either side of the case behind her. "Come on, Hannah, level with me. You're just scared to admit you—"

"Sorry to keep you waiting, sir." A bright-eyed salesclerk stepped out of the back room of the bakery department, drying her hands on a towel. "Can I help you?"

"He's too far gone for help," Hannah muttered, stepping down hard on Rook's toe. With a muffled curse he dropped his hands and stepped back, giving her the opportunity to escape.

The saleslady tilted her head to one side and beamed a friendly smile. "Would you like to try our frosted buns? They're on special tonight."

Rook glanced over his shoulder at Hannah's retreating figure. "Uh...I think I've seen enough frosted buns for one night," he said with a wry smile. "Just give me a dozen doughnuts."

Hannah, seeing that he was occupied, slipped down the canned-goods aisle, heading for the front doors. As she reached the end of the green-bean section, she darted a quick look behind her. The aisle was empty. Breathing more easily, she began to sprint past the creamed corn—ahead lay the exit and freedom. Unexpectedly, her way was blocked by a careening cart and Rook was there, a look of something akin to madness in his eye.

"Aha, headed you off at the peas," he chortled.

"Very funny."

"I can do better," he stated. "Bet you never thought I'd turnip here, did you?" He started toward her.

"Get away from me," she warned. "This is crazy. *You* are crazy!"

"Whose fault is that?"

A large woman bustled around the corner, her pushcart nearly colliding with Rook's. Her look of disapproval vanished as he favored her with a broad smile.

"Excuse my carelessness, ma'am. Let me get this cart out of your way. I was just helping my wife here pick out some lima beans."

"That's perfectly all right, young man," the woman simpered.

Hannah barely had time to frown in disgust before Rook shoved the shopping cart to one side, then whipped around to reach for a can of lima beans. His maneuver proved quite successful. Because the beans were on the top shelf right above Hannah's head, he was forced to reach up and over her, flattening her beneath him. Hannah shrank away, but she was very much aware of the metal shelves at her back, and even more aware of his equally steely physique pressing intimately along the front of her body. She gasped in outrage when he deliberately ground his hips against her own, and practically breathed fire when he casually dropped one hand to brush her breast.

"Sorry, hon," he lied glibly, "I lost my balance."

"If you don't get off me, you may lose something else," she quietly hissed.

"God, I love fierce women." He laughed softly, right in her ear. Louder he said, "Two cans enough?"

"Plenty," she replied, through tightly clenched teeth.

Reluctantly, Rook moved away to drop the cans into the cart. The older woman was still observing them. "How lucky you are to have such a...helpful husband," she commented with an envious smile. "I do hope you appreciate him."

"Oh, I do." Hannah glared at Rook. "And I'm sure I'll find some way to reward him for all he's done."

The woman rolled her eyes. "Oh, Lord, I've no doubt."

As soon as she was gone, Hannah turned on Rook. "You maniac! Get away from me and leave me alone, do you hear?"

"Not until you agree to talk to me."

"There's nothing to talk about."

"Don't give me that."

"Ha! I don't intend to give you anything—ever again!" Hannah flounced down the aisle.

"What in the hell is that supposed to mean?" he demanded, following close on her heels. "Would you mind making a little sense?"

"I think I'm making perfect sense."

As they passed the meat counter, Rook seized a couple of T-bone steaks and tossed them into the cart.

"Look, I haven't had dinner. Have you? Why don't we take these steaks and go back to your place—I'll fix us something to eat and maybe we can work this out."

"Not interested."

"Afraid to be alone with me?"

"Yes...no! I don't want to be alone with you."

"Then let's go out to the Red Coach Inn for supper. There'll be lots of people there."

"Can't you just leave me alone?" she cried, stalking off.

"No!" In two long strides, Rook had gripped her arm, whirling her around, pulling her tight against his chest. "Hannah," he groaned, "you are driving me crazy. Please...let's talk about this."

An employee rounded the corner, registering surprise at having disturbed a romantic interlude.

As she caught sight of the badge he wore, Hannah exclaimed, "Oh, good, you're the night manager! Look, this man is annoying me. Will you please tell him to stop?"

Rook's hold on her tightened momentarily, then fell away and she nearly laughed as she saw a faint blush stain his cheekbones.

"Rook McAllister!" boomed the manager. "Long time, no see! How the hell have you been, man?"

The two of them shook hands. Rook, pausing to give Hannah a victorious wink, turned back to his long-lost friend. "I've been great, Ken. And yourself?"

God, Hannah snorted silently, the whole town dotes on the man. He could rob an orphan on Main Street and they'd fall all over themselves patting him on the back.

At least the chance meeting was giving her time to make an escape and that was exactly what she did, scrambling in her purse for car keys as she raced out of the store. Once inside her Mustang, she drove out of town as fast as she dared. Her only hope was to reach the cottage and barricade herself inside before he could catch up with her. There was no place else to go. His less-than-gentlemanly instincts gave him no qualms about tracking her down in public, and she didn't want to create any more scenes for the hometown folks tonight.

As she sped down the highway she fought panic, her eyes watching the rearview mirror constantly. It wasn't until she was only two or three miles from the cottage that a pair of headlights appeared in the mirror and her heart lurched. It was Rook, she was sure of it! And from the way he was closing the distance between them, she realized he was ignoring every driving precaution. In response, she stepped down on her own accelerator and with a shuddering roar, the Mustang sprang forward. She was glad the road was relatively straight, but the night was so dark she almost missed the corner. She hit the brakes and slewed around, making the turn with tires slithering on the loose gravel. She skidded to a stop in front of the padlocked gate, leaping out to fumble with the lock, her heart hammering in her throat.

Calm down, she told herself sternly. There is absolutely no reason to let the man terrify you so. You'll soon be safe inside the cottage.

She had just driven through the gateway and snapped the padlock shut when she saw Rook's lights and knew he was turning off the highway. Thank God, he hadn't caught up with her as she was trying to unlock the gate.

She drove the rutted road as fast as she could, bailing out of the car and scurrying to the cottage. Once inside, she re-locked the door and switched off the porch light. Weak-kneed with relief, she sank down on the couch and buried her face in her hands.

Good heavens, what was she going to do? She was a grown woman, supposedly a responsible adult, and yet Rook McAllister had ways of bringing out her most childish characteristics. It was silly. She had to stop acting this way.

After a while, she realized she had not heard the sound of his truck approaching. Had he given up the chase at the gate? Maybe he didn't have a key to the padlock with him and had to drive to McAllisters' Acres to get one.

She crossed the room to the window, pulling back the curtain to peer out into the darkness. There were no lights; nothing was moving. Breathing more easily, she dropped the curtain and shrugged out of the windbreaker she'd worn to town.

It really doesn't matter what tactic he tries now, she thought, I'm safe for the time being.

Though it was barely eight o'clock, Hannah felt exhausted and decided the best thing she could do was to keep the lights off and go to bed. Stifling a yawn, she entered the bedroom. The yawn turned into a shocked half scream. There, lying on her bed, arms crossed behind his head, was Rook.

"How did you get in here?" she stormed, backing away. "I didn't hear your truck."

"I walked from the lake." He slowly unfolded his long frame and got to his feet. "And you may remember I once told you that as a kid I crawled in the bedroom window with the broken lock. Well, would you believe that lock has never been fixed?''

"You sneak! I want you to get out of here right now." She stamped her foot. "I want you..."

He leaped across the floor, grasping her shoulders. "I want you, too, Hannah. So what's the problem?''

"I didn't mean it that way and you know it," she cried, twisting away. "Leave me alone!''

"Why?"

"Because I said so. Because I don't want this...this to go any further.''

"This?"

"Yes, this...relationship. I'm calling a halt to anything...well, to anything between us."

She walked into the next room and he followed, pausing just long enough to seize the grocery sack sitting at the foot of the bed.

Hannah switched on a lamp, then stepped in front of the fireplace, staring at the empty hearth. Involuntarily, she shivered. Rook carelessly tossed the sack of groceries onto the couch, scattering the contents, and came up behind her, putting his hands on her upper arms to pull her back against him.

"What in the hell is going on?" he asked in a tight voice. "The other morning I thought things between us were pretty damned fine. Since then I haven't understood your behavior, at all. I think you owe me an explanation.''

"I'm sorry," she sighed. "It's my fault, really. I should have found some way to put a stop to things before they got so involved.''

He turned her around to face him, holding her at arm's length. "I could have sworn you were just as interested in...in involvement as I was. You didn't exactly fight me off.''

She refused to meet his eyes. "I know, you're right. I made a mistake.''

"You think our making love was a mistake?"

She dared a look. "Of course, it was. One of the biggest mistakes of *my* life, anyway.''

"Honey, that's hardly flattering.''

"I'm not trying to be flattering, only truthful. Look, Rook, I don't want an affair with you—or anyone else, for that matter. I was wrong to let things get out of control."

"What do you have against an affair? And for God's sake, as far as what happened the other morning, what could you possibly find wrong with that?"

"Wrong?" she cried. "Everything was wrong."

"It was not! It was great—fantastic!"

She pulled away from him and began pacing the floor. "Of course it was, to you. Men have different ideas about these things. They welcome physical gratification at any time and place."

"Physical gratification? Isn't that putting it a little coldly?"

"It's an accurate term, I believe." Hannah's chin came up. "And that is where male and female differ. A woman isn't interested in mere sex."

"Mere sex? Is there such a thing?"

"See? You prove my point. Sex in itself is enough for you, for almost any man. But a woman wants more than that. Love...at least affection, should enter into it somewhere. And what about romance?"

"What about it?"

"Did you think grappling in the back of a rusty pickup truck was romantic?"

Rook's eyes gleamed dangerously. "Yeah, for your information, I did. I also thought it was pretty damned amazing."

"Me, too," she sneered. "Amazing that I could be so gullible as to fall for your cheap seduction. I'll never forgive myself!"

"Cheap?"

"Sure! Orange juice instead of champagne! Melon balls instead of fresh peaches!"

"What the hell are you talking about?"

"Never mind, you wouldn't understand anyway."

"No, if it's like most of your screwy ideas, I probably wouldn't."

"Just like you'd never see anything wrong with giving yourself to a man in a...my God, in a sleeping bag!"

"Well," he drawled, "it isn't exactly something I've planned on."

"Go on, make fun of me," she fumed. "It's the only way you know to deal with the truth of what I'm saying."

He ran a hand through his thick hair. "All right, Hannah, I'll make an effort to figure out your problem. Until I do, we're never going to get beyond standing here and yelling at each other."

"That's the point. We aren't going to get beyond it anyway. In plain language, there is no future for us. I want you to please leave me alone."

"It's beginning to sound more attractive all the time," he warned. "But at least make a stab at explaining your reasoning. I've always liked knowing why I'm getting the brush-off."

"I'm willing to bet you've never gotten a brush-off before and that that's the only reason you're hanging around me. The male ego is a funny animal."

"Let's not get into that. Just tell me what's going on in your strange little mind."

"I'm trying, but you won't listen."

He walked around the couch to confront her, hands on his hips. "I'm listening now. Go ahead and make your speech."

"I've made the speech before, as you very well know. Trouble is, apparently neither of us was listening. In the last few days I've tried to get back in tune with what I want from life, and unfortunately it's just not what you are offering."

"Which is?"

"Fun and games. A brief, sexy fling—no strings attached."

"Sounds good to me," he commented dryly. "But how did you determine I'd be offering something like that? I don't recall proposing any such thing."

"You didn't have to. I know your type better than you think."

"Better than I do, it would seem."

"You are a reasonably good-looking man with a big—"

"Why, Hannah, I didn't think you'd noticed!"

"—bank account. At this stage of your life, you're free to do as you please. Why should you be interested in tying yourself down to a serious relationship? And anyway, even if you were, the two of us are terribly ill-suited. We simply don't belong together.''

"Says who?'' he demanded.

"Says me. I have certain standards.''

"Ah, yes, I do seem to remember something about that. Aren't you the impractical dreamer who longs for a perfect life?''

"Laugh if you want, but why shouldn't it be possible?''

"Because, love, it just isn't. Nothing is perfect.''

"Not if you aren't patient and willing to work at it.''

"Tell me this, what if you wait all your life and it doesn't happen?''

"It will! I'll make it happen.''

"Then, if you believe it is possible to make perfection happen, make it happen with me. I'll gladly work with you.''

"There has to be some common ground,'' she cried. "There isn't anything between us on which to build.''

"Yeah? What about the other morning? I'd say that was something pretty exciting and wonderful between us.''

"That was purely physical. It takes more than that. For instance, where is the mental alignment? We could never reach a meeting of the minds.''

"As long as everything else is meeting, does it really matter?''

"See? That's the trouble with you, Rook McAllister. You turn everything into a joke. You can't be serious for five minutes—how could I ever expect you to sustain any kind of important involvement?''

"Okay, okay. Even though it sounds boring, I'll prove I can be just as serious as the next guy.''

"It's too late for that. I already know how being around you is. Whenever we're together, it's a disaster. Things break or fall or run away... or catch on fire! I usually end up acting like a fool, embarrassed within an inch of my life, and you come off virtually unscathed. We're an impossible match.''

"Bull! You're afraid to give me a chance because you think I might prove a better man than your precious Matthew."

"Leave Matthew out of this."

"Why? So you won't have to face what a wimp he really is? So you don't have to analyze why he would let you get so far away from him if he was such a hotshot lover?"

"No, of course not. Matthew doesn't need me to defend him. He's perfectly able to do that himself."

Rook's jaw jutted. "Pardon me, I keep forgetting how often the word *perfect* comes up where Matthew is concerned."

"We need not discuss Matthew, at all. We can talk about my parents' marriage—another reason I don't want an entanglement with you."

"Okay, let's talk about that. Believe me, that's something I haven't forgotten. It made a big impression on me that night you told me about their romantic dinners for two, about how you sat on the stairs and watched them."

"So you see why I want the same thing for myself?"

"Hannah," he sighed, "can't you understand...? Oh, what's the use? You are so hellishly stubborn you aren't going to listen to anything I say. That's why I resort to caveman tactics—it's the only way to get through to you."

Rook reached out and easily pulled her into his arms, despite her efforts to fend him off. "You only seem to pay attention to the things I *do*."

With those words, his mouth swiftly came down on hers, angrily yet with an ardency that denied that anger. His big hands roved over her back, pressing her against him, kneading her shoulders, stroking the curve of her buttocks. Her hands, knotted into fists and caught between them, slowly relaxed and crept free, to encircle his waist. The fresh-laundry scent of his sweatshirt combined with the headier fragrance of his after-shave to swirl around her, rendering her weak and nearly helpless within his embrace. Her lips sought the sweet firmness of his, and she stood on tiptoe to arch her body closer. Self-disgust flickered through her, then trickled away like the last grains of sand in an hourglass; and she knew she was, once again, on the verge of surrender. Damn the man! Damn the strange power he had over her.

Rook raised his head and stared down into her eyes for a long moment before setting her away from himself. "Lord, I'm sorry, sweetheart. How could I have inflicted something as...as imperfect as that kiss on you? How thoughtless of me."

Hannah felt an inner trembling that she preferred to believe was rage. "You are the most sarcastic man I know," she retorted. "That's just another of the reasons I never want to see you again."

"You're lying," he challenged. "About not wanting to see me again. And we both know it."

"I know nothing of the kind. And I'll prove it."

"Sure you will." He started toward the door, stopping halfway across the room to say, "That's fine. You just sit here in your little ivory tower and dream of a perfect lover and life in never-never land. In the meantime, I'll be out associating with other people like a normal human being. And when you get lonely and bored, you come and find me, and I'll show you some of the real joys of life. They may not be perfect, but they sure as hell beat mooning over things that can never be!"

"Don't flatter yourself thinking I'd ever come to you for anything."

"Don't flatter yourself by thinking you'd be strong enough to stay away!"

The truth of his statement made her cheeks grow crimson. "Will you please just get out of my house?" she spit. "And here, take your stupid groceries with you! Find someone else to share your steak with."

"I will."

"Good."

Together they threw the scattered grocery items into the sack and Rook, hoisting it into the crook of his arm, gave her one final glare before unlocking the door and flinging himself out into the night. With his free hand, he slammed the door behind him.

Hannah's eye fell on a can of lima beans he'd left lying on the couch, and in an uncontrollable burst of temper, she picked it up and threw it after him. "Take your damned lima beans, too!" she shouted.

With a dull crash, the can struck the stone wall and clattered to the floor. Hannah gave it a kick that sent it spinning to the other end of the room.

"I hate lima beans, anyway," she declared in a tearful whisper. "Almost as much as I hate you, McAllister!"

Chapter Nine

A week later the weather turned hot, and Hannah had a taste of the sweltering summer to come. She threw open all the windows in the cottage and left them open, even at night. She enjoyed long, aimless walks across the pastures, picking a variety of prairie wildflowers. She visited the Bookworm to purchase a guide to birds and wildlife, then spent hours looking for both. In the cool early-morning hours she often saw deer grazing in the field behind the cottage or stopping to drink at the lake, and once or twice she had caught sight of a small flock of wild turkeys as they crossed her property.

Rook had disappeared from her life so completely that she sometimes had a difficult time believing she hadn't dreamed him in the first place. At those times, therefore, she would mentally list all her grievances against the man, and eventually the anger she harbored in her heart would flare up and consume any fledgling feelings of loneliness or forgiveness.

Motivated by her ire, she had spent several days doing some much-needed work on her property. She weeded the flower beds and struggling with the borrowed mower, cut the grass. That done, she turned her attention to the out-house. She painted it inside and out—the outside to match the green trim on the cottage, the inside a pale eggshell color. She hung frilly print curtains at the one window and covered the floor with a small shag carpet. She put up a wall shelf to hold tissue, books and magazines, and completed the decor with plants and a framed Grandma Moses painting.

Oddly enough, she didn't feel the same pleasure she had experienced with the earlier renovations. She knew it was probably because she had no one with whom to share her accomplishments and for a time considered inviting Bev and Janice over for lunch and an afternoon of gossip. Finally she scrapped the idea because she knew the conversation would eventually get around to the McAllisters and she wasn't up to that just yet.

She could only assume that by not coming around, Rook had taken her at her word and had given up. She ignored the definite pang she felt at that thought, telling herself it was what she wanted and that it would, in the long run, be all for the best. Still, there were times in the middle of the night when she would awaken, and before she could discipline her mind, think of Rook, wondering where he was and if he was with someone else.

Not that she cared, she would hastily assure herself. She only wondered...

On one particularly stifling afternoon, having spent a couple of hours sorting through her grandmother's belongings with only two sleeping cats for company, Hannah decided to walk down to the lake. Remembering that her grandmother had once told her she often went there to read, she took a book, a blanket and a pillow.

A deep blue sky with cushiony masses of snowy clouds was precisely reflected in the waters of the lake, though the narrower end was darkly shaded by graceful willows that trailed along the shore. Hannah tossed the blanket onto the sandy beach and stretched out on it. She observed a jet streaking noiselessly overhead and heard the faint hum of a vehicle traveling the nearby highway. The only other sound or movement in the afternoon heat was an occasional listless stir of wind that rattled the dry leaves of the cotton-wood trees.

Hannah sighed and opened her book. Then, realizing the sound of an engine was getting closer, she laid the book aside and sat up. Appearing on the rutted lane that passed through the old farmyard was Rook's slate-gray pickup, and, as she watched, Rook himself stepped out and started toward her, leaving the truck parked alongside the road-way.

His arrival was so unexpected that she didn't know how to react. She judged her chances for a successful escape and knew her only choice was to simply stand her ground.

As Rook approached, his avid gaze never left Hannah. Instead it flickered over her, making certain she was not going to run away. After the first cursory inspection, he allowed himself a more leisurely look.

His mouth went dry as he acknowledged she was even more beautiful than his tormented memories had recalled. Her dark hair was full about her heart-shaped face, slightly mussed, softly clean and shining. As he drew nearer, he could see the streaks of paler color among the brown and thought she must have spent considerable time in the sun lately. A new crop of freckles across her straight nose and her tanned arms and legs bore out his theory. She watched him through wary gray-green eyes, keeping her mouth stubbornly firm and unsmiling. Her whole body seemed tense beneath the peach-colored shorts and top she was wearing, and he wondered how close she would let him get before she either ordered him off her land or got up and fled herself.

He had missed her in the past week, missed her more than he could ever have imagined. In his less rational moments, he swore he missed her more than he'd miss breathing, if it came to a choice. He almost smiled at that thought, but it hit too close to the truth.

Since the argument with Hannah, he'd been so wrapped up in his own unhappiness he had failed to see how impossible to live with he had become. His own mother was refusing to speak to him because he'd snapped at her one too many times, and now she walked around the house in aggrieved silence. The household help they employed tiptoed about, avoiding him whenever possible. And then two nights ago Dusty, acting as spokesman for the rest of the hired hands, had braved a meeting with him in Rook's office.

His words still stung. "Look, old buddy," Dusty had said, "I don't know what's gotten into you, but you've been a real bastard to work for lately. The men sent me to tell you that if you can't keep your personal life separate from business they'd just as soon move on. You're in a mood to kick butt, and they don't like it. And while I'm at it I might as well remind you that Gerald Overton has issued a standing job offer to most of them, so they're not bluffing."

It was a long-winded speech for Dusty and it hit Rook hard. Suddenly he knew everyone else was right and he was wrong. He *had* been a bastard. And it was time to do something about it.

Two dozen hothouse roses and an abject apology to his mother was the first order of business; secondly, a promise that he would henceforth restrict his personal life to after-business hours, accompanied by a peace offering of a few kegs of beer and a night off, regained the approval of his hired hands. Then he'd had to face up to the fact there was only one other problem to tackle. The problem of Hannah Grant.

It was incredible that someone he hadn't even known two months ago could create so much chaos in his life. He had, it seemed, plunged headfirst into one of the worst situations known to man: he couldn't live with Hannah, but, as the past week had proven, he couldn't live without her, either. That reality severely limited his options: he could go on trying to ignore his feelings for her, making himself and everyone around him miserable in the process, or he could swallow some of his damnable pride and try to deal with the infuriating little witch on her own terms. He'd mulled over that idea for a long time and now, having made his decision, here he was.

Only one thing made it any easier. He was in love with Hannah, and it happened to be his personal belief that love warranted any sort of sacrifice necessary.

Rook had found the two paperback romance novels in the grocery sack Hannah had thrust at him the night of their fight, and suspecting she must have worked as editor on them, he'd sat down and started to read. Somewhere between the first chapter and the last, he began to understand her. And he knew he loved her. Of course, it hadn't been the book itself that made him fall in love with her—it had only made him realize the truth. He'd probably been head-over-heels since the first minute he'd seen her in the dusty cottage, frightened by his shotgun but determined not to show it. If not that particular moment, then no doubt when she had seen the snake and thrown herself into his arms. Or possibly even when she'd hit him with the broom.

Just thinking of Hannah and reliving those memories cheered him up, giving him hope she would at least listen to him and consider his plan. He vowed to be calm, reasonable and unendingly patient. But now that he was actually facing her he felt none of those things.

"Hello, Hannah," he said quietly.

"Hello."

"Uh . . . how have you been?"

"Fine, just fine. And you?"

"Oh, I've been fine. Keeping busy."

"Me, too."

"Oh?"

"Yes, I worked in the yard, and . . . and I painted the outhouse."

His laugh was warm, unexpected. "Did you? What color?"

"Green."

"Green, huh? Don't think I've ever seen a green outhouse."

From habit, her chin rose defiantly, but before she could speak, Rook rushed on. "Bet it's real pretty, though."

After that, they stared at each other for a long, silent moment. Finally clearing his throat, Rook said, "I see you're doing some reading. I . . . uh, read the books you got at the grocery store the other night. I liked them both."

"I'm glad," Hannah replied.

"You did a great job with the editing."

"Thank you. Those were among the last romances I worked on. Actually the two authors are very professional, so it was relatively easy."

"I brought the books back. They're in the truck."

"Oh, good."

Rook glanced out at the lake, fighting the frustration welling up inside of him. This stilted conversation was getting them nowhere. True, they weren't fighting but, then, they really weren't communicating, either.

"Hannah, I'd like to talk to you," he blurted. "About—now, don't get mad—about us."

"What about us?"

He walked closer to her. "About the fight we had, the things we said to each other."

"Is there really anything more to discuss?"

It took sheer effort on Hannah's part to keep her voice steady as she glanced up at him. Lord, she had forgotten how magnificent he looked. He was wearing the brief cutoffs he'd worn at the barbecue and an unbuttoned cotton shirt that hung open to reveal the swirling black hair on his chest. She attempted to drop her gaze to his battered tennis shoes, but her undisciplined eyes refused to behave and traveled lingeringly down an unbelievable length of muscular leg hazed with dark hair. By the time they had arrived at their intended destination, one of his feet was tapping the sand impatiently. Quickly she raised her eyes to his face and knew by the tight look of his jaw that he was struggling to keep his emotions in check. What those emotions were she could only guess.

"There's plenty to talk about," he replied. "At least I think there is."

"Well, all right. Start talking."

She sensed that though he thought her statement was flippant he was not going to answer in kind.

"Let's go for a boat ride," he suggested suddenly. "I can think better when I'm busy doing something."

"But we don't have a boat," she pointed out.

"Sure we do. Didn't you know? There's an old rowboat pulled up in that clump of willows over there. It's been here for years. I used to go out in it as a kid."

She watched as he strode down the beach, then turned to grin at her. "It's here, but a little worse for wear. We'll grab that cushion off the swing—the seat in the prow has rotted away. Bring your blanket and pillow."

Hannah just stared at him.

"Come on, Hannah, don't get muley on me now," he pleaded, coming back to face her. "I'm not planning anything. I just thought you'd be more comfortable."

He seemed entirely sincere, so Hannah shrugged and gave in. This was a different Rook than she had seen before, and she decided that maybe she owed him the benefit of a doubt.

Until he reverts to his old tricks, she thought, tossing the blanket and pillow into the boat on top of the vinyl cushion he'd placed on the warped-looking bottom.

She felt a little weak-kneed when he reached out and took her hand, but he was only assisting her into the boat, and as soon as she was safely on board he released her abruptly.

As he pushed the boat through the sand and into the water, Hannah settled back against the pillow she had propped in the prow. Rook jumped into the boat, using a cracked and splintered oar to push them out into deeper water before sitting down on the one remaining wooden seat and fixing the oars into rusted oarlocks.

He kicked off his wet shoes, then grasped the oars and propelled the boat into open water, away from the shore.

Lazily Hannah trailed a hand in the cool water and watched him, fascinated by the bunching of muscles in his arms and thighs. Unexpectedly she remembered being with him in the sleeping bag and blushed.

"I missed you, Hannah."

Rook's words followed her thought so closely that she almost believed he had been reading her mind. She bent a suspicious look at him, but he was merely gazing at her, an earnest expression on his lean features.

Finally, she nodded. "I . . . I missed you, too."

"I've done a lot of thinking in the past week," he continued, smoothly pulling the oars through the still water. "I was sort of hoping you'd be willing to listen to some of the conclusions I've reached."

"All right."

He smiled, a dimple appearing in one cheek. "Great."

"You seem surprised that I would listen to you. Didn't you think I could be reasonable?"

Instantly a few hundred caustic responses flitted through his mind, but he resisted the urge to exchange barbs with her. That had once been an amusing and challenging part of their relationship, but no more. He and Hannah were going to have to move on, strive to reach some new plateau of understanding.

"I was hoping you would be," he finally replied. "As I said, I've really missed being with you. Because of that, I've come to the conclusion that whatever I have to do to convince you to let me hang around is worth it."

"What are you saying?"

"Look, I know I'm not the man of your dreams but I think you like me, and I'm sure we have fun together. Why not put up with me until someone better comes along?"

"I've told you I don't want an affair—"

"I'm not talking about an affair," he broke in. "I'm talking about spending time together—whatever time you'll give me." He stopped rowing long enough to run his hands through his hair, tousling it wildly. "Damn it, I'm serious about this."

"Stop it, Rook," she said uneasily. "I don't want to hear you talk like this. I've never wanted you to grovel, and it seems to me that is exactly what you are on the verge of doing."

He studied her with a bemused look, then took up the oars and began rowing again. "What's wrong with a little honest groveling?"

"It's demeaning," she snapped. "And a man like you shouldn't have to resort to such things."

"A man like me?" One black brow quirked upward. "Care to explain that?"

"You know perfectly well what I mean. I shouldn't have to recount all your many attributes again. You're well aware that you're attractive and sexy...."

"You find me sexy?" he asked, with such a disarming smile that she couldn't summon a single iota of irritation. Instead, she ignored him.

"You have a good personality, a number of talents, lots of financial clout. You could have your choice of females, Rook, and not have to chase after someone who...well, who..."

"Doesn't want me?" he asked quietly.

"I didn't say that. What I meant was, someone who isn't your type. Someone who is just too different from you to appreciate what your life is all about." She gave him a crooked smile. "Someone who truly doesn't deserve you."

"Let me be the judge of that, will you?"

"For some reason, your judgment in this matter appears to be flawed. I can't figure out why you would subject yourself to...to this."

"Because I lo...like you! A hell of a lot more than any other woman I've ever met. I think we'd be good together."

"For how long?"

"For as long as you're willing to put up with me. Maybe a little longer, if I'm lucky."

"But, Rook, what's the point? At the end of the summer, I'll go back to New York and you'll stay here."

"The point is, in the meantime, for the next two or three months, we can have a good time together. If it grows into something more than that, terrific—if not, I promise I'll be a gentleman, say goodbye and not bother you again. All right?"

"And yet, you claim you aren't interested in an affair."

He leaned forward to fix her with a piercing gaze. "I never said I wasn't interested," he corrected. "I just said an affair was not the issue right now. Believe me, I'm interested...but only if and when you say the word."

"I don't know what to say. The whole idea just seems so hopelessly complicated. Wouldn't it be much simpler if we didn't see each other again?"

"Haven't you been listening? Honey, I'm already in so deep that that idea isn't at all appealing. I'm ready to run up the white flag and surrender, for God's sake. What else do you want?"

"I really don't want anything from you, Rook."

He sighed. "I know, and it irks the hell out of me. Don't you think I'd prefer that you were pleading with me for my attentions?" His grin was wry. "Unfortunately it hasn't worked out that way, but I'm willing to take what I can get."

"Stop it, you're making me feel guilty," she declared, only half joking.

"No need," he said lightly. "That wasn't my intention. As I said before, I'm serious about this."

"But it isn't fair that it should be so one-sided. And it certainly doesn't make sense, either. Why should you settle for a situation where all the advantages will be mine? Don't you expect to get anything out of our involvement?"

"Naturally. I feel sure there will be *some* fringe benefits. I'm not greedy, and it doesn't take much to make me happy."

Gravely she asked, "What would it take right now? To make you happy, I mean."

His white teeth flashed in an impudent smile. "Hardly anything at all."

"Name it. I'm curious to know."

"Well, I'd be happy as a little meadowlark if you'd come over here and give me one small kiss. I'd even promise to keep my hands to myself."

With an odd expression on her face Hannah got to her knees and moved toward him, stopping just short of touching him, positioned between his bare legs. She leaned forward and put her mouth on his, touching him nowhere else. The first tentative meeting of their lips had the same impact as a lightning bolt wrapped in cotton batting. The boat lurched as Rook released the oars and she saw his hands, knotted into tight fists, come to rest on his thighs. She opened her mouth slightly, rubbing against his, eliciting a small but very masculine moan of pleasure. A little experimentation with her tongue brought forth an even more fervent moan, accompanied by a shudder so violent she could feel it, even though she was touching no part of his body. She drew back to look at him. His eyes were smoldering so hotly she thought they could surely scorch.

"See, one kiss made me very happy," he said with difficulty. "Two would make me positively delirious."

Hannah inched closer to him and putting her hands on either side of his jaw pulled his face down to hers and initiated a kiss that surprised even her with its ferocity.

Could she have forgotten in a mere week how compelling the taste and feel of this man could be? How his very nearness excited and challenged and thrilled her? In that moment, though she still believed there could never be anything lasting between them, she knew that on a deeper, more basic and primitive level, they were ideally suited. Each desired the other with such total abandon, that when they were clasped together like this, personalities and backgrounds and ambitions became meaningless. The only thing that mattered would be the mad and passionate scramble toward sensual pleasure and ecstatic fulfillment. It might be wrong or selfish, but it was a life urge more powerful than either of them. At this instant, her mouth fused with his, it was beyond her capabilities to deny it. Feeling foolishly invulnerable, she had flirted with danger and now felt herself being drawn inexorably into the heart of the storm, lost in a whirlwind of breathtaking emotion.

Rook's hands unclenched, then moved to splay across her back, pressing her ever more deeply into his embrace. Her breasts flattened against his chest, her hips nestled within the spread of his legs. Her own arms went around his neck as she rocked against him.

Struggling for breath she broke free of the kiss, resting her face alongside his neck. His palms continued their massage of her back, his fingertips sliding erotically up and down her spine.

"I thought you were going to keep your hands to yourself," she chided with a throaty laugh.

"Oh, God, Hannah," he gasped, "I tried. Remember, I'm new at this—it may take some time before I get it right. Forgive me?"

"Mmm, definitely," she murmured, returning her lips to his. Tightening her hold on Rook's neck, she arched her body and pulling him with her, fell backward onto the cushioned floor of the boat. Sprawled upon her, Rook raised his head.

"I must be dreaming," he said with a sheepish grin. "I'd almost swear you were trying to seduce me, Hannah Grant."

"That humble act just got to me, I guess," she said tartly.

"Lord, I should have tried it sooner."

"Was it just an act?" Her silvery eyes probed his.

"No, sweetheart, I meant every word I said." He placed a light kiss on her chin. "I was so damned miserable without you that I was acting like a jackass with a burr under his tail. My men were ready to lynch me, and my own mother wanted to furnish the rope!"

"That bad, huh?"

"Worse." He dropped a kiss on each eyelid, then brushed her mouth gently. "I can't tell you how bad."

"Then, Rook how will it be...at the end of the summer?"

"I'll worry about that when the time comes," he replied. "Besides, with the whole summer ahead I may just be able to win you over."

"Oh, yeah? How do you intend to do that?"

"I've got a few tricks up my sleeve."

"Such as?"

"Such as this..." He relaxed his big frame, shifting her so she lay against his side. Firmly his mouth reclaimed hers, kissing her until her breath came in short, ragged gasps and her senses clamored for something more. "And this..." One hand stroked her knee, then continued upward along the smooth skin of her thigh to settle on the hard flare of hipbone, drawing her closer into the curve of his own hips. "And this..." He lowered his mouth to her breasts, lips caressing her through the thin material of her shirt, teeth gently grazing the nipples that so boldly demanded his attention. Hannah felt a start of sheer, frantic pleasure and almost unaware of what she was doing she removed his hand from her hip and guided it beneath her clothing to the place where his mouth was generating such a riot of sensations. His fingers stroked the satin-soft flesh.

"No bra?" he whispered in surprise.

"Too hot."

"Why, you little pagan. I'd have never..."

His words died in a surprised sigh as, impatiently, she fumbled with the metal button on his jean shorts.

"You *are* a pagan!" he cried in delight as she started tugging the brief bit of denim over his hips.

"Any objections?" she queried, her restless mouth seeking his.

"No, none whatsoever. It's just that . . ." His hands busied themselves with her clothing, which provided no substantial obstacle. "I only . . ."

Her hands clutched at his shoulders, urging him on, and as he lowered his body to hers he gave up. "Oh, what the hell! I'll talk later."

No matter what their other differences might be, physically they were very much in tune. They moved together with unstudied ease, alternately giving and demanding, soothing and provoking, their bodies expressing what words never could.

Their little boat might just as well have been caught in the jaws of a devastating hurricane, for its inhabitants were experiencing a storm of similar proportions. It seemed to swirl and spin beneath a savagely rising wall of water; when the water struck with shuddering force, the helpless craft was swept along to teeter precariously on the edge of the world for a long, timeless moment before plunging over. With the return of reality, they realized they had not crashed upon some rock-strewn shore but were, instead, freely drifting upon a beautiful sea of tranquility.

"That really didn't solve a thing," Hannah said some time later, as she nestled sleepily within Rook's arms. She felt a laugh rumble deep in his chest.

"I don't know. It seemed to take care of my most pressing problem."

"And this is the man who swore he could forestall the physical side of his nature?"

He rubbed his chin against the top of her head. "Yes, this is the man. The only thing is, he's a hell of a lot happier a man right now than he'd planned on being for a long time."

"It doesn't mean that I've accepted your offer of a summer of fun, no strings attached, with a double-your-money-back guarantee if not satisfied, you know."

"Why not? It sounds like a good offer to me. Especially that part about being satisfied."

Hannah groaned. "Can't you ever be serious?"

He tilted her chin with two fingers, putting his face close to hers. "All right, I'll be serious ... but just this once. As far as I'm concerned, I've already lived the 'serious' part of my life. That was when I was an insecure kid who only wanted one thing—his father's approval. I damned near killed myself trying to get the man to *like* me. We're not even talking love, here. Hell, I'd have settled for being noticed, most of the time.

"No matter what I did, it was never enough. It took me a lot of years to figure out he wasn't worth the effort, but once I did, I decided no more gloom and doom. I'd spent too much time feeling insignificant and unimportant; the next step was self-pity or self-loathing, and neither gets you anywhere.

"Tragedies and unhappiness are going to happen at least a few times in every life, and when they do we all have to handle them as best we can. But the rest of the time why not enjoy whatever pleasure is available? Why not laugh every chance you get? Do you understand what I'm trying to say?"

"Yes. And it makes a lot of sense. I think it explains a great deal about you."

"Fair enough."

"You know, the strangest part of this whole thing is ... well ... oh, never mind!"

"Come on. Finish what you started to say."

"I'd rather not."

"For God's sake, would you just say whatever is on your mind?"

"I was merely puzzling over the fact that while we don't have another thing in common we do ... well, strangely enough, we do seem to have this physical ... uh, attraction."

"You noticed that?"

"The thing is, I've never experienced similar feelings with anyone else. I think it's so odd that—"

"Not even with Matthew?" he interrupted.

She looked away quickly. "No, not even with Matthew."

"What is it with you and this Matthew guy? Every time I bring him up you get very cool and uncommunicative. Why is that? Is he too damned *sacred* to discuss with me or what?"

His sudden show of temper surprised her. "No, it's not that."

"Then what? What's so special about him that you can't talk about him? Don't you think I have a right to know a little about the competition?"

Despite herself, Hannah's mouth curved upward. "He isn't..."

Rook gave her a small shake. "Don't you dare laugh at me, Hannah Grant! I want to know everything there is to know about this goddamned paragon! And I want to know right now!"

"He isn't real."

"And don't try to change the subject... What? What did you just say?"

"I said, Matthew isn't a real person. He's someone I made up."

"Made up?" Rook shot into a sitting position and dragged her up with him. His eyes were fiercely black. "Do you mean to tell me I've suffered every sort of ego-bruising, gut-wrenching jealousy over an imaginary man?"

"I don't know about the jealousy part but, yes, Matthew is imaginary."

"Honey, I could kill you!" he rasped, and at that moment she didn't doubt it at all. Instead, he caught her in his arms and pulled her against his chest, his mouth coming down on hers in a kiss that combined definite elements of triumph, relief and unbounded joy.

"You don't know how many times I wished I could meet that bastard face-to-face and see what I was up against. I should feel like a fool finding out I wasted all that mental energy on a figment of your twisted imagination but I don't.

I'm too damned glad!'' He kissed her again. "But honey, why? Why would you have to make up someone?''

"Because the real men I kept meeting were so inadequate," she said defensively. "Matthew simply became a symbol for the type of man I wanted to meet. He was everything I was looking for—suave, sophisticated, romantic. And he didn't have weird hobbies or sinus problems or..."

"Whoa, you lost me there. Sinus?''

"Suffice it to say, Matthew is what I'm looking for. True, I haven't met him yet but I will.''

"I take it I don't begin to qualify?''

"Do you want the truth?''

"Lies will do, if they'll make me feel any better.''

She touched his cheek. "You have one or two of the qualities I attribute to Matthew. More than any other man I know, if that's any consolation.''

"I'm not sure it is. Maybe it would help if you'd tell me what those qualities are.''

"Well, you are basically kind...and honest, I think. And you're..." She dropped her eyes and her hand to his chest, where her fingers began to twine restlessly through the sworls of black hair. "You're a very adequate lover.''

"Adequate? Oh, great! I suppose I should quote Shakespeare on being damned by faint praise, but I think I'm too devastated!''

"It wasn't an insult," she protested, giving his chest hair a little tug. "Perhaps adequate wasn't the proper word.''

He nuzzled her neck, breathing in the scented warmth of her skin. "How about marvelous?''

"Mmm, maybe.''

His lips grazed her throat. "Incredible?''

"Not sure.''

"Fantastic?'' His hand moved to caress her sun-heated body, lazily at first, and then with growing ardor.

Hannah moved her lips against his. "How about insatiable?''

"Or irrepressible?''

"Or inexhaustible?''

"Or," he murmured, sliding back down onto the bottom of the boat and taking Hannah with him, "how about impatient?"

"Incorrigible," she whispered with a smile.

"And just remember, sweetheart, I do have one advantage over good old Matthew. He can't do this...or even this...and definitely not this. I'm inarguably, undeniably, irrevocably real."

Hannah sighed deeply. "Oh, yes, you are. Undeniably, irrevocably, wonderfully, *gloriously* real!"

Hannah and Rook fell asleep in each other's arms, rocked by the gentle motion of the little rowboat as it drifted idly. It finally came to rest on the far side of the lake, where it bumped softly against the grassy bank until a slight breeze sprang up, pushing it back into open water. A blanket of sunshine covered their entwined limbs and feeling warm and content Hannah began to dream.

A boat on a beautiful lake had to be the most romantic setting in the world for making love!

Hannah, twirling the lace parasol she held, leaned back against the satin pillow in the prow of the boat and sent a secret smile to the man facing her. As he rowed, his shoulder muscles rippled beneath the white suit he wore, adding a touch of rugged masculinity to his usual cool, sophisticated look. She could not see his face because the panama hat he wore cast it into shadows, but she was certain he was Matthew. After all, there was no one else with whom she'd dare be so abandoned, so... naughty.

With a smug little smile, she glanced down at the bodice of her white cotton dress, remembering with pleasure how it had gotten so disheveled. Matthew was such an impetuous man. She frowned—it was Matthew, wasn't it?

She was so drowsy! She stifled a ladylike yawn and stretched languorously. The ruffled hem of her gown lifted to reveal her bare feet and she blushed to recall how impatiently her lover had removed her shoes and stockings. With a sigh, she closed her eyes and began drifting off to sleep.

Suddenly she became aware of a softly annoying sensa-
tion. Opening her eyes, she found that Matthew was tick-
ling one of her feet with the waxy petals of a water lily. He
smiled a crooked, inviting smile and, pleased, she went to
him....

Hannah's bare foot twitched, then jerked, waking her.
She sat upright in the boat, disoriented and more than a little dazed.

The chilly sensation creeping over her toes and up her legs
demanded immediate investigation.

"Oh, my God!" She couldn't believe her eyes. "Rook,
wake up! Oh, my God!"

Rook stirred, reaching for her. Ruthlessly she clutched his
shoulder, shaking him. "Wake up! The boat is filling with
water. We're going to sink!"

Rook was instantly alert, and the truth of her statement
was all too evident. "The old tub must have sprung a leak.
She's going down fast." He seized his cutoffs and scrambled into them.

There was a faint splintering sound and the boards along
one side of the boat buckled and gave away. Water poured
in through the gaping hole. As it swirled around Hannah's
knees she uttered a small yelping scream and grabbed
frantically for her clothing. Rook caught her in his arms just
as the boat capsized and sank, spilling them into the lake.

Minutes later, cold and bedraggled, Hannah stepped behind a clump of willows to struggle into her wet shorts and
top. Too chilled to go back into the water, Rook was using
a long tree limb to snag a floating tennis shoe and drag it to
shore. He looked up as she approached, obviously reluctant to face her.

"I'm sorry about this, sweetheart," he said.

"I've decided to take you up on your offer," she said
abruptly, hiding a smile at his astonished look.

"Even after this?"

"Yes. I guess even this disaster had merit. It reminded me
that while you have much to offer in the way of intriguing
diversion, life around you is completely devoid of romance. Therefore I can be free to enjoy a purely physical

affair this summer and walk away emotionally unscathed in the fall. And believe me, that is exactly what I intend to do.''

"Fine. Agreed. At least we know where we stand.''

But as they started off on the long walk around the lake he couldn't resist one last shot.

"But you'd better not be so damned sure of yourself, lady,'' he muttered. ''This is one good man who's far from down.''

Chapter Ten

Hannah's grumpiness waned quickly, to Rook's amusement and her own surprise. It hadn't taken much longer than it had for her to get into dry clothes. The whole boating incident was rather like her disastrous dinner party—once she stepped back and took a good look, what seemed an intolerable situation had actually provoked some rather entertaining moments.

And if he offered nothing else, Rook did provide a wealth of entertainment. For the summer, she promised herself, that would be enough. She would just relax and stop searching for perfection, long-term commitment or heart-stopping romance. For the first time in her twenty-six years, she was simply going to take life as she found it and enjoy it, even if it killed her. And the way things went when she was around Rook McAllister, that was a definite possibility!

Rook was planning an overnight stay in Wichita for the boys from the detention home, and Hannah agreed to go with them. She had never gone away for the weekend with a man before and it seemed ironic that, when she finally did, there would be ten energetic chaperons.

As strange as that would be to her, she had to chuckle thinking of Rook's predicament. She wondered if he'd given any thought to what he'd be facing. Knowing him, it was certain he'd be in the mood to take immediate advantage of her new compliance and yet, in the constant company of his young friends, how could he? His conduct would have to be exemplary, for they were also going to be accompanied by two adults from the home. Besides, she was aware that Rook himself had a pretty well-developed code of honor, which would keep him firmly in line.

Oh, it was delicious! She could flirt and tease and torment—subtly, of course—and there wouldn't be a thing he could do about it. Until later, at any rate, and by then she'd have had her little laugh and would be willing to take up where they had left off.

As she drove to McAllisters' Acres, where she was leaving Tom and Jerry in Helen McAllister's care, she indulged in a delightfully wicked fantasy of herself as Delilah, calmly rejecting a Samson who knelt at her feet pleading for her favors. It was surely no coincidence that Samson's lean, craggy features bore a striking resemblance to Rook McAllister's.

At the farm, Hannah chatted with Helen until Rook, who had come in late from working cattle, was ready to go. When he appeared, dressed in khakis, a print shirt and loafers, Hannah was frankly surprised at his preppie look.

Expecting him to drive the gray pickup, she had been admittedly impressed when he roared out of the garage in a dark, hunter-green Jaguar. Something told her that Rook fully intended to use the upcoming weekend to prove to her he was something more than the simple Kansas cowboy she wanted to believe him to be.

They drove to the boys' ranch near Augusta and from that point a van carrying the youngsters and their sponsors followed them on the highway to Wichita.

The boys had taken a vote, deciding to spend the afternoon at a Wichita State University baseball game. As they drove, Rook told Hannah that the Wheatshockers almost always had an exceptional team, but in addition to the enjoyment of seeing them play he hoped the college atmosphere might be attractive to the boys.

"It won't hurt them to see some of the fringe benefits of higher education," he reasoned. "Anything to get these kids interested in school."

"Is that also the point to the expensive clothing and driving the Jag? Pretty fancy for an old dirt farmer."

"The boys know my financial situation. I've been honest with them. They know I had an advantage none of them had—a rich father. By the same token, they also know I put in my time at college and that my mother and I have worked damned hard to build up a successful farming operation of our own. My dad was mainly interested in cattle and later oil. The Boss and I saw the potential for alfalfa and soybeans, not to mention wheat. I want these guys to know that even when times aren't the greatest there's money to be made if you're willing to work hard and use the brains God gave you." He flushed slightly. "End of speech." Then he reached out to lay a hand on her knee. "Thanks for coming with us, Hannah. I appreciate it. By the way, the clothes and the car were to impress you." With a broad wink, he removed his hand and turned his attention back to the road.

It was evening by the time the game was over, and everyone was starved. They swarmed into a McDonald's like a horde of hungry locusts, and from there drove to the motel where they were spending the night. Hannah sat back and enjoyed the sight of Rook assigning rooms and sorting overnight bags. The boys were placed three in a room, each pair of older boys to be responsible for one of the younger ones. It was decided that the youngest, seven-year-old Teddy, who sometimes suffered from nightmares, should stay with the sponsors in a room at one end of the corridor.

"I don't mind taking the single room at the other end," Rook said nobly. "That way the boys' rooms will be in between, in case there are any problems."

Hannah was amused to find she had a single room just across the hall from Rook's. It was obvious to her that he had done some serious planning. She wondered if the men from the ranch noticed it, too.

Her cynicism over Rook's strategies was short-lived, eclipsed by her admiration for what he was giving the boys. It was painfully apparent that most of them had never stayed in a motel before, especially not one with two levels overlooking a covered courtyard with swimming pool and a video arcade. Most of the youngsters stowed their gear in their appointed rooms, then emerged with awed expressions, entreating Hannah to come look at their quarters. There were color televisions, she was told, and Jacuzzis and free chocolates.

Ooh-ing and ah-ing, she dutifully toured each room in turn, until Rook rescued her by suggesting everyone get into swimsuits so they could go down to the pool.

"Of course, you know very well whose swimsuit *I'd* like to get into, don't you?" he murmured conspiratorially, as he walked Hannah to her door.

"I'm sure I don't have a clue," she replied with a toss of her head.

He grinned and started to walk off, but paused as she said his name. One black brow shot up in question.

"Changed your mind already?"

She had to smile. "No, I just wanted to tell you that...well, I think it's really wonderful what you are doing for these kids. They are having a ball!"

"This is the first time the governing board has agreed to let us stay away overnight. We fought long and hard for this weekend."

"Then I'm glad it's going well."

"Your being here has helped, you know. The guys like you a lot."

"Rook, I feel guilty thinking what all this is costing you. It might not help much, but I'd be willing to..."

"Unless you're getting ready to tell me you'd be willing to slip into my room about midnight, don't say a word! There's no need to worry about money, sweetheart. Just remember, the cost of this weekend is nothing compared to the pleasure it gives me. Besides, I always take the money for these outings from my father's personal business accounts. It helps me feel an old score is being settled."

He came back to stand in front of her, putting his hands on her shoulders.

"And speaking of old scores, I want you to know that our family attorney is checking into the sale of your grandmother's property. I had an appointment with him the day we watched . . . or rather *didn't* watch the sun come up. As soon as he knows anything, he'll contact me."

Hannah shrugged. "It doesn't seem to matter all that much anymore."

"It does to me."

She gazed up into his dark eyes, knowing he was going to kiss her, and trying desperately to summon resistance.

"Whooee! Look who's gettin' mushy," cried a skinny twelve-year-old named Jason, flipping Rook with his towel as he raced past on the way to the pool.

"Yo, Rooker!" cried Billy, grinning broadly. "Get it on!"

With a wry expression, Rook shrugged apologetically. "We'll continue this . . . discussion later, okay?" He glared at Billy. "When we have a little privacy."

The boy laughed. "You guys comin' down to the pool?"

"We'll be there as soon as we change clothes," Rook replied. "And then, hotshot, you'd better watch out."

The evening passed rapidly, with Hannah taking full advantage of the boys' presence. She stayed just out of Rook's reach, and even though he appeared to be totally occupied with the exuberant youngsters she often saw him watching her, the look in his eyes becoming noticeably grimmer as the hours went by. Once, as he sat on the edge of the pool, she walked by, feathering her fingers across his bare shoulders, and he'd flinched as though he'd received an electric shock. In the arcade, as he'd stood behind her attempting to help her blast alien invaders, she'd innocently pressed back against him, slightly twisting within the circle of his arms to ask, "Is my aim accurate enough?"

Rook rolled his eyes heavenward. "Lord, yes. Right on target," he'd assured her.

He might have completely lost his composure when they both squeezed into the minute front seat of an electronic race car, had not Brian approached at that moment to inform them that Jason was setting a new record playing pinball and wanted them to come watch.

Ten-thirty had been decided upon as the curfew hour, and by that time everyone was tired and ready to go back to the rooms. Rook told Hannah goodnight in full view of the boys, promising to see her the next day, though the look in his eyes promised something of an entirely different nature.

She put on her nightgown and robe and got into bed, intending to read a while before turning out the light. Two chapters later, she was startled by a knock on her door.

Rook must have been even more eager than she'd thought, if he would risk visiting her room with the boys so close at hand. She'd have to find a way to placate him yet firmly turn him away, she decided. She didn't want to jeopardize his relationship with his young friends.

"Just a minute," she called softly, throwing back the covers and getting to her feet.

She unlocked the door and swung it open. To her astonishment it wasn't Rook, at all. Teddy, round eyes huge in his freckled face, was standing there, clutching a book.

"Teddy! What are you doing here?"

"Mr. Wallace and Mr. Jenkins are both asleep already," the child explained gravely, "but I wasn't tired yet. Could you read to me so I can go to sleep? Sometimes I don't get nightmares if somebody reads to me."

Hannah smiled. There was no way she could refuse such an earnest request.

"Of course I'll read to you, Teddy."

Within twenty minutes, Teddy, propped against her pillows, was sound asleep. She tucked the blanket around him, brushing tousled reddish-brown hair off his smooth brow.

Just then a second knock sounded on her door and she eased off the bed, starting across the room. She only made it halfway before the door opened and Rook stepped inside.

"What the hell, Hannah? This door was unlocked. Isn't that pretty careless for a city girl—?" In quick succession, his attention was arrested by two things: first, the sight of her standing in the center of the room in a sheer robe and gown of ivory Victorian lace, and second, the sleeping child in the bed. A crooked grin lighted his face as he approached her.

"I should have known I couldn't trust a woman," he sighed dramatically, putting his arms around her and pulling her close. "Here we've just made an agreement to commence a torrid affair, and you've already got another man in your bed."

"But surely you can see why he replaced you in my affections," she countered, drawing back to nod her head in Teddy's direction. "He's so cute, so intelligent, so..."

"Young," he finished for her. "That's where I have the advantage, surely."

"In what way?" she questioned.

He leaned down to kiss her, deliberately touching only her lower lip. "In all the ways that count." He kissed each corner of her mouth, then let his lips encompass hers in a deeply sensual caress that easily set her pulse racing.

As his arms tightened around her, she struggled for some semblance of good sense and placed her own hands against his chest. "We can't ... do this," she gasped, feeling real dismay. "Not with Teddy in the room and apt to wake at any moment."

"We could go over to my room," Rook suggested halfheartedly, already knowing what the answer must be.

"We can't leave him alone."

"Damn!" he sighed. "Damn, damn, damn, *damn!*"

"I agree."

"Sure you do," he accused. "I'll bet this was just another part of your fiendish plan."

"Fiendish plan?"

"Yes, to torment me. And don't deny it, you little tease. You've played games with me all day. Hell, you probably paid the kid to come here!"

She had to laugh. "I did not."

"No? I can see it now. You spent the day enticing me, just so you could put on this elegant, sexy nightgown, lure me to your room and then crush all my hopes! What did you pay Teddy? A couple of dollars and a new slingshot?"

He raised a hand, letting his long fingers casually stroke her neck through the stiff lace collar of her robe. He lowered his head....

Another knock on the door sent them leaping guiltily apart.

"Who is it?" Hannah managed to ask.

"Pat Wallace. I'm looking for Teddy. He isn't in there, is he?"

Hannah shot a frantic look at Rook. "Uh...yes, as a matter of fact, he is."

"Good. May I come in?"

"Oh, my God!" she whispered. "Rook, he mustn't find *you* here!"

"I can't get out the door, that's for sure."

"Then hide somewhere! Quick!" She raised her voice. "Just a second, please."

Rook crossed to the sliding glass doors that opened onto a balcony. "I'll wait out here."

Hannah slid the glass door shut, closed the draperies, then rushed across the room to open the door to the hall. A highly agitated Mr. Wallace looked over her shoulder, reassured to see Teddy sleeping peacefully. "Thank heavens," he muttered. "I feel so guilty falling asleep before Ted did. I never dreamed he'd leave the room."

"He's fine, really. He just wanted someone to read to him," Hannah said. "I don't mind taking responsibility for him, if you'd like to leave him here tonight."

"That's very kind of you, Miss Grant. I believe it might be better if we didn't disturb him...if you're sure you don't mind."

"Not at all. Goodnight, Mr. Wallace. See you in the morning."

When he had gone, she tiptoed past the sleeping child and slid open the balcony door. Rook, arms crossed over his chest, glared at her.

"I don't mind taking responsibility for him if you'd like to leave him here," he mimicked.

She laughed and he groaned. "Hannah, how could you?"

"There really was no need to wake him. You shouldn't be here and you know it. Even if he'd taken Teddy away, you couldn't stay."

"But how can I leave? Wallace might still be in the hallway."

"No problem," she smiled. "That next balcony connects with a flight of stairs. You can go down them and come in the front door of the motel and back up to your own room. Very simple, actually."

"Sure, if I don't slip and fall trying to leap onto the next balcony."

"It's only three feet away. You'll manage just fine."

"And if I don't? Think of the headlines—'Frustrated Farmer Falls from Frigid Female's Fire Escape'!"

"Or," she chimed in, "how about: 'Careless Casanova Crashed on Concrete...more than his heart was broken!'"

He gripped her shoulders, one corner of his mouth quirking upward. "How about this: 'Sex-starved Swain Strangles Sweetheart'?"

She leaned forward to kiss him. "I really think they should read: 'Propriety Prevents Passion; Properly Platonic Pair Postpones Playtime."

He returned the kiss. "All right, Hannah, you win this round. But honey, don't underestimate the champ. I plan to come out fightin'."

"I'll remember that. Goodnight, Rook."

As he threw a leg over the balcony railing, he smiled and said, "Good night...until the next round."

He stepped across to the neighboring balcony and with a wave disappeared down the stairs.

Saturday was Billy's fifteenth birthday and he had asked to spend the day at the Wichita Zoo. After another swim and a late breakfast, they arrived at the zoo and spent a pleasurable afternoon there.

Celebration of the birthday was continued with supper at the Pizza Hut where, following the consumption of countless pizzas, Billy was surprised with a huge chocolate cake studded with candles. From the look on his face, Hannah suspected it was the first time anyone had ever made such a fuss over the boy. She sensed his usual swaggering bravado hid a very lonely, insecure personality. Again, she silently blessed the black-haired man who watched the proceedings with a pleased smile.

From nowhere Rook produced a large, gift-wrapped box and, eyes shining, Billy ripped it open to reveal a 35-mm. camera and a dozen rolls of film.

"How'd you know?" he exclaimed.

"Oh, a little bird mentioned something about you being interested in photography," Rook answered. "He also told me you'd like to have a real darkroom, so we're setting one up in the storage closet next to your room."

"Geez," Billy said, obviously awed by the news. "I . . . I never had such a good birthday. Thanks, Rook. Thanks a hel . . . heck of a lot!"

Rook clamped a hand on the boy's thin shoulder. "You are entirely welcome, buddy. However, there's one stipulation I've got to warn you about."

Sudden distrust showed in the boy's face.

"Oh, it's nothing you can't handle, Billy, believe me. I'm just letting you know right now that if you continue to break some of the rules that you have been—like smoking and ignoring homework—darkroom privileges will be revoked. Fair enough?"

"Fair enough," Billy said promptly. "I'll do better, I promise."

"See that you do," Rook said gruffly. "Now, how about cutting that cake?"

At promptly nine o'clock, the men from the boys' ranch announced it was time for them and their charges to start home. The van departed in a confusion of noise as each boy loudly expressed his gratitude for a wonderful weekend.

Rook turned to Hannah. "Did you bring your western jeans?"

"Yes."

"Good. We'll stop at another hotel where I have reservations and change clothes, and then we're off to find a cowboy bar and I'm going to teach you to do the Texas two-step. After that . . . who knows?"

Hannah had expected another super-modern motel and was caught unaware when he pulled up in front of a small, Elizabethan bed-and-breakfast inn.

"This is charming!" she cried, admiring the arched doorways and leaded window panes. "How did you know about it? Have you ever stayed here before?"

"Once or twice."

Something in his tone grasped her full attention and her eyes narrowed. "With a woman?" she demanded.

He nodded. And grinned. "My mother."

Hannah expelled a deep breath, realizing she had sounded very much like a jealous female. A mistake she must not make again, for all that it seemed to please Rook. It didn't please her in the least to find herself thinking like that.

The bar was small, crowded, smoky and dark, filled with cowboys in outrageous hats and cowgirls who looked as if they were engaged in fierce competition for the Miss Rodeo Queen title. Hannah was frankly surprised that she ended up having such a good time.

Self-conscious at first, she gradually relaxed and began to enjoy Rook's dancing instructions, mastering the basics of the two-step with no difficulty at all. Later, as they slow-danced to a George Strait song, Rook's hands riding low on her hips, her face nestled into the curve of his neck, she realized she was like an alien in a strange new world. Rook felt her silent laughter and demanded to know the cause.

"I was just thinking how far from New York I've really come," she replied. "Look at me! Instead of spending an evening in a café drinking coffee and listening to Broadway tunes I'm in a western bar, dancing to a song about someone with baby-blue eyes. I feel as if I'd been dropped right in the middle of a foreign country, like . . ."

"Like Dorothy?" he supplied.

"Who is she?"

"You know, Dorothy and Toto... in *The Wizard of Oz*. Yellow brick road and all that."

"Oh, yes, of course. The Land of Oz—exactly how I feel about Kansas."

"Bet you didn't know *we* refer to it as the 'Land of Ahhs'. Spelled a-h-h-s, by the way."

"What's the meaning of that?"

"Most people think it's a promotional idea thought up by a tourist board so the rest of the country will know we have some awesome scenery here. But, if you'll remind me later, I'll show you what it *really* means, okay?"

"Okay."

Arriving back at the inn in the early morning hours, Hannah thought it was more quaint than ever. The very fact that Rook would have chosen to bring her some place like this was mind-boggling, and she wondered if she would ever figure him out.

The two of them slipped quietly up the spiral oak staircase to their rooms on the second floor. Hannah unlocked her door to reveal a rose-and-ecru room awash with soft lamplight. The bed covers had been turned back and lying across the pillows were her robe and gown. Rook cast a pointed look in their direction.

"All day I've been picturing you wearing that nightgown," he whispered. "Put it on for me?"

"It's late...."

"I know," he said. "Time to go to bed."

He gently pushed her into the room ahead of him, closing the door.

"But you're paying for a room of your own," she protested.

"Don't try to distract me, lady," he warned, laying a finger against her mouth. "After the way you've treated me for two days, you've got a lot to make up for. We might as well get started."

As he kissed her, he slowly unbuttoned the Western-style blouse she wore, easing it off her shoulders and tossing it aside.

"I knew what you were up to all the time," he informed her, pushing her back onto the bed to remove her boots. Then putting a knee on the edge of the bed, he bent forward to unsnap her jeans and undo the zipper with maddening slowness. "You ought to be ashamed of yourself, tormenting a poor, helpless man like that." He seized the bottom of each leg of her jeans and walking backward tugged them off, dropping them on the carpet.

He reached for the nightgown and handed it to her. "Do you want to take it from here or shall I continue?"

"I'll put it on," she said, snatching it away from him and making a dash for the bathroom.

When she came back into the room Rook was already in bed, his hastily discarded clothing in an untidy heap by her own. Propped against the pillows, his arms crossed beneath his head, he let his appreciative gaze wander from the crown of her swirling dark hair past slim shoulders encased in lace, over breasts half revealed by a deeply plunging neckline and along a satiny skirt that hinted at the loveliness of the legs underneath. Wordlessly he held the covers aside for her, and she came into his arms.

"So far we've had romantic interludes in the back of a rusty truck and in a not-very-seaworthy old boat. I thought maybe we ought to try something a little more conventional tonight—say, like a bed. What do you think?"

"It sounds like an idea with merit."

"Oh, it is. Believe me, it is."

He pressed her back into the pillows, instigating a slow, deep kiss that quickened her breathing. When he raised his head, she draped her arms about his neck.

His white teeth gleamed in a devilish smile. "It's now my pleasure to tell you why Kansas is called the Land of Ahhs," he said, one hand stroking the lace edging lying between her breasts. "This is one reason...."

His hand shifted subtly, capturing the rounded flesh beneath the satin and lace, his thumb moving in unhurried circles.

Hannah arched against him. "Ahh..." she breathed.

The hand slid lower, caressing the curvature of her hip, the swell of buttocks. "Another reason..."

Hannah kissed his neck and snuggled closer. "Ahh..." she softly repeated.

Raising himself above her, Rook let his exploration continue down to her knee, then beneath the silky fabric of her nightgown and upward again. "Another..."

"Ah, Rook!" she gasped. "Ahh..."

Breakfast the next morning was leisurely. The inn's obliging proprietress sent the meal up to the room on a white wicker tray and they ate sitting up in bed. They sipped chilled white grape juice and hungrily devoured omelets, frizzled ham and buttery croissants. Hannah laughed aloud as she uncovered a small dish of sliced kiwi fruit.

Rook met her amused look with a bland one of his own. "You can have mine," he offered. "I don't need them. In fact..."

She warded him off with her butter knife. "Behave yourself for once, can't you?"

"I'll try," he conceded. "But only because we need to finish eating and get dressed. We've got places to go and things to do."

"Oh, really? Where *are* we going today?"

"How would you like to see Cowtown? It's a replica of Wichita in the 1860s and '70s. I'm thinking of taking the boys there, and I want to okay it with the management first."

"It sounds like fun, I guess. I'm not really sure what a cow town is."

"You'll find out soon enough."

When they arrived at Cowtown, Hannah decided to browse through some of the gift shops near the entrance while she waited for Rook to make his stop at the administrative offices.

Twenty minutes later, just as she had given in to the temptation of buying a leather vest, fringed and beaded in Indian style, Rook rejoined her.

"All set," he told her. "I can bring the boys next month. They'll even arrange reenactments of a train robbery and a shoot-out for us." He rubbed his chin. "Though I'm not sure it's a good idea to glamorize that sort of thing. Not with those guys. What do you think?"

"Oh, it'll be all right," Hannah assured him. "They'll see good triumph over evil, remember." It amused her to hear him fuss about the boys like a mother hen over her chicks.

"I suppose it can't be as bad as those video games they play," he conceded. "Hey, look at that."

His attention had been diverted by a pair of silver spurs hanging near the cash register.

"What are they?" Hannah asked uncertainly.

"Spurs. You know, they're worn on your boots."

"What for?"

"To get your horse to moving," he explained, taking them down to examine them more closely.

"What if you don't ride a horse?"

His dimple appeared briefly. "Then they just jingle and look sexy."

"Very practical," she said dryly.

"Indeed they are, and I think I'm going to buy them. I've always wanted a pair like this . . . and what better place to wear them?"

"I'm beginning to think you may be a little kinky, Mr. McAllister."

"Just keep thinking that way and you may inspire me," he promised, pulling out his wallet. "Here, give me that vest and I'll pay for it."

"Oh, no, you don't. You've already spent more than enough on me this weekend."

"But I'd like to buy you a gift. Especially one that is going to knock 'em on their ears back on Fifth Avenue."

Depression swept over Hannah for a few seconds. It was, she realized, the first time since their argument that he had spoken of her return home. And spoken of it so casually that she thought he must have resigned himself to it. Funny, she'd thought he'd argue the point more.

"Thanks, but no thanks," she said quietly.

"Well, when's your birthday?"

"Coming soon—June fifteenth, but you can buy me a *small* gift then, not before."

He placed a quick kiss on the tip of her nose. "Believe me, I won't forget."

Outside the shop, he sat down on a bench to put on the newly purchased spurs; and when he took a few tentative strides, they did indeed make a pleasant jingling sound. Stepping off the boardwalk, he propped one boot against a hitching rack to adjust the rowel on the spur, and Hannah watched him with an odd mixture of emotions.

She supposed a tall man in a cowboy hat always drew more than his share of attention. But lean-hipped and long-legged besides, moving with easy effort, Rook was destined to stand out in any crowd. His broad shoulders strained the yoke of the faded plaid shirt he wore, and the rolled-up sleeves revealed sinewy, sun-browned forearms and strong hands. Hannah was fascinated by him, by the flash of his smile, by the casual way he shoved his hat back, by the proprietary arm he slipped around her waist. But she was afraid of him, too. Or rather, afraid of her reactions to him, her awareness of his overwhelming masculinity.

"Come on," Rook was saying as he led her past the other shops and through a pair of wooden gates into the Western town, "let's get this show on the road."

Cowtown, with its boardwalks and false-fronted buildings was located along the Arkansas River, not far from the heart of modern-day Wichita. But as soon as she stepped onto the dusty main street, Hannah's vivid imagination was captured. She was, for all intents and purposes, transported back to the 1870s, when Wichita was a bustling cattle town. Though she had edited dozens of popular Western romance novels, they had never been her particular favorites. Now she glimpsed something of what made them appealing to so many readers. It was a simpler time, yet fraught with an almost naive excitement long lost in today's complicated existence.

They strolled along the walkways, stopping to look through windows into the old bank, the pharmacy, the undertaker's establishment, a pioneer home. Men, women and children in costume peopled the town, endowing it with a certain authenticity, and Hannah felt reality slipping away. The austere wooden buildings and the unpaved streets filled with horse-drawn wagons and carriages made her world of concrete and steel seem very distant.

At the end of the street was a white frame church and as they approached they could hear boisterous organ music. Suddenly the front doors burst open and in a shower of rice a bride and groom dashed out. The groom was dressed in blue jeans, the bride in calico, carrying a bouquet of prairie flowers; every other member of the wedding party was also in Western dress.

"I wonder if this is for real," Hannah whispered, enchanted by the romantic idea of an Old West wedding.

A man with a camera and a press badge pushed past her. "It's for real all right," he said, "and my butt will be out of work if I don't get at least one good shot of it!"

"What a wonderful idea," she breathed.

"His butt being out of work?" Rook asked.

"No, silly, the wedding!" She looked up at him with glowing eyes. "I love romantic weddings."

Rook threw an arm around her shoulders and tucked her close against his side. "They always make me thirsty," he declared. "How about going into the saloon for a sarsaparilla or something?"

With mugs of cold beer, they sat down at a small wooden table in the corner to watch gaudily dressed saloon girls dance the cancan.

"I've never seen a pioneer wedding before," Hannah said after a few minutes. "I wonder where they'll go on their honeymoon."

"To the nearest Best Western?" he quipped.

"Lord, Rook, you have about as much romance in your soul as . . . as that spittoon over there!"

"Are we back to that issue again?" he asked.

"I guess so. It seems to be a major one between us."

"It's not. I have plenty of romance in my soul—you just refuse to believe it."

"You? Romance? Why, you've never had a romantic thought in your life."

"I have, too. Plenty of them."

"About what? *Your* wedding, for instance?"

Unbelievably, the man blushed. Hannah's eyes grew wide and the corners of her mouth twitched. "You have! Tell me about it, Rook...please!"

"I'm not subjecting my personal plans to ridicule," he snapped, taking a swig of beer and thumping the mug back down on the table.

"I won't make fun of you, I swear. You should know that I, of all people, would enjoy hearing something like that. Oh, please tell me. I'll hound you until you do."

"I can believe it. Oh, all right, I'll tell you, but you'd better not say one word."

"I won't."

"First of all, I want to be married in Scotland...."

"Scotland?"

"Hannah," he said in a severe tone, "are you going to listen to this or not?"

"Sorry."

"Okay, I want to be married in Scotland, preferably in a castle, and I want to spend my honeymoon touring the country."

"Wouldn't your wife get an opinion on the matter?"

"Of course, but if she wasn't the sort to think it was a wonderful idea I wouldn't be marrying her in the first place."

"Why Scotland?"

"I'm a McAllister, remember? My grandparents came from Scotland and I still have relatives there. Besides, I've always fancied seeing myself in a kilt."

"You'd get married in a kilt?" Hannah couldn't contain her surprised laughter.

His black brows drew together in a fierce line. "I knew you'd think it was funny."

"Oh, no, I don't think it's funny, at all. I think it's a lovely idea—but I must admit, I'm utterly shocked hearing it from you."

"There's more to this ol' cowboy than you thought, huh?"

She made a face at him. "What about your mother? How would she feel about missing your wedding?"

"Who said she'd miss it? I'd want her there. In fact, I'd take my family with me."

"On your honeymoon?"

"Well, I had planned on that being a rather private affair," he said, his look something between a leer and a smile. "So I would send my mother and aunties off on a guided tour after the wedding."

"I must say, it all sounds wonderful."

"Then I'll let you know when I start taking applications."

Before she could think of a stinging reply, he pushed away from the table and stood up. "Come on, let's go over and see the demonstration at the blacksmith's shop."

As they threaded their way through the crowded saloon, Rook saw someone he knew and stopped to talk a few seconds. Hannah, still bemused by Rook's confession, wandered dreamily out the front door, stepping off the boardwalk and pausing to gaze up and down the street.

As she did so the image of Cowtown gradually faded, and she no longer saw tourists in modern clothes, no longer heard the drone of an airplane overhead. There was only the eternal prairie wind sweeping through the town—that and the steady drumming of a horse's hoofs.

Hannah brushed the dust from the full skirts of her blue-and-lavender calico gown and tucked a loose strand of hair back into the soft knot she wore at the nape of her neck. She shielded her face from the sun with one hand, smiling expectantly as she waited for the rider to approach. The man, wearing a dark hat and a long duster coat, came into sight at one end of the street. As soon as he saw her, he raised a gloved hand and started her way.

Even riding in off the range, Matthew retained the look of a gentleman. Chestnut hair ruffled by the wind, strong jaw shadowed by an unshaven beard, he sat ramrod-straight in the saddle, his bearing as aristocratic as ever. He reined in and sat looking down at her, a tender smile on his lips.

"I missed you," he said. There were deep sun creases around his wonderful blue eyes, she noticed. "I've come back to get you."

She didn't know what to say, and in the sudden silence there was a new sound—the metallic jingling of a pair of spurs.

"She isn't going anywhere," said a deep and ominous voice.

Hannah glanced up to see Rook, dressed completely in black except for a silver hatband, silver spurs and the six-shooter strapped to one thigh. With a thumb, he pushed his hat farther back on his head and calmly met the fierce glare of the man on horseback.

"Hannah, who is this?" Matthew demanded, and her heart sank. She had never heard him use that tone of voice before.

"It doesn't matter a damn," Rook replied for her. "I say she stays and that's how it's going to be."

Hannah looked from one to the other of them. How could she have known something like this would happen? And what in the name of heaven was she going to do?

"Please..." she began, but neither man was listening.

"Hannah is mine," Matthew stated. "She's going with me."

"Over my dead body."

"As you wish..."

Hannah screamed as she saw Matthew's hand reach for the gun he wore. From the corner of her eye she saw the swift movement of Rook's arm and knew he had drawn first. Matthew's face grew pale and his jaw clenched tightly.

She held her breath as she waited for Rook to fire the gun he held, but he merely kept it leveled at Matthew and said quietly, "I suggest you tell Hannah goodbye and leave town. Now."

Frantically, she tried to decide what she was feeling. Did she feel outrage at Rook's high-handedness...or relief? Did she feel remorse at the thought of never seeing Matthew again...or did it no longer matter as much as it once would have?

"I seem to have the advantage of being on horseback," Matthew said grimly, unexpectedly spurring his stallion. As the startled animal reared up onto its hind legs, a sharp hoof struck Rook, sending him sprawling in the dust where he lay unmoving, a trickle of scarlet blood staining his temple.

"You've killed him!" she heard herself cry, shocked by Matthew's uncharacteristic ruthlessness.

"Not yet, I haven't."

Her heart seemed to stop as she saw him pull his gun from its leather holster and aim it at the defenseless man on the ground.

"No!" she cried, and somehow Rook's gun was no longer lying in the dust at her feet. It was grasped in her shaking fingers and pointed at Matthew. "I won't let you do it!"

"But you love me, Hannah, not him." Matthew's wheedling voice grated on her nerves. Slowly he raised his gun.

"Don't do it," she said on a sob. "Don't make me shoot you. Oh, God, don't make me shoot you, Matthew!"

"You love me, Hannah—not him."

Something in his eyes told her he was going to pull the trigger and with a muffled groan she jerked Rook's gun up and fired first. She closed her eyes as the explosion of gunfire rocked her entire body.

"Hannah!" A hand was gripping her shoulder, shaking her firmly. She opened her eyes to look into Rook's concerned ones.

"W-what?"

"Honey, what's going on?" He bent close to her, one arm going about her waist. "You were standing in the middle of the street screaming at the top of your lungs."

"I was not," she protested, looking about guiltily. Several people were staring in such a way that she knew he'd been telling the truth. Her face flamed.

"Oh, my Lord," she muttered. "Did I say anything?"

"I heard you calling for Matthew," he said, a little stiffly.

"Get me out of here," she begged in a whisper. "Please!"

He tightened his arm around her and tossed a quick look at the bystanders. "She doesn't get out much," he explained blandly. "If you'll let us through, I'll just take her back to the Home now." The onlookers parted silently, watching as Rook hastily led her away, out the main gateway.

As they crossed the parking lot, Rook stopped and faced her. "What happened back there?" he asked.

Hannah looked away. "For Pete's sake, why are you making a federal case of it?"

"Because normal people don't suddenly freak out like that and start yelling at nonexistent men."

Her chin jutted stubbornly and she walked a few steps away from him.

"Oh, I get it—you were having one of your damned fantasies, weren't you?" he accused. "You're so wrapped up in your dream world that you can't stay out of it. I'm right, aren't I?"

She took half a dozen more steps, desperately searching for his car.

"That's where you go when you tune everything else out. Like the time we were horseback riding or when we were playing softball. Admit it, Hannah. That's it, isn't it?"

She turned and looked at him. For a moment she was tempted to just sit down and bawl. She blinked rapidly and went back to scanning the parked cars.

Oh, Matthew, she thought, I have loved you for so long. And yet I was actually willing to kill you! Willing to raise a weapon against you...in defense of that...that...

She finally saw the green Jaguar and headed in that direction. Behind her, Rook was still storming.

"Why won't you tell me what goes on in that weird mind of yours?"

She whirled around, eyes blazing. "Because it's none of your damned business, that's why!"

With that she turned her back and flounced away, leaving him to follow, swearing softly and fervently in time to the rhythmic jingling of the spurs he wore.

Chapter Eleven

Hannah had begun to have serious doubts about the dreams that had always motivated her. Had they been as screwy as Rook often implied? She wondered if she had been led astray by an overactive imagination and a childish disregard for reality.

And, she thought with a sigh, if I have, where does that leave me now? I'm a little old to be redefining my priorities, as they say.

She stretched a rubber band around the stack of old letters she held and placed them in the cardboard carton on the table in front of her. A jewelers' box and a manila envelope of photographs went in also, but a sheaf of legal papers was relegated to a second, larger box. Closing the lids, Hannah secured them with Scotch tape and identified the contents with a felt-tip marker. At last she had finished going through her grandmother's things, sorting the important from the merely sentimental. In the process, she had learned even more about her grandmother's life . . . and, possibly, something about her own.

Looking at the neatly labeled boxes, it occurred to her that that was what she had been trying to do with her own existence—compartmentalize it. She'd expected everything to fit into tidy, alphabetized niches, to be perfect and correct and predictable. And it might have worked if it hadn't been for one arrogant, irresistible cowboy-type who refused to conform and in so doing threw every other aspect of her life into chaos.

She shook her head in despair and picked up the largest box. She didn't know what to think or expect any more. It was like walking on an ice floe; even when the footing seemed solid, dangerous chasms could appear without warning.

As she approached the door to her bedroom, she saw that its feminine prettiness had been spoiled by the appearance of a pair of dusty, battered cowboy boots beside her bed. She blinked hard and the boots disappeared.

"I'm really losing my mind," she muttered, shoving the box into the back of the closet. For the past few days, every time she came into the bedroom those damned imaginary boots had been there, their foreign presence conjuring up Rook just as surely as if he'd been standing there in person.

She supposed her subconscious was trying to tell her something, but she wasn't entirely prepared to heed it. She was afraid the message might be as revolutionary as the daydream in which she had found herself facing Matthew with a gun, ready to destroy all her illusions of ideal love.

Since coming back from the weekend in Wichita, Rook had been busy helping his men put up hay and Hannah had not spent much time with him. After one such day, when he had logged nearly ten hours in the hay fields, he had shown up at the cottage. When she found out he'd only taken time to bathe and shave before coming over she'd insisted on fixing him a sandwich, but by the time she returned from the kitchen he'd been sound asleep on the couch. He looked so exhausted she didn't have the heart to disturb him until midnight, when she awakened him and sent him home—despite his sleepy protests.

"I'll stay here," he'd suggested.

"Your mother would worry about you."

"She knows I'm a big boy, Hannah. She'd probably figure out where I was."

''But she might not. She might think you'd gone to sleep and driven your truck into a ditch somewhere. There's no sense in making her anxious. Go on home and come back when you've finished the hay.''

He groaned and pulled her close, resting his face against her hair. ''Promise we'll make up for lost time?''

''I promise. Now, go on.''

When he'd gone, Hannah remained in the yard watching until a short while later she saw his headlights on the distant hill and knew he'd made it home safely.

She'd looked around at the night, awed by its beauty. In the heart of New York, it was impossible to see the stars, but here they were sprinkled across the onyx sweep of sky for everyone to admire. Cautiously, Hannah allowed herself to wonder how many other things that had once seemed beyond belief might just be possible in this vast, wind-carved . . . land of ahhs.

Hannah heard the old pickup rattling across the pasture and walked out to the front gate. Rook leaped from the cab and in three long strides was clasping her in his arms and swinging her around.

''Lord, I've missed you,'' he breathed, setting her on her feet and stepping back to look into her face.

''Is the haying done?'' she asked hopefully.

''Not yet. I got a short break from it because someone needs to fix the windmill in the west pasture. I volunteered for the job, thinking maybe you'd keep me company. That way I'll get to see you a few minutes, at least.''

When they got into the truck, Rook rested one hand on the gearshift and gave her a long look. Unexpectedly, he grinned.

''I can't get over it,'' he said, shaking his head. ''Whenever I'm away from you, I have a constant picture of you in my mind. But then, when I see you again, you're always so much more beautiful than I remembered . . .'' He traced the curve of her cheek with a forefinger, letting it trail across her jaw and down the side of her neck, coming to rest just at the top button of the blouse she wore. ''Honey, if you get much prettier I'm going to have to stop letting you out of my sight.''

"Rook," she began uneasily.

"You know," he said lightly, "whenever I say something like that, you get a worried little frown that isn't the slightest bit flattering." He hooked his finger into the neckline of her blouse and pulled her closer. "Humor me, Hannah. Just because I say things like that doesn't mean I don't intend to honor our agreement. When you get ready to go, I won't try to stop you."

She felt a momentary pang of disappointment, but it was immediately replaced by an influx of different emotions when he bent his head and laid his mouth upon hers. The hand at the opening of her blouse moved to cover one breast, his other arm slipped around her waist and he used his upper body to gently push her backward onto the dusty vinyl seat of the truck. The kiss deepened, became urgent and demanding, and Hannah responded with ardor. She didn't know about the rest of their relationship, but she had definitely missed this! The weight of his mouth on hers, the weight of his body holding her captive sent a sharp thrill piercing through her.

"What is there about this old pickup that affects me so?" Rook's rueful chuckle sounded in her ear. She felt a soft kiss that lingered very near the vulnerable spot on her neck before he released her and sat up. "But I won't make love to you here," he vowed. "Not this time. We've been apart too long to indulge in mere...gratification." His grin was wicked. "I want it to be something special." He pulled her up and into the circle of his arm. "How about Saturday night? The baling will be done by then and we could have dinner at my place."

"Dinner?" she murmured, feeling dazed.

Rook made a wry face. "Actually, I'm scheduled to have one of those obligatory parties—you know, business associates and people I just generally owe. There's a small group coming over for drinks and swimming. But we could have a nice dinner for two before they get there, and an even nicer celebration after they leave. What do you say?''

"I guess it would be all right. The party, I mean. As for the other, what about your mom?" Her gray eyes shone. "There are rules, if I remember."

He nuzzled her neck. "Honey, there are rules and there are rules. Besides, my mom has gone to Kansas City to visit her sisters. We'll have privacy...and a water bed."

She rolled her eyes heavenward. "I bet you say that to all the girls."

He didn't respond to her teasing. "Actually, Hannah, you're the first woman I've ever invited to my bedroom. And as far as the rules go, there never were any. Even if there had been you'd soon learn that my mother is extremely open-minded."

He winked and she laughed. "I can't believe you," she said. "In fact, sometimes I can't believe myself."

"Hmm, that sounds interesting. Care to tell me what you meant by it?"

"Not really. Now, don't you have a windmill to fix?"

A few minutes later, Hannah sat on the truck fender and watched as Rook prepared to climb the narrow metal ladder to the top of the motionless windmill.

Sometimes, she realized, he looked even more attractive in work clothes than when he was dressed up. Something about denim and faded chambray made him seem so excitingly rugged, so devastatingly male. There was a casual virility about him, enhanced by an old shirt, loosely hanging open to reveal a chest that was the answer to a maiden's prayer; the masculine image was definitely aided and abetted by the worn denim of his jeans, enticingly stretched over hard thighs as he squatted to rummage through a toolbox. He'd pulled on a pair of scarred leather gloves and just the sight of the fine black hair springing from his forearms above them was enough to send a wave of heat undulating through her.

Lord, she thought, there is something so wonderfully primitive about a hairy man!

"Hannah," he drawled, pulling his hat brim down to shade his eyes from the sun, "what on earth could there be clear out here in the middle of nowhere to make you blush like that?"

Hannah almost choked. "I'm not blushing. It's probably the heat or something. Uh, what's wrong with the windmill, anyway?"

Rook gestured toward the blades. "The head's not moving around into the wind, so it's not pumping water. I expect the spring that connects to the tail is broken." He stood up and jammed a crescent wrench into the back pocket of his Wranglers. "Want to go up with me?"

"No, thanks," she replied emphatically. "I'll watch from here."

"Chicken," he softly taunted, bending to place a tantalizing kiss on her bare knee, just below the hem of her cotton shorts.

He swung onto the frail-looking ladder and began climbing upward, one hand grasping the rungs, the other clutching the materials he needed for the repairs. Halfway up, he stopped and looked down at her, flashing a brilliant smile.

"You exhibitionist!" she chided. "You love having an audience, don't you?"

"You're the only audience I'm interested in, Hannah, and I promise you will be present at all my best...performances!"

"Just fix the windmill, will you?"

She couldn't help but smile at his antics as she leaned back on the sun-warmed hood of the truck and gazed at him. He scrambled onto the narrow platform below the windmill blades and gave the task at hand his full attention. She let herself enjoy the sight of his broad-shouldered body silhouetted against the cloudless sky.

From the top of the mast the half-naked pirate scanned the horizon in every direction, then skillfully shimmied down the ship's rigging, a dagger clamped between his straight white teeth. As he strode arrogantly toward her, he removed the knife and held it so the blade flashed dangerously in the sunlight. Hannah gasped in fear as she cowered before him.

The pirate laughed triumphantly. "Ah, my beauty, don't be afraid. True, there are no ships coming to rescue you, but, my sweet, you have nothing to fear from me." His black, bold eyes raked over her, from the windblown mane

*of dark hair to the bare feet below jewel-green skirts. His
rapacious gaze missed no detail: the deep ivory curves of her
bosom, heaving beneath the low-cut peasant blouse, the
wide leather belt that nipped her waist to nothing, the
strands of hemp that bound her hands before her. He
stepped closer and raised the dagger.*

"Please!" she cried out. "Please don't hurt me!"

*In one swift motion, he slashed her bonds, then watched
in amusement as she tore away the shreds of hemp and
rubbed her chafed wrists with trembling fingers.*

*"Thank you," she murmured in a small voice. "I did not
like being your prisoner."*

*One side of his beautifully seductive mouth lifted in a
carnal smile. "Make no mistake, milady. You are still my
prisoner. But I have no need of bonds to keep you under my
control."*

*Sudden fear rekindled within her silvery eyes. This time
when he raised the dagger, he placed the point between her
breasts. "You are completely in my power . . . and well you
know it. If I wish to ravish you, there is no one to stop me."*

*He slit the blouse she wore from the neckline to the waist
and the ruined fabric fell away to reveal the smooth flesh
beneath. Shamed and frightened as she was, Hannah found
she could not tear her eyes from the man before her.*

*He was magnificent—a vision of splendid manhood
clothed only in black trousers and high-topped boots. As he
tossed the dagger aside and stood surveying her, hands
moving to rest on his hips, the corded muscles of his chest
and arms flexed and rolled. Black curls blew wildly about his
head, a gold hoop shone in one ear. He threw back his head
and roared with laughter.*

*"Do I pass inspection, then? Blast me for an infidel, but
I think your fear is being replaced by . . . dare I hope, passion?"*

*"Never!" She flung the words defiantly, causing him to
laugh louder.*

"Come, wench, I shall wait no longer to have you!"

*He grasped her arm and pulled her close to him, so close
she could feel the heated warmth of his bare skin. One of his*

large hands fondled her breast, and a hot, liquid melting began within her. She had no will to fight her captor.

"I will make love to you," he stated, "but not here. I prefer privacy. Come with me."

"No, I won't!" Her protest sounded feeble even to her own ears.

Without a word, he leaned forward to toss her over his shoulder, then crossed the deck to the door of the captain's quarters and entered the cramped room, kicking the door shut behind them. He insolently caressed her buttocks through the skirt she wore before dropping her onto a pillow-strewn bed. Towering over her, he let his burning eyes brand her flesh.

"You are mine, Hannah, and I will keep you a prisoner until you realize that fact. Even if it takes forever."

He knelt and placed a possessive hand on her knee, moving it upward with deliberate slowness. His lips followed his hand, leaving scalding kisses in their wake.

"This can't be happening. It must be a dream," Hannah whispered. "Only a dream..."

"It's another one of those goddamned dreams, isn't it?"

The deep voice intruded on her thoughts, rudely jolting her out of the disturbing reverie. Rook stood before her, brandishing the crescent wrench and swearing.

"What?" she mumbled, trying to collect her thoughts. "Oh, well... the sun made me drowsy. I must have dozed off for a moment."

He tossed the wrench back into the toolbox and heaved an aggrieved sigh. "I don't believe you were asleep."

She slid off the fender. "Why would I lie about something so silly?" she evaded.

"You tell me," he countered, unable to keep the anger from his tone. "And while you're at it, tell me why you were sprawled all over the truck looking like you were dying to be kissed."

"That must have been your imagination."

"It was not my imagination," he retorted. "Remember, you're the one who thinks I don't have an imagination."

She shrugged guiltily. "Rook, I don't know what to say."

"Isn't this the point where you remind me that I have hay to bale and that we really should be going?"

"I suppose so. Yes, that's probably a very good idea."

He slammed the lid of the toolbox. "Get in the truck, Hannah."

All the way back to the cottage, she was in a state of shock. Not because Rook was perturbed at her—heaven only knew, that was the usual state of affairs—but because of the pirate fantasy. It had been dramatically different from any of her others.

First of all, Matthew hadn't figured in it in any way. My God, had she effectively killed him, after all? And that pirate! That brash, licentious, lascivious man. There was absolutely no doubt about it: he had been Rook McAllister in black tights and an earring.

She groaned inwardly. She was starting to have daydreams about Rook now, and they were daydreams of an entirely different nature than any she'd had before. There was no gentleness, no romance. This fantasy had fairly pulsated with raw sexual overtones and, damn it, she had enjoyed it!

She stole a quick look at the man beside her. She could never let him guess how thoroughly he was destroying her illusions and ideals. If he ever had a clue to the effect he was having on her he'd never give up. One hint of victory and he'd move in for the kill. The hopes, dreams and plans of a lifetime would be finished. No, he must never know....

After he'd left Hannah at her cottage, Rook drove the truck hell-bent for leather, slamming in the clutch and grinding the gears, hurtling over every spring-jarring bump and rut in the lane. It didn't help at all in easing the black mood into which he had fallen.

Damn! Things had been going so well lately. Why did she have to resort to another of her stupid love dreams about Matthew? He gritted his teeth.

The man was imaginary, for God's sake. How was it possible for him to be so jealous of someone who didn't even exist? But then, how was it possible for a grown woman to get so starry-eyed over a figment of her own imagination? Any man seeing that look in his woman's eyes would be jealous, no matter what the cause. Real or not, the threat he posed was tangible. She had been so reluctant to admit she had been thinking about Matthew, so evasive when he'd questioned her, that Rook knew the daydreams were taking on new significance. Like a three-hundred-pound woman hiding chocolates in the closet, Hannah was becoming defensive and secretive. He felt it was a danger signal—he could be close to losing her to an idea, a dream. He struck the steering wheel with a gloved fist.

"But, by God, I'm not going to," he growled. "I will not lose out to some jerk who doesn't even have the decency to be flesh-and-blood."

He loved Hannah, loved everything about her, from her odd little back-East accent to the most irritating habit in her vast repertoire. He'd never known anyone like her, never even guessed there could be anyone like her. Good Lord, he wasn't about to give up on her now. Not when the vague plans he'd always had for his own future were beginning to swim into some kind of focus. Not when he suspected that she was there at the heart of those plans.

A pleased grin lit his face as he thought, Hannah, girl, I'm gonna give your precious Matthew one hell of a run for his money.

Saturday night, he decided, would be an ideal time to start. First, over dinner, he would confess his real feelings for her—she had the right to know how he felt—but he wouldn't beg or plead or even try to reason with her. No, he'd simply use the method that succeeded best. He'd begin with a small erotic kiss on the neck and gradually work up to the biggest damned tidal wave a water bed had ever seen. One night, one week . . . he didn't care. He'd keep her there as long as it took to *love* some sense into that stubbornly independent mind of hers!

Leaning close to the mirror, Rook slapped after-shave on his newly smooth face. He was feeling on top of the world! The haying was done for a few weeks, his mother had called to say she was having a wonderful time in Kansas City, and Hannah was waiting for him down by the pool.

"Tonight, tonight," he found himself singing as he took the stairs two at a time. Lately, those old Broadway tunes had a way of insinuating themselves into his mind.

He nearly collided with the cook's helper, who was carrying their dinner to the table set up at poolside. Apologetically, he stepped aside to let the woman pass and waited until she had emptied her tray and gone before dropping a light kiss on Hannah's bare shoulder.

"You look fantastic tonight, sweetheart," he said, his admiring gaze sweeping over the pale yellow sundress she was wearing. "And so does this meal. I love chicken in wine sauce."

Hannah smiled up at him as he pulled his chair close to hers. A candle in a glass globe illuminated her face, bathing her features with a soft, golden glow.

"On second thought, forget the chicken," he muttered, leaning forward to brush a kiss against her smiling mouth. "You can't know how much I've looked forward to this evening."

"Yes, I can," she stated. "I've... ah... ah-choo!" Her head snapped back with the force of the sneeze. "Oh, my heavens, I'm sorry! I didn't know I was going to do that." She seized her napkin in time to stifle a second sneeze.

"You haven't caught cold, have you?" His voice was filled with concern.

"No, I don't think so. I've been fine...ah! ...all day. Ah-choo!"

"You don't sound fine now," he fretted.

"I don't know what's...ah! Ah! Ah-choo! Ah-choo!" Tears stung her eyes as she fumbled in her purse for a tissue.

"Maybe you should try to eat something," he suggested lamely. "I mean... well, feed a cold, they say."

"I don't have a cold," she insisted. But she picked up her fork and speared a bite of chicken. "Please don't just sit there and watch me. You eat your dinner, too."

"All right," he agreed doubtfully.

After a few bites without any further sneezing, Hannah brightened up. "I guess there was dust in the air or something. I'll be okay now."

Rook winked at her over the rim of his iced-tea glass. "Good. I've got something important to say to you tonight, and I think it will be easier if you don't sneeze after every word."

"Something important, huh? Sounds intriguing."

"It's a confession I want to make."

"A confession? Well, well. That's more intriguing than ever."

"Stop looking at me like that or this excellent meal is going to get very cold." He picked up her hand. "And I am going to get very warm."

She leaned toward him, blatant invitation in her eyes. "How warm is warm?" she asked.

"Would you believe...?"

"Ah-choo!"

Rook drew back and mopped his face with his napkin.

"Oh, Rook, I'm sorry!" she cried. "How embarrass...ah-choo! Ah-choo!"

"What the hell is the matter? You weren't sneezing until I got close to you. Is this some kind of joke?"

"It's...ah-choo...no joke," she gasped. "I think...ah-choo...I must be al...ah-choo...allergic to...ah-choo!"

"To me?"

"Ah-choo!" She nodded miserably.

"You never have been before."

"I know. Is there...ah-choo...anything...anyth...ah-choo!"

"Different?"

"Yes."

He started to shake his head, then paused. "The aftershave. I'll bet it's this damned after-shave."

"But I've never been ah-allergic to it before."

"It's a new brand."

"That must be it...ah-choo!"

"I'm going to go wash it off right now."

"A-choo! Too late." Dabbing her streaming eyes with a tissue, she nodded toward the back door to the house. At that moment several people were strolling through it onto the patio. Rook swore beneath his breath.

"Sorry we're a little early," Gerald Overton called out, "but we were anxious to get the party started."

"Obviously."

"Rook, don't be rude," Hannah counseled softly. "You can take a shower later . . . when everyone has gone."

One black brow shot upward. "Now that gives me several pleasant ideas."

"I thought it might . . . ah-choo!"

Of necessity, Rook and Hannah avoided each other for the rest of the evening, forced to be content with the exchange of charged glances from safe distances. About twenty people of Rook's acquaintance had gathered for the party, and though some of them swam the majority spent the night chatting over drinks or dancing to soft music at poolside. Rook grew so frustrated as he watched Hannah dance with several of the other men present that he finally disappeared upstairs to shower and change clothes. Hannah watched him go, a faint smile on her lips.

"You and Rook have it pretty bad, I guess," Gerald Overton observed, swirling the ice cubes in the drink he held. "You haven't heard a word I've said for staring at him."

"Oh, I'm sorry, Gerald . . . really. I didn't mean to be so unattentive."

"We're all used to being ignored when Rook's around," he said glumly. "Don't worry about it."

"Well, I apologize, and I'm not ignoring you now. What were you saying?"

"Strangely enough, I was talking about Rook. About the fact that he keeps things pretty stirred up in our little backwater."

"What has he done now?" Hannah took a sip of her fruit punch and gave the man her polite attention.

"Well, all this fuss over your grandmother's property. Hell, Rook was so cussed mad when he found out how his father had engineered that deal I thought he might go up in smoke."

"Engineered?"

"Yeah. Rook came into the bank a few days ago to talk to my dad about some report he'd gotten from his attorney. Guess he couldn't believe my old man would have fallen in with a scheme like that but, shoot, his hands were tied. What else could he do?"

"What scheme?" Hannah asked carefully.

"J.W. wanted your family's land, wanted it bad. But like a real businessman he wanted it cheap. He made an offer your grandmother said was laughable, but as luck would have it he had the last laugh. Seems there'd been offers from some of the other neighbors, but J.W. queered the deals by threatening to withdraw his money from Dad's bank if he approved any loans to buy the Grant property."

"And eventually my grandmother needed the money so badly she was forced to sell to McAllister?"

He looked uncomfortable. "Something like that. But," he hastened to add, "it was all perfectly legal."

"Though not particularly ethical," Hannah said. "Or humane."

"J.W. wasn't big on humanity," Overton commented. "He drove a hard bargain."

"Yes, quite a shrewd businessman, obviously."

"Can't say that Rook is anything like him, though. If it wasn't for his damned incredible luck, he'd have gone broke more than once. Dad says he's too soft to be a true businessman, and I expect he's right. J.W.'s probably spinning in his grave these days."

"Why is that?"

"Oh, the money Rook throws away on those boys, for one thing. J.W. would never have spent money like that without getting a return of some kind. Of course, Rook will realize quite a profit when he sells your lake property to them. But if I know him, he's probably planning to share the proceeds with you in some quixotic effort to make up for what his father did in the past."

Hannah didn't think she could have heard him correctly. "Would you mind repeating that?"

Her words were so strained that he shot her a quick look. "Which part? About Rook sharing the profits? Now, I don't know that for sure. I shouldn't have said . . ."

"No, the part about selling my property...to the boys?"

"Not the boys themselves. The ranch. Rook thinks your ten acres would make a great camp for the boys' ranch."

"I...I thought he wanted my land for himself," Hannah said, thinking aloud. "I had no idea he intended to sell it to someone else."

"Look, maybe I spoke out of turn. I assumed the two of you had talked it over."

Across the pool Rook was just emerging from the house dressed in fresh clothing, his hair damp from the shower.

"No, he never mentioned his plans," she said. "I had no idea..."

Overton saw Rook approaching. "Uh, Hannah, maybe it would be best if you didn't tell him about our conversation. I realize now that it really wasn't my place to discuss his personal business affairs with you."

"Don't worry, Gerald. I won't say a word."

Noticing that a pretty redhead had waylaid Rook, Hannah murmured an excuse to Overton and made her escape. She slipped around the side of the house into the yard, leaning against a tree until her eyes had adjusted to the darkness. Then she wandered down the sloping lawn toward the duck pond. She sank down onto a wooden bench, hands clasped in her lap. Despite the warmth of the summer night, she felt cold.

How could Rook have deceived her so? All this time she had trusted him to tell her what his lawyer had discovered. Oh, not for any reason other than the satisfaction of knowing her grandmother had been right. She had no desire for revenge, nor any need to force the McAllisters to make restitution. J.W., the real villain, was beyond the reach of earthly laws, and it would be ridiculous to hold Helen or Rook responsible for his misdeeds. But why hadn't Rook told her what he'd learned? The obvious reason was that he was ashamed of what his father had done, but even that did not explain his failure to tell her about his plans for her property.

She had thought he felt the same love for the old cottage and the lake that she did. That she could entrust them to him and know he'd always take care of them. How could he have been arranging for their sale behind her back? Before he'd even gained control of the property himself?

Sadly she acknowledged the fact that there must be more of J. W. McAllister in his son than anyone realized. The worst part of all, to her, was that he could genuinely care about her yet so casually defraud her through dubious real-estate dealings. She'd been an easy mark, for she'd never thought Rook would betray her. She still found it difficult to believe....

When Rook finally found her, she was lost in thought, staring intently into the night-shadowed pond. When he said her name, she jumped nervously.

"What are you doing clear out here?" he asked, concerned and a little angry when she intentionally kept the bench between them.

"Just thinking," she answered.

"About what?"

"Nothing important."

Matthew again, he thought glumly. She'd rather sit here in the dark and fantasize about him than stay with me and my friends.

"Hannah, do you think it's wise to let yourself—?"

"Rook," she broke in, "I think I'll go on home. I ... I don't feel very well. Maybe I am coming down with a cold."

"I'll drive you."

"No, there's no need. I have my car. You go on back to your guests."

Before he could insist, she turned and walked away. He started after her, then stopped. What was the use?

Shoulders slumped in dejection, he watched her go, bitter that his hopes for a special evening had been so brutally dashed. He didn't know whether to blame her or himself or the untimely urge that had caused him to purchase the new brand of after-shave.

Eventually he returned to the party, doing his best to maintain an unconcerned smile, though his jaws ached with the effort and his friends, exchanging worried glances, weren't fooled for a minute.

Chapter Twelve

During the next week, both Rook and Hannah were constantly aware of the strange new undercurrents in their relationship—and neither knew exactly what to do about them.

Hannah was disillusioned by Rook's deception concerning the plans for her property and, yet, she didn't want to confront him about it. She had almost decided it would be best to pretend ignorance until the feelings between them died a natural death. Then she would quietly sell him the land and go back to New York. She couldn't afford to keep the property herself, and it wasn't going to help anything to find another buyer. No matter how unscrupulous his methods seemed, if she sold to Rook at least the boys would someday benefit from the deal.

Under the circumstances, Hannah no longer looked forward to her birthday celebration. Rook had promised something special, but she knew from experience his plans often went awry and, anyway, how could she relax and enjoy herself when every time she looked into his eyes she'd be remembering how untrustworthy he had turned out to be?

* * *

Depression was a new emotion for Rook McAllister. Always before, his natural enthusiasm had bailed him out when things got rocky. Not this time, though.

It made him mad as hell that the most important thing in his life was slipping between his fingers and every move he made seemed to be the wrong one. Since that night at his house, he'd sensed defeat within himself. Trying to compete with Hannah's fantasies of perfection was like shadowboxing—there was nothing substantial for him to challenge. He could have done battle with another man or the many differences in their life-styles. He could even have dealt with Hannah's desire to return to New York or with her general mistrust of the McAllisters. But it was impossible to combat something he couldn't see or understand. And he'd only been prolonging his own misery to think he could. Hannah was a warm, lovely, sexy woman and, damn it all, he adored her. But he feared she was mentally immature, living in a dream world designed for her alone. A world in which there was no room for him.

Rook had gone to a lot of trouble for Hannah's birthday; it was, in a sense, one final, last-ditch effort. He intended to use the evening to prove something to her, and if he failed he'd know for certain there could be no future for them. In that case, her birthday would mark the end of their time together and not, as he had hoped, a special new beginning.

Having seen the headlights coming down the lane to the cottage, Hannah ran into the bedroom to get her purse. There, in masculine disarray, were those damned dusty cowboy boots. She blinked hard, then blinked again, and as usual they disappeared.

She couldn't believe her state of mind these days! Rook had completely replaced Matthew in her fantasies, for whatever reason, and even in more lucid moments she found her thoughts turning to him with maddening regularity. Lord help her, she was beginning to wonder if she might not be a little in love with him . . . as rough-edged and imperfect as he was. No, it simply couldn't be. She was merely dazzled by his splendid physicality, that's all.

When she opened the front door, she couldn't prevent her mouth from dropping open in stunned surprise. Talk about physical splendor!

"Rook, you're absolutely beautiful," she gasped.

He was wearing a black tuxedo with an elegantly pleated dress shirt that looked snowy against the bronze of his skin. His newly clipped hair had been brushed until it shone and the hand he raised to straighten his burgundy bow tie had been neatly manicured. In his other hand he held a bouquet of lilies of the valley which he presented to her with a courtly bow.

"Happy birthday, Hannah."

"My favorite flower—you remembered. Thank you."

She leaned toward him, inclined to express her pleasure with a kiss, but he stepped back quickly. Her smile died.

"What's wrong?" she asked. "I...was only going to kiss you."

"Hannah, you look so beautiful tonight. I wouldn't want you to ruin that perfection by smudging your lipstick." He had to bite the inside of his cheek to prevent a smile at the priggishness of his words.

"Oh." She gave a small, uncertain laugh. "Of course. Well, I'll just put these in some water and we can go."

When they left the cottage, she caught her breath again. Rook had come for her in a chauffeured limousine, its elegant black sleekness almost comic by contrast to the prairie track and humble cottage. With a grave smile, Rook carefully assisted her into the car, closing the door and going around to the other side to get in. He exchanged a few murmured words with the chauffeur and the vehicle began moving smoothly across the pasture, the hum of its powerful engine barely audible. Hannah looked around the luxurious interior, stroking the tufted velvet upholstery.

"This is the most beautiful car I've ever seen," she said, laying a hand on his sleeve. "Believe me, I never thought I'd ever be riding in a chauffeured limousine through a barnyard! This is really the most outrageous thing you'd done yet, Rook." She leaned closer. "But I love it, I really do!"

"Careful, sweetheart," he warned softly, "you don't want to crush the skirts of that pretty dress."

She wanted to tell him she didn't give a damn about her stupid dress, but she held her tongue. Something about the distracted expression in his eyes made her simply smile faintly and remove her hand from his arm. What was wrong with him tonight? He didn't seem angry, only very, very distant.

Once they were on the highway, Rook leaned forward to press a button. A small refrigerator was revealed, containing a plate of fruit and cheeses, as well as a chilled bottle of white wine, which he uncorked and poured into etched crystal wineglasses.

Hannah felt deliciously decadent sipping wine in isolated luxuriousness as the limousine purred quietly through the night. Several humorous observations crowded into her mind, but she was reluctant to break the silence in the car by voicing them. What a good time they could be having if only Rook wasn't so restrained and withdrawn. She discovered that she missed his usual spontaneity.

Eventually she realized they were cruising through the city streets of Wichita, and not long afterward they came to a stop in front of a tall, fanciful building. The brick facade, Moorish in tone, was painted pale blue with white trim; a marquee with flashing lights proclaimed it the Crown Uptown.

As Rook helped her from the limousine she exclaimed, "It's a theater!"

"Yes, a dinner theater. I think you'll like it."

Hannah more than liked it, she fell in love with it, even though the posters and theatrical displays in the lobby were painful reminders of her fateful dinner party. She'd never forget the reaction she had gotten when she'd asked what plays her guests had seen. They'd let her believe the Midwest was totally devoid of theaters, and now here she was, being ushered into a very sophisticated little playhouse of the kind she liked best.

Eyes shining, she took in the old-time elegance of the theater's interior—the graceful balconies, swagged draperies and, most charming of all, a high ceiling that sparkled with stars, like the prairie night.

"This is wonderful," she breathed. "But why aren't there any other people here?"

"This is your evening, Hannah. I didn't want anyone else to spoil your good time."

"Are you saying that you rented this entire theater?"

He nodded, taking her elbow. They followed the usher to the only table in the room set for dinner. Arranged on pale pink linen, china and silver gleamed in the light of two mauve tapers; a centerpiece of white gardenias filled the air with heavenly fragrance.

As Rook seated her, Hannah saw a gift-wrapped box beside her plate. She touched it with her fingertips and looked up at Rook.

"It's a birthday gift," he explained, sitting down across from her. "Go ahead and open it."

"But you've done so much," she said. "All this extravagance..."

He waved away her protests. "Don't worry about that. I just want you to have the perfect evening."

She lowered her eyes quickly, lest he get a glimpse of the uncertainty she was feeling. Why did he keep using the word *perfect*?

Inside the slim white box was a bracelet and earrings of square-cut green stones in old-fashioned gold settings. Hannah caught her breath sharply.

"Oh, these are gorgeous, Rook!" She held them up and they caught the fire of the candle flames. Her eyes widened in disbelief. "Oh, my God...are these...?" She raised her eyes to his. "They're real emeralds, aren't they?"

"You should expect nothing less from the Land of Oz. The Emerald City only stocks the real thing, you know."

"And you know I can't possibly accept such an expensive gift."

"Hon...Hannah, I chose them because I knew they'd match your eyes perfectly. I've waited a long time to see you wear them, so please don't argue. Put them on, and we'll discuss the details later."

She decided not to make matters worse by being obstinate. She'd wear the jewelry tonight, but tomorrow it had to go back to whatever exclusive shop it had come from.

She removed the earrings she was wearing and replaced them with the emeralds. She distinctly heard Rook's indrawn breath and saw the motion of his hand as he reached across the table toward hers. Then, as if he'd suddenly regretted the action, his fingers stopped just inches from hers, though he couldn't quite smother the fire that leaped within his eyes. Hannah thought his lips formed the word, "Beautiful," but he didn't say it aloud. Tears stung her own eyes, and she felt as miserable as she ever had in her life.

"Good evening and welcome to our humble little establishment."

The man who had come to stand beside their table rocked back and forth on his toes, smiling pleasantly. Rook introduced him as the owner of the dinner theater, informing her that he often took part in his own productions.

"Yes, if you watch closely, you may see me tonight. I'll be the handsome one in the second act."

"We're going to see a play?" Hannah asked, astonished. "Just the two of us?"

"Certainly. And one I hope will entertain you."

"But . . . it hardly seems worth your while."

The man winked broadly. "Rest assured, Rook has made it well worth our while. Ah, here is your dinner. I'll go get into my makeup and talk to you later. Enjoy!"

Over cream of broccoli soup served in delicate china, Hannah decided to try to draw Rook out. She felt as if they were two tongue-tied teenagers on a first date! Why, when everything was otherwise so special, did she persist in thinking something was disastrously wrong?

"This is a lovely place," she began. "I've never been in such a unique theater. Especially one hired exclusively for me."

He smiled politely and went back to his soup. With a small jolt, Hannah realized he had abandoned his usual exuberant eating style, making no move that was not socially correct. He was even dipping the soupspoon *away* from himself, something no one else she knew bothered to do anymore! Consternation clouded her eyes. What was he trying to prove? She'd never faulted him for his table manners—they were more than adequate. In fact, she'd always liked to watch him eat because he did it with such obvious appetite, the same way he approached . . . well, other things they had done together. With a tinge of rose on her cheeks, she attempted further conversation.

"You know you have gone to too much trouble and expense over tonight, don't you?"

"Not at all. I've looked forward to it." When he glanced up at her she could swear he was deliberately shuttering a warm expression.

"It really isn't fair, though. I don't even know when your birthday is."

"January 25," he replied, nodding at the hovering waitress who then began clearing away the soup plates.

Trying for some kind of reaction, Hannah commented, "January? See, I won't even be here to repay you for this wonderful evening."

She didn't know what she had expected, but it wasn't a look so totally empty of emotion.

"I don't expect you to repay me, Hannah. That wasn't the idea behind this celebration, at all."

A prickle of irritation went through her. "Then just what was the idea behind it?" she asked with asperity.

Blandly he answered, "I simply wanted you to have a perfect time. No fires, no shipwrecks, no musk after-shave."

When his usual teasing smile didn't materialize, she wouldn't let herself admit how much she had hoped to see it. The little imp was back in her mind, urging her to try harder to provoke a more satisfactory response from Rook.

"January 25, did you say? That makes you an Aquarius." She toyed with her fork. "Of course, you probably wouldn't believe in anything as unfounded and unscientific as astrology, would you?"

She could see that he sensed her challenge; and for a few seconds, she thought he was going to react to it. There had been a time, she knew, when he would have taken the opposite side in an argument, no matter what he truly believed, just so they could enjoy the verbal sparring.

"To tell the truth, sweetheart, I don't actually know enough about astrology to have an informed opinion one way or the other."

Damn, she couldn't even goad him into a disagreement!

When he placidly started on the endive salad just being served, she had to resist the urge to upset the dinner table. She wracked her brain for the reason behind his odd behavior. Perhaps he was still disgruntled about the awkward timing of her sneezing attack; she knew he'd planned an intimate evening that hadn't worked out. Still, that was the night she'd found out about his dishonesty, and it seemed to her that she had more reason to be angry then he. If she was prepared to overlook what he had done, what was his problem? Of course, he didn't really act angry...in fact, she was simply unable to define his mood.

Following the salad they were served the main course, a specialty of the house: Beef Morris—beef, baby carrots and pearl onions simmered in wine sauce and covered with a flaky pastry. It was accompanied by hot bread, cold wine and, on Rook's part, lukewarm courtesy.

Halfway through the course, Hannah was fighting the urge to start babbling just to break the intolerable silence when, to her relief, a trio of violinists stepped through the stage curtain and began to serenade them. The relief was short-lived, for she soon realized they were playing all her favorite songs, one after another. Her emotions were in a turmoil; she was touched that Rook had done this for her, but she was also unhappily aware that she must have talked an excessive amount about herself for him to know her so well. Her self-esteem plunged. What a selfish witch she must be! Was that what Rook was trying to tell her?

By the time their plates were cleared away and they were having coffee and fruit, she was positively morose. The combination of sentimental music and self-disgust was having an adverse effect on her. She was beginning to doubt she could survive the rest of the evening without a major bout of hysterics. Whatever nefarious purpose Rook had had in mind, things were definitely going his way.

The violinists finished their last song with a flourish, then bowed deeply and took their places in the orchestra pit, along with the other musicians now filing in from the wings.

A short time later the curtain went up, and Hannah's mood lightened considerably. The haunting overture and misty hills of Scotland depicted by the stage setting told her the Crown Players were going to perform *Brigadoon*, her favorite musical. It never failed to enchant her, and tonight was no exception. There was a distinct pleasure in emptying her mind of her own problems and immersing herself in the love story unfolding on the stage, letting the familiar music soothe and relax her.

Rook was, as always, impressed with the talent and professionalism of the Crown actors, but tonight he simply couldn't keep his mind on the play. His stubborn eyes, bored with the bright costumes and plywood village, strayed to Hannah's face again and again. Willfully, they traced the contours of her delicately carved profile, resting on her slightly parted lips and the dark hair winging back to display the sparkling earrings. Rivaling the glow of the jewels, her green eyes contained a rapt expression that he suddenly, fiercely wanted to see turned upon himself. His fingers tightened around the stem of the wineglass he held. If he gave vent to his frustrations now it would spoil the evening and, for once, he was determined that was not going to happen.

After the performance, when the players came to their table to meet Hannah, Rook invited them to stay for drinks, and the next hour was passed in animated conversation. Later, as they left the theater, a bagpiper in tartan stood outside and piped them away in fine Scottish tradition. Instead of the limousine, they were met by a horse-drawn carriage which took them for a midnight drive along the river.

"The perfect romantic touch," Hannah assured Rook, resting her head against the high curved back of the carriage. This time when she reached for his hand, he didn't pull away. They rode in silence, their fingers lightly entwined, resting on his thigh.

The limousine was waiting for them in a riverside park and only moments after the ride home began, Hannah was fast asleep, her head nestled on Rook's shoulder. Far from feeling sleepy, Rook himself gazed moodily out the window at the darkness.

"You're home, Hannah," he said, shaking her gently to rouse her. "Come on, I'll walk you to the door."

He helped her from the car and after speaking with the chauffeur in low tones, took her arm and led her down the front walk to the cottage.

"There are lights on," she said in alarm. "I didn't leave any lights!"

He opened the door and a rush of cool, fragrant air enveloped them.

"Oh, good Lord!" she gasped, one hand flying to her mouth in stunned surprise. The living room was a mass of blooms. Flowers of every imaginable kind covered the tables, the mantel, the bookshelves and the window sills. There were huge bouquets of roses, lilies, carnations and baby's breath, their combined scents overpowering in the tiny room. On the polished dining-room table was a three-tiered birthday cake decorated with violets and pink rosebuds. Pastel streamers and pink balloons festooned every doorway.

Eyes brilliant with unshed tears, Hannah turned to Rook who was quietly closing the front door. "You shouldn't have done this . . . it's too much!"

"Don't you like it?"

"I love it! It's a fairy tale come true, but . . ."

"You keep waiting for the prince to turn into a frog?" His lips quirked upward, but there was no humor in the smile.

She brushed her fingers over the fluted edge of a bowl containing an arrangement of irises. "That's not what I meant."

"Don't tell me—you got the same thing for your birthday last year."

"No one has ever given me a roomful of flowers before. I've never even heard of such a thing."

"Whoa. Isn't that the sort of gesture heroes from romance novels make all the time?"

"Oh, so that's why you did it?" Disappointment sounded in her voice.

"Isn't that reason enough?"

"No," she cried, "it isn't. Obviously you've gone to a lot of trouble for something that doesn't mean a thing to you."

"Strangely enough," he said, "it means everything in the world to me."

"I don't understand...."

"Let me ask you a question, Hannah. Did you enjoy yourself tonight?"

"Of course. It was an extravagantly romantic evening. A dream come true."

She saw him wince at her words and hastened to reassure him.

"Rook, really, it was the kind of night every girl fantasizes about. I've had the best time of my life."

He sighed. "I was afraid of that."

"Afraid? What do you mean?"

"Let me ask you something else. What if I'd suggested going on a picnic down at the lake for your birthday? Maybe some fried chicken and cold beer, a blanket on the sand. We could have gone swimming or danced to music on the radio."

"I wouldn't have objected," she said slowly. "It sounds like fun."

"But it wouldn't have been the same, would it? It wouldn't have been grand or romantic."

"What difference does that make?"

"I think it might have made a lot of difference to you. It would probably have rained; or there'd have been sand in the potato salad. Or I'd have eaten the fried chicken with my fingers."

Hannah sank down on the couch. "So?"

"So?" He crossed the room to stand in front of her. "So...you hate imperfection, remember? You'd have been upset if we couldn't find Broadway music on the radio...or if the only flowers were cowslips or Queen Anne's lace. And, God knows, making love on the beach would have been absolutely sordid! You couldn't have seen anything fun or exciting or adventurous about an evening like that, could you?''

She pressed trembling fingers to her aching forehead. ''Am I really that demanding? That spoiled?''

''In a way,'' he said slowly. ''But, honey, I think you're mostly just confused.''

''What do you mean?''

He started pacing back and forth in front of the couch. ''All your life you've been handed a bill of goods where love is concerned. Your ideas of that particular emotion are based on notions as insubstantial as . . . as a desert mirage. All you know about it is what you've read in a book or seen in some old movie. Or dreamed up in your own imagination.''

''That's not true! What about my parents?'' she cried. ''Do you think I made up their happiness? Don't I have the right to want that for myself?''

''What is so wonderful about a love that shuts everyone else out? Tell me that.''

''I . . . I don't know what you mean.''

''The night you told me about sitting on the stairs and watching your mother and father enjoy an intimate dinner for two, I got damned mad. What kind of parents, I wondered, would be so wrapped up in themselves that they would shut out their own daughter? Make her watch their happiness from a distance? My God, a family is supposed to *share* their love! I was sorry for you, Hannah, because I went through the same thing. I knew how you must have felt.''

''How dare you pity me? Our circumstances were nothing alike! And you don't know anything about my feelings.''

He turned to face her. ''Are you sure? I think you're still that same little girl, always standing on the outside looking in, afraid to let yourself experience real life for fear someone else will reject you. Your damned dreams are a defense mechanism, sweetheart, if only you'd admit it. I think you really want perfection because you know it's never going to be possible. No matter how long you look, you won't find it, and in the meantime you're safe from any potentially hurtful situation.''

"I don't care to be lectured by an amateur psychologist," she spat, leaping to her feet.

"No, I'll just bet you don't. If you look too closely, you might see some truths you don't want to face."

"Such as?" she challenged.

"Such as the fact that perfection isn't really as wonderful as you've led yourself to believe."

"That's crazy. How could perfection not be...perfect?"

"I did everything I could to make tonight perfect, and I don't know about you but I was pretty damned bored. It isn't much fun when you can't say or do what you want because it might not be gentlemanly, or when you can't enjoy a meal for minding your manners. When you can't relax and get carried away by an excellent play because you might forget and make some spontaneous remark or laugh at the wrong time. Tonight was so elaborately engineered that it was exhausting. Frankly, I'd rather have worn myself out rolling around in the sand."

She glared at him. "You are so crude!"

"So you've told me several times. And now I see how silly it is for someone like me to attempt to be something I'm not. Wearing a tuxedo and renting a fancy car just doesn't get it. I'm a plain Kansas cowboy who likes bumping across the pasture in my old pickup with Hank Williams, Jr. on the radio and a few beers in the cooler. I don't mind getting dressed up once in a while to show my lady a good time, but I don't want to live that way."

"Meaning?"

"Meaning that I'm not Matthew or anyone like him. And I'm through trying to be."

"I've never asked that of you," she pointed out.

"True enough. You're too big a coward to ask anything of me. I might just manage to succeed at it, and then you'd have to deal with me on a more permanent basis."

"That's your opinion," she snapped.

"And we both know you don't want my opinion or my help and advice. In fact, there's only one thing you seem to want from me...."

He gripped her arm and jerked her against his chest, his mouth hard and angry as he took hers in a devouring, almost savage kiss. Both hands dropped to her waist, pulling her tight into the grip of his thighs. She struggled briefly, her hands flailing against his shoulders, but when he raised his head and looked into her eyes his expression was so tormented that she felt her wrath give way to surprised compassion. With a muffled groan, he touched her lips with a mouth now soft and coaxing, gently persuading her to surrender. As if she had no will of her own, her mouth opened to his and she pressed against him, her hands beginning a slow massage of his shoulders.

She loved the heat of his hands as they spread across her back, effortlessly holding her prisoner. She loved the feel of his hard body, the scent of his skin. She loved...oh, God, she loved *him*. She did! Why had it taken her so long to know what was really in her mind?

The sensation of warmth flowed through her as his hands slid to her waist again, then upward to thrust aside the thin fabric of her evening gown. She regretted the removal of his mouth from hers, but reveled in the feel of its heat on her breasts. She moaned his name and arched closer.

It's going to be all right, she thought. Whatever is wrong is going to be all right....

Rook scattered sweet, feverish kisses from her breasts to the pulse thrumming at the hollow of her throat; he placed a soft kiss on the sensitive curve of neck and shoulder, then lovingly grazed the skin with his teeth. Lightly, he nipped at her earlobe, and she could hear his ragged breathing. Her own breath was coming in short excited gasps. Her fingers wove themselves through the thick hair at the back of his neck and forced his mouth back to hers.

Rook lifted his head, gazing into her eyes for a long moment. He saw the passion reflected there, felt the heavenly rise and fall of her breasts against his chest. He brushed a kiss at each corner of her parted lips.

"This is the one area where I'm able to please you," he murmured. He touched her bottom lip with a thumb.

"Oh, yes," she breathed, "you please me very much."

"Even though I'm an old plowhorse instead of the thoroughbred you wanted?"

"Don't start that corny farm talk with me, Rook... please!"

"But I've got something to say, love, and I don't know any better way to express it than to relate it to what I know best." His smile was slow, rueful. "It's this way—I think I've got the heart of a champion, but if I'm not good enough to run the whole race with you, I'll be damned if I'm going to stand at stud."

When his hands fell away from her, she stumbled and nearly fell. His words made her face flame, but the wave of pain enveloping her was icy cold.

"By the way—before I go, I have another gift for you," he said calmly. He drew an envelope from an inside pocket and dropped it on the couch. "You were right about my father. He was more of a bastard than even I knew."

"Rook, wait," she cried pleadingly as he started toward the door.

"There's really no point in continuing this conversation," he said. "I've learned what I needed to know."

"Would it help if I said I'm sorry? If I said I wanted to talk things over?"

A rueful smile played over his lips. "I'd say it's too late. And then I'd advise you to conjure up good old reliable Matthew—see if he won't take you to bed. Wouldn't that be the perfect ending to a perfect day?"

When the door slammed behind him, Hannah ran to the window, half expecting him to regret his haste and come back. Instead he climbed into the limousine and soon all she could see were the red taillights bouncing along the rutted road.

Absentmindedly she lifted the sheaf of white roses lying on the windowsill, pressing her face into their glorious fragrance. Thoughts of the evening just past flitted wildly through her mind, but the most persistent was the image of Rook—that crooked smile masking the hurt in his eyes. Her fingers tightened convulsively on the roses, bringing an unexpected stab of pain. Thorns! Even something as flawless as a rose had its imperfections. Suddenly she thought she knew what Rook had been trying to tell her for so long.

Chapter Thirteen

Hannah wasn't sure she ever wanted to smell flowers again! Even with the windows wide open, the scent was almost overpowering. But she appreciated their visual beauty and, after some serious thought, the reason Rook had made the gesture in the first place.

The night of her birthday, when he had turned his back and walked away, her immediate inclination had been to throw every blossom in the room out after him. Then she had picked up those white roses and just that easily her perspective had changed. Instead of destroying the flowers she had labored to take care of them, putting the individual blooms into vases and watering the plants and arrangements faithfully. Only after a bouquet had wilted and faded beyond recognition did she throw it away.

It wasn't until the second day that she found a small envelope from the florist's shop stuck in the leafy ferns surrounding a dozen crimson rosebuds. Scrawled on the card in Rook's distinctive handwriting was a simple message: "Happy birthday, Hannah. I love you. Rook."

She read it over and over, unaware she had started to cry until the tears fell on his words, making the ink blur. How like him that message was! Plain, simple and to the point. No beating around the bush, no equivocating. No caution. He'd written the note before their evening together, uncertain how things would turn out. He'd been courageous enough to put his heart on the line, even knowing she might walk all over it. She read the card again. She'd give a lot to be that brave.

Rook was right when he called her a coward. Though she'd denied the words when he spoke them, in her soul she knew it was true. Why had she never recognized her hidden resentment? Or faced up to the fact that she had been so close to her grandmother because that dear woman had really been the only one with time to spare for her?

The feelings of inadequacy and insecurity engendered by forever being the one left behind when her parents were off on some thrilling new adventure had almost surely given rise to her dislike of reality. And as she had grown older, the daydreams had virtually taken over her life. She had slowly but surely wrapped herself in an insulating cocoon of fantasy, magical in its ability to protect and sustain her.

Now she was faced with an ugly realism. At twenty-seven years of age, the cocoon was being stripped away and she was about to emerge into the real world. What if instead of a beautiful butterfly she discovered she was only a plain brown moth?

She had known instinctively that when Rook closed the door behind him he had not been saying a final farewell. In some way, he had laid his cards on the table and now it was her play. He was willing to back off and let her consider the alternatives, then make her decision. With equal surety, she knew that if she chose to end matters between them and go back to New York he would say or do nothing to stop her. But she didn't know what his reaction would be if she elected to stay—if she told him she'd be around as long as he wanted her. Had she misread him? Would he, at this point, merely laugh and coldly reject her offer? Somehow, from somewhere within herself, she was going to have to summon the courage to find out.

She crossed the room to the bookshelves and picked up the white envelope Rook had left with her just before his departure that night. Its contents were another matter that must be put right, though that bit of business would not require any undue heroism. It had been a sweet and sentimental act on Rook's part, and though she loved him for it, she could never accept what he so generously wanted to give.

With sudden purpose, she dropped the envelope into her purse. She would take care of it first, then turn her mind to the resolution of other, more difficult dilemmas.

Driving toward the McAllister farm, she experienced an unexpected thrill as she passed acres of wheat on either side of the road. The fields looked like golden oceans, the sun-ripened grain undulating in the hot wind like waves. It was fascinating, hypnotic. Some fields stretched away as far as the eye could see, an awe-inspiring reminder of the incredible space and freedom to be found in Kansas. Easily, her mind turned to Rook and she thought how like this state he was—rugged, even fierce at times, but gentle and nurturing, as well.

A scene that might have come directly from her coffee-table book of Kansas photographs now loomed before her. Three dusty red combines moved in perfect symmetry across a field, felling the tawny wheat in matching swaths. She knew with certainty that Rook was inside one of those combines, and the very thought of his nearness suddenly strengthened her, urging her mind down the long path to decisiveness. In a burst of self-truth, she realized her heart had raced ahead and was already waiting there.

Helen McAllister opened the front door and regarded Hannah with an uncertain smile.

"It's good to see you, my dear."

"Thank you. I...I came to bring this back...." She held up the long white envelope, then took a deep, unsteady breath and finished her speech in a rush of words. "...and to tell you I love your son and need your help in figuring out how to convince him of that."

Mrs. McAllister's smile broadened. "Thank God," she murmured, reaching out to draw Hannah inside.

Hannah unburdened her soul over iced tea and sugar cookies. She told Rook's mother about the night of her birthday, about what she thought Rook had been attempting to prove.

"Now I see how he must have hated my daydreaming and my...obsession with perfection. He could have raged at me about it, but instead he chose a calm, sensible way to point out the errors in my thinking. I believe he did everything in his power to give me a perfect evening, but he really didn't want me to enjoy it, did he?"

Helen McAllister retreated behind her glass of tea.

"He wanted me to see that everything can be perfect...and yet, meaningless. The best food, the best wine, the best entertainment are nothing without a spark of...what? Life? Joy? I don't know exactly how to define it."

Hannah couldn't sit still a moment longer. Setting aside her glass, she began to pace up and down in front of the bay window. "There we were, having a spectacular evening and yet something was all wrong. Rook didn't laugh or tease or even smile much." She grinned. "He knew exactly what he was doing, didn't he?"

"It may seem that way to you, Hannah," the other woman said, "but he was really quite terrified about the whole thing. Of course, Winston would strangle me if he knew I was telling you that, but it's true. He agonized over whether or not he was doing the right thing. You see, on the one hand, he wanted to be subtle—in order to find out your true feelings. On the other, he was so certain you'd choose Matthew and your daydreams over him that he almost backed out several times. He kept saying, 'What if she doesn't see? Or worse, doesn't care!'"

"I should have admitted that all the money and effort he put into my birthday couldn't compensate for the lack of enthusiasm on his part." She fixed Rook's mother with a slightly dazed expression. "Helen, your son is very special."

"Yes, I know. Oh, you may think that sounds very smug and complacent but, Hannah, I've known it for a long time. All those years I saw him struggling for some kind of warmth or recognition from his father proved it. He was never bitter or defeated, and he never lost the respect he had for J.W. I have to wonder if my husband ever sensed what he had missed by not allowing Winston to love him.''

Hannah shuddered. "It scares me to think how close I came to doing the same thing to Rook! To myself!"

"But you're not going to, dear, and that's the important thing."

"You're right. I want to clear up this little matter," she declared, waving the envelope, "and then I am going to get down to the serious business of humbling my stubborn pride."

"You don't have to worry about that," Helen said, indicating the envelope. "It was a birthday gift, one we want you to accept."

"The deed to a section of ground I have no legal right to? No, I'm sorry, I can't take it. Your husband may have used less-than-honorable tactics to acquire the land, but that was between him and my grandmother. The property belongs to you and Rook now, without obligation to me or anyone else. I realize Rook was probably very upset when he learned what J.W. had done...but I never wanted this." She picked up the envelope containing the deed and handed it to Helen. "Please, give it back to him and tell him thanks, but no thanks. Will you?"

"I'll give it to him, but I can't promise to make him understand your reluctance to regain your family's land."

"I'll make him understand that later. There are more important issues to be dealt with first." Hannah returned to her chair, sitting on the edge of the seat, her knees close to those of the older woman. "I saw Rook and his men in the wheat fields."

"Yes, the harvest is in full swing. They've been working long hours."

"When will they be finished?"

"Oh, by the end of the week, I'd say. Why?"

"I may be from the city, but I've learned enough about life on the farm to know that everything waits for the baling or the planting or whatever! But if you will send word the minute the harvest is over, I have a plan...."

* * *

Ominous charcoal-colored clouds had been building all afternoon, massing high in the west to gradually spill out over the rest of the cobalt sky. The first faint ripples of lightning had just begun to dance along the horizon, accompanied by the low brass rumble of thunder.

Rook shoved his begrimed cowboy hat farther back onto his head and wiped his brow with a dusty forearm, leaving streaks of dirt on his forehead. He was hot and tired, his back aching from hours of bouncing over rough ground in the combine. But he knew he was no worse off than the rest of the harvest crew, and if they could all keep up the pace they'd have the last of the wheat cut before the storm broke.

He reached for a jug of ice water and took a deep swallow, thinking longingly of the air-conditioned cabs on the other two combines. The drivers took turns, but as luck would have it, this had been his day to drive the old machine.

At least it has a radio, he thought, turning the dial. Ironically, the cab was immediately filled with the sounds of a Hank Williams, Jr. song. Rook's jaw clenched in angry pain as he leaned forward to shut it off.

If there was one thing he didn't need right now, it was another reminder of Hannah. Lord knew, there had been enough of them already. For an instant, his mind dwelt on the evening three days ago when he'd come in from the fields to find his mother waiting, the deed to Hannah's property in her hand. As soon as he saw it, his heart went into a nosedive, plummeting to the worn soles of his old boots.

"Hannah brought this by, son," his mother had said carefully. "She says she can't accept it, that she doesn't want the land."

He'd known that what she really was saying was that she didn't want anything from him. He also knew it probably meant she'd soon be going back east, putting him and their whole miserable relationship behind her.

Face it—you screwed up, ol' buddy, he'd told himself, shoving the envelope containing the deed into the back of a dresser drawer. You should have left well enough alone, but no, you wanted to prove a point. Well, you sure as hell proved it!

And still, he couldn't give it up. At night he'd lie in bed and stare at the ceiling where a shimmer of light reflected from the pool below created a fascinating display, inducing a relaxed state of near-sleep. With relaxation came thoughts of Hannah—thoughts that teased and tormented, urging him to find a way...any way...to change her mind.

Now that the harvest was nearly over he would have the time and energy to deal with those thoughts, he promised himself.

A louder, more threatening roar of thunder sounded, causing him to cast an appraising glance at the stormy sky. They were going to have to push it to beat the rain. With effort, he forced his mind away from the temptation of Hannah and back to the reality of the bright golden wheat falling victim to the churning reel at the front of the combine.

Two hours later Rook watched as the last truck loaded with wheat rumbled out of the field on its way to the grain elevator. Harvest was officially over. All that remained to be done was to get the combines under cover in the machine shed where the mechanics would check them over thoroughly before putting them in storage until fall.

He flexed his tired arm muscles, then swung the water jug onto a shoulder, turning his head to take a long swallow. As he did so, he saw the old pickup rattling onto the field and was relieved that Dusty had come to take him home. The sky had darkened considerably and a cooler wind had sprung up. The increasing thunder and lightning were evidence that rain could not be far away.

Calling some last-minute instructions to the mechanic who was climbing into his combine, he went to meet Dusty.

Tossing the plastic water jug into the back of the pickup, he opened the door on the passenger side and got in.

"My butt's really dragging," he commented, sliding down in the seat and stretching out his legs.

"It looks fine to me." The quiet alto voice was definitely too feminine-sounding to be Dusty's!

Rook straightened up so fast he hit his head on the roof of the truck, knocking his hat askew.

Hannah, arms draped over the steering wheel, was observing him with amusement, though there was a hint of uncertainty in her silvery-green eyes. She looked as out of place in the scroungy old pickup as a Hell's Angel at Sunday school, but he was so glad to see her he had to clamp his hands on the edge of the seat to keep from grabbing her then and there.

"What are you doing here?" he forced himself to ask calmly. "I was expecting Dusty."

"I hope you're not disappointed." Her smile was a little wobbly. "I came to get you because there are some things I have to say."

He studied her. "What kind of things?"

"Oh," she said airily, "important things. Things that should have been said a long time ago."

He drew a deep breath. "It sounds interesting, I have to admit. But why don't you drive me home so I can get cleaned up and I'll come over to your place later?"

She shook her head. "No chance." Clumsily she shifted gears, wincing as they ground noisily. "Now that I've got your attention, I'm not letting you out of my sight."

"I'm not trying to give you the slip," he countered. "But I'd really like to take a bath...."

"Sorry, Rook, but I've been patient as long as I can. You might as well sit back and relax. Consider yourself at my mercy."

He quirked one dusty brow. "Honey, the way it looks to me, that's where I've always been."

As the truck bumped out of the field and onto the gravel road, he found he could not keep from staring at her, his eyes greedy for glimpses of what they had been denied too long. She looked cool and fresh in a white sundress that laced up the front from a narrow waist. A full skirt was bunched over her knees, leaving an enticing view of slender legs and feet encased in ridiculously feminine white sandals. She had pinned her hair on top of her head, and Rook was filled with an almost ungovernable urge to kiss the spot where loose tendrils curled against the nape of her neck. He tightened his hold on the seat, his knuckles showing white through their griminess.

Hannah sneaked another quick look at the man beside her. Rook seemed tense, she thought, and a little wary, but he made no objection as she turned in at the gate on the lane to her cottage, stopping to padlock it behind them.

She couldn't believe her own reaction to his nearness. Her pulse was racing, her heart hammering unsteadily. All the words she had so carefully rehearsed had fled her bemused mind leaving her unable to think of anything but how much she had missed him.

He looked wonderful, even beneath a layer of good Kansas soil. His jeans were old, faded nearly white in all the interesting places where jeans tend to fade. He was wearing a red-checked cotton shirt whose sleeves had been ripped off at the shoulder seams. It was so thin and threadbare she could see through it in places, and it didn't take much imagination to envision it falling to shreds beneath her marauding hands.

No, she cautioned herself, you can't think like that! Coming on too strong would be the worst possible thing to do. You've got to talk to the man, not attack him.

She dared another look and this time caught him looking at her. Their eyes locked for several long seconds, and then he smiled, causing her to very nearly drive the truck through the fence surrounding her cottage. She slammed on the brakes, rocking them to an abrupt stop.

Somewhat breathlessly she said, "Let's go inside where we can . . . talk."

At that moment the first raindrops streaked across the windshield.

The cottage looked somewhat bare to Rook and it took him a moment to realize why. The last time he'd seen it, it had been crammed with Hannah's birthday flowers. Now all that remained were a dozen or so plants scattered about the room. The cloying floral fragrance was gone, replaced by a decidedly savory aroma. He sniffed appreciatively.

"Your mother gave me the recipe for your favorite pheasant and wild rice casserole," Hannah explained. "As well as a pheasant from her freezer."

"So," he queried, tossing his hat onto the coat rack in the hall, "you intend to feed your prisoner?"

"When the time is right. Would you like to sit down?"

"I'd like to wash up."

"You can do that in a minute. Right now I have to get something off my chest."

His eyes shifted with undisguised interest to the low-cut neck of her sundress with its inviting lacing, and Hannah blushed.

"Sit down, please," she said, a trifle brusquely.

He dropped onto the hearth rug to sit Indian-style.

"I meant on the couch."

"I'm too dirty to sit on the couch," he pointed out. "And anyway, I'm very comfortable right here."

"I guess I can't expect you to make this any easier for me," she said, gripping the back of the wicker chair. "I..." She cleared her throat nervously. "It seems I've made things pretty hard for you from time to time."

His grin was positively lewd as he straightened out his legs and leaned back to look up at her. "From time to time," he agreed dryly.

Hannah concentrated on a piece of loose wicker on the chair back, not wanting to let him see the effect his smile was having. It was so good to have some sign the old Rook still existed!

"I'm sorry about that," she began.

"I'm not. I never was."

Now her head came up, and she was warmed by the tenderness in his dark, dark eyes. She took a step toward him.

"You don't hate me, then?"

"No, love, I don't hate you."

"You can't know how glad I am to hear that."

With sudden determination, she reached down to unbuckle one of her sandals, letting it drop carelessly to the floor. Her eyes still on his, she undid the second one, allowing it to slide slowly from her fingers.

"Hannah?" Rook's expression was puzzled, his mouth twisted in a faint half smile.

"Hmm?"

"What did you want to talk to me about?"

She walked close to him, so close her bare feet were tucked between his thighs. She rested a hand on each of his shoulders.

"I forget."

He turned his head and kissed the inside of her wrist.

"Rook?"

"Hmm?"

Her fingers slid along his shoulders and up into his thick hair. "Do you think we could talk . . . later?"

She bent her head to kiss him and felt him pull away.

"Honey, I'm filthy," he protested.

She smiled and brushed a light kiss on his upturned mouth. "I know. That's one of the things I like best about you." She gave him a second, slightly less fleeting kiss.

"You know what I mean," he said sternly. "I'm all sweaty and dusty. . . ."

"I don't care."

He looked shocked. "What did you say?"

"I said, I . . . don't . . . care." She rested her cheek on the top of his head and breathed in his male essence. The odors of earth and sun-warmed cotton mingled with the slightly acrid tang of sweat creating a surprisingly pleasant effect. Hannah raised her head and gently cupped his jaws with her hands, lifting his mouth for a lingering kiss. With an anguished moan, he rose to his knees and his arms went about her hips as he pulled her close, his face against her rib cage.

"I've missed you," she said simply, stroking the back of his neck with trembling fingers. "Please, Rook, let me show you how much."

"Hannah, your dress. . ." He looked grim as he noted the streaks of dirt his face and hands had left on the white cloth. "I need a bath."

She dropped to her knees, too, evading his feeble attempt to stave her off. Nestling close to his body, she pressed a kiss beneath his chin, feeling the rapid drum of his pulse against her lips.

He groaned, his hands gripping her shoulders. "Sweetheart, stop it! You don't want to do this."

"Who says I don't?" she whispered.

"But we were going to talk . . ." His words were muffled as she covered his face with a series of sweet kisses.

As her mouth explored his, she found he tasted like the smell of summer-ripe wheat, the discovery startling an intense earthiness to life within her.

"I can't remember a single thing I was going to say," she confessed with a smile, her fingers wandering to the lacing at the front of her dress. With deliberate slowness, she untied the small bow between her breasts and let the neckline gape invitingly. Rook turned such a burning gaze on her that she fully expected to burst into immediate flames. His hands stilled hers.

"Let me," he said in a voice so huskily roughened that it sent shivers up and down her spine.

She watched as his lean fingers deftly unlaced the ribbons of her bodice, infinitely stimulated by the sight of his tanned hands against her own paler skin. He pushed the loosened sundress off her shoulders and let it drift into a crumpled heap at her knees, leaving her clad only in a skimpy white lace bra and bikini panties. A tingling sensation erupted each place he touched as he unhooked her bra; the sensation spread throughout her body as he brushed aside the scrap of lace and caught her eagerly thrusting breasts in his hands. His fingers moved to caress their rounded sides, letting the weight of each breast rest on the arc of thumb and forefinger. She clutched his shoulders, wildly excited by the bold touch of his heated mouth on her sensitive nipples, the brush of his hair against her neck. Shocks of sensual enjoyment streaked through her, conducting an electricity she had never felt before.

"Oh, Rook!" she gasped, arching closer, her hands moving restlessly across his wide shoulders and down his back. Her fingers, impatient with even the thin shirt that now separated them, gripped handfuls of cloth, tugging until she heard the satisfying sound of rending fabric. Burrowing beneath the shredded remains of the garment, her searching fingers found bare flesh, feverish to her touch.

One of Rook's knees insinuated its way between her thighs as he crushed her body to his, his own reluctance forgotten. He'd tried to keep himself under tight control, fearing she might, in a moment of passion, initiate a sexual encounter that would later spark disgust when she regained her senses. He'd fought to ignore temptation, refusing to think of the solace her willing body offered, denying the sweet promise of her searing kisses. But now, with her frantic hands touching him, he could do nothing but succumb. He was beyond rationality, lost in overwhelming sensation and ready to surrender to the raging desire to possess this woman, despite the eventual cost.

Caution be damned! he silently vowed, stretching out on the rug and pulling her down beside him.

"You asked for this," he muttered fiercely between clenched teeth, his eyes burning into hers.

"Yes, I did," she said demurely. "Thank you for not making me beg." She smiled serenely. "Though, of course, I would have. Gladly." She laced her hands behind his neck. "Rook, I just remembered one thing I meant to tell you." She drew his head down and whispered against his parted lips, "I love you."

He went perfectly still, as if uncertain he had heard her correctly. She laughed throatily and repeated the statement, punctuated with tiny kisses.

"I . . . love . . . you."

Suddenly Rook moved away from her, lying back on the rug, eyes closed. For one horrible moment, Hannah thought he was rejecting her and an icy terror gripped her heart. Then he opened his eyes, which were suspiciously moist, and fixed her with an intense gaze.

"You had better be telling me the truth, Hannah Grant, or so help me I won't be responsible for my actions."

Relief made her flash-fire temper flare. "Are you accusing me of lying about something that important, you . . . you plowboy-cowboy?"

"Don't think I haven't heard about fast women like you," he drawled, dark eyes twinkling. "You'd say anything just to get your hands on my body."

"Oh!" she spit, scrambling to her knees. "Let me suggest what you can do with your damned precious body...!"

His face was lighted by a huge grin as he seized her wrist and pulled her back into his embrace. One hand closed around the back of her neck, the thumb lightly brushing the curve of her cheek. "God, you're a snotty bitch," he murmured in a voice so tender it brought tears to her eyes. "And I love you more than anything in this world."

He raised her face to his, allowing his mouth to worship hers. He kissed her so thoroughly that her breath caught in her throat and she was once again ensnared by the all-pervading passion of a few minutes earlier.

Shamelessly she whispered in his ear, her hands roving over his chest and ribs to linger at the fastening to his jeans. His own hand moved to cover hers and assist in the removal of the last of his clothing. She sighed in unconcealed admiration as her eyes swept over him.

"You are a beautiful man," she breathed. "A beautiful, beautiful man."

"And you are overdressed," he pointed out, one finger hooking into the elastic at the top of her lace bikini panties.

Driven by an overriding urgency, they melted together, their bodies fitting perfectly. Motivated by the desire to bestow every pleasure imaginable on each other, they were, by turns, vigorous and gentle, tender and teasing. But as their feelings mushroomed, bringing them to some sort of climactic breaking point, they were no longer in command—they became hapless victims, randomly tossed by imperious currents of emotion, able to do little more than cling to each other, whispering small encouragements.

"I love you, Rook."

"I still can't believe it."

"It's true. I swear."

"Then say it again, sweetheart. Never stop saying it!"

"I love you...love you...oh! God, I love you!"

"I love you, too."

They experienced an emotional release that was shattering in its pure animal pleasure, soul-searing in its intensity. Dazed and humbled by the awesome depths of their feelings for each other, they lay quietly together and listened to the contented beating of two hearts in complete accord.

After a while, Hannah fashioned a makeshift pillow from her wrinkled, grimy sundress and the ruined shirt, and tucked it beneath Rook's head. Then she snuggled closer within his encircling arm and placed a warm kiss on his shoulder.

"You know," Rook remarked softly, "for an old plowhorse, I feel like I just won the Triple Crown."

Hannah smiled. "Well, it *was* a championship performance but, then, I think I've always known you were a thoroughbred."

"Championship?" he teased. "That good?"

"It was perfect," she mumbled drowsily. "Absolutely perfect."

Lulled by the peaceful sound of rain on the roof and fatigued by their emotional expression of passion, they drifted into a serene sleep.

Some time later Rook awoke to the smell of burning rice and the sound of scraping metal. He sat up and ran a hand through his tousled hair.

"Hannah?"

Stark naked, she was dragging the copper bathtub into the room. She straightened and flashed him a comical look. "I scorched the casserole," she announced, then shrugged. "I'm really not a very good cook."

His eyes smiled at her. "Nobody can do two things at the same time and do them well. And since you were definitely excelling in...other areas, I really couldn't care less about the casserole."

"How nice of you to say so." She turned beneath his admiring gaze and disappeared into the kitchen. When she returned, she was carrying a pail of steaming water.

"Good God, Hannah," he cried, leaping to his feet. "You'll scald yourself!"

He crossed the room and took the water from her, favoring her with a reproving look.

"I was only going to fill the tub so you could have a bath," she said in defense of her actions. Then, more meekly, "There are two more buckets of water in the kitchen. And your boots and clean clothes are in the bedroom."

"How'd they get there?"

"I had an accomplice—your mother."

"I figured as much."

She watched while the tub was filled, enraptured by the sight of Rook's splendid nudity as he moved about the cottage.

"Now what?" he asked, setting the last empty pail aside.

"Climb into the tub, and I'll get some soap and towels."

When she returned from the bedroom, she had to laugh at the sight of the long-legged man dwarfing the copper tub. He grimaced.

"This isn't going to work, honey. There isn't even room for a bar of soap in here."

"Don't you worry," she said, dropping to her knees beside the tub. "I'll manage somehow."

"You're going to bathe me? Well, I'll be damned. This has been one surprising day."

She dipped the washcloth into the water covering his flat midsection, then lathered the cloth with clove-scented soap. "Lean forward and I'll do your back first."

When he had complied with her brisk command, she moved around behind him and began applying soap to his shoulders. "We really do have business to conduct, you know."

He leaned his head back to look up at her. "Actually, I prefer the sort of business we *just* conducted," he said.

With an indulgent smile, she pushed his head forward and swept the soapy cloth down across the breadth of his back. "Yes, that was nice, but . . ."

"Hannah, what's wrong with you? Aren't you going to give me hell for not being serious?"

She reached around to douse the washcloth in the water again, leaning close to his ear. "Never again, I promise. You took care of that the night of my birthday."

"I did?"

"Don't pretend you didn't plan it that way," she laughingly scolded. "Your method was quite successful."

"Oh?"

She busied herself rinsing his back, then moved around to lather his chest. "I decided that I have more fun when you're your usual self. I missed your laughing and teasing that night. When I think how much more fun we could have had if only..."

"But you said the evening was perfect."

"Yes, and you said perfect wasn't all that wonderful and set out to prove it. You were so right, Rook—I know that now."

She paused in the washing of his arm. "Just as you were right about a lot of other things. My mother and father, for one. My own lack of courage, for another. My need for perfection." She sighed. "There, that's what I wanted to tell you. You were right about everything, and I was wrong."

"Honey, I wasn't just trying to be right for the principle of the thing, you know. I was fighting for...well, for some kind of future for us. I realized I had compromised my own pride when I made that ridiculous bargain with you. I could no more have let you go back to New York without a fight than I could have flown."

"But you weren't going to argue if I told you I never wanted to see you again after my birthday." She reached for his other arm.

"That's what you think." He grinned sheepishly. "I was already planning my strategy, sweetheart. I was a fool to think I could let what was between us die."

"Maybe we've both been fools in some ways," she said quietly. "But I think we have learned a few things. I'm not going back to New York until you throw me out."

"And I'm not going to do that until hell freezes over...twice."

She leaned forward to kiss him and his soapy arms closed about her. She softly shaped her mouth to his.

"I still don't understand about this evening," he said, gently nuzzling her neck. "I mean, my God, I was grungy and then some. How could you...well, I guess I'm trying to say I was far from being the perfect man. Why did you even let me touch you?"

She moved out of his embrace to resume the bath, trickling water over his chest and arms to rinse them. "Because I have finally learned that a man doesn't have to be perfect to be *perfect*. It can be the little imperfections and idiosyncrasies that make someone special. You made me realize I wouldn't change one thing about you." Face rosy, she grasped his foot and rubbed it briskly with the washcloth. "Besides, I loved being with you tonight. A bit of honest dirt can be downright ... exciting."

"Hannah, look at me," he softly ordered. His dark gaze roamed tenderly over her even features. "You aren't the only one with confessions to make, you know. I should have told you what I'd found out about my dad ... and not just made some stupid grand gesture that ended up insulting you."

She laid a hand on his knee. "Oh, no, I wasn't insulted! I didn't consider it necessary, that's all. If my grandmother could have met you and your mom, I'm sure she'd have felt the same way. That land is yours now and I know we can trust you to take good care of it. I'm going to trust you to do what is best with the cottage, too."

"Ah, the cottage," he said slowly. "That's another matter I'd like to get straightened out. I talked to Gerald Overton the other day, and he told me about certain information he'd passed on to you. Information about a deal I had made with the officials at the boys' ranch."

"Rook, it doesn't matter ... really."

"It does, sweetheart. I want you to know there was no deal. I never intended to sell this property to the ranch or anyone else. I wanted it for myself."

"But Gerald...."

"Was thinking like a banker. I'd often said I thought it would be a good camping site for the boys—and it will be— but I never meant I would sell it. The Overtons tend to forget I like to be a human first and a businessman second."

"Second, huh?" She swirled the dark hair on his chest with a soapy hand. "Funny, I can think of a number of your other attributes that definitely take precedence over your business acumen—in my book, at least."

"And I'd be interested in hearing them. But first, love, may I point out that you seem to have forgotten to wash one very important part of my body?"

Her smile was brilliant. "Why, so I did! Let me rectify that mistake immediately."

He settled back in the tub. "Be my guest."

"How could I have been so careless as to neglect your... face!"

She swiped the dripping cloth over his mouth and he spluttered indignantly.

"We have a saying here in Kansas," he muttered. "'Paybacks are hell!'"

She screamed in mock fright as his arm snaked around her waist, tumbling her into the tub with him. Sprawled across his lap, she splashed and struggled until he subdued her with a masterful kiss. "Besides," he whispered against her ear, "you really could use a bath. You're as dirty as I was!"

Due to circumstances completely within their control, her bath was brief. In a very short time, Rook was rising from the tub with her in his arms, streaming water as he strode across the floor to the bedroom beyond.

It was nearly midnight when Hannah, wearing her thin Victorian robe, finally made it into the kitchen to get their supper.

As she returned to the bedroom, she saw a pair of leather cowboy boots at the end of the bed. She blinked hard, then blinked again. This time the boots didn't disappear. They stayed stubbornly in place, looking very much as if they belonged there.

"They do add a certain macho charm to a room that is altogether too feminine," she murmured. "A very nice touch, indeed."

"What did you say, sweetheart?" inquired Rook from the bed, where he sat propped against the pillows.

She studied him, captivated by the golden sheen of lamplight on his muscular shoulders, and by the warm and loving glow in his onyx eyes.

"Oh, nothing... I was just warning you that this casserole doesn't look too appetizing."

"No big deal. My appetites have been efficiently taken care of for a short while, at least."

"Lecher," she chided fondly, handing him the tray containing plates of pheasant and scorched rice so she could climb in beside him. "Anyway, if this is too awful, we can always have dessert. My freezer is full of birthday cake!"

As he studied her smiling face, his ardent eyes grew serious. "Hannah," he said slowly, "how would you feel about getting married in Scotland?"

Ignoring the dinner tray, she leaned forward to press her mouth lovingly against his. "I'd adore it."

"But what would you think of living here in Kansas?"

"The Land of Ahhs, you mean? Oh, I think I could handle it."

"They don't have many book editors in Kansas," he warned.

"I don't mind. I've been toying with the idea of writing a novel based on my grandmother's life, anyway."

"A romance?" he questioned.

"What else?" she replied.

"I'd be willing to help with the research," he offered.

"How very generous of you," she accepted.

His gaze caressed the ivory skin barely concealed by the robe she wore, moved upward to her softly parted lips, and finally came to rest on her huge silvery-green eyes. "God, I love you, Hannah."

She grazed his chin with her fingertips. "Even if I am a lousy cook?"

With a devilish smile, he set the dinner tray aside and reached for her, pulling her into his arms.

"Honey," he said, his kiss warm on her mouth, "nobody's perfect."

"Yes," she breathed with a contented sigh. "I know."

Epilogue

Hannah lifted the sheer white-silk nightgown from its tissue paper and, folding it carefully, placed it in the open suitcase. It was followed by a more substantial robe of white velvet. Rook had warned her that castles in Scotland were chilly, even in summer.

She stuffed the last pair of panty hose into the suitcase and shut the lid.

Reaching for the list she had made earlier, she began checking off items. Tom and Jerry and three cases of cat food had already been left at Bev and Arlo's; Rook had called the carpenters and plumbers to order the installation of an indoor bathroom and new plumbing while they were gone; Dusty and Janice, who were to supervise the remodeling, had offered to water the plants and mow the grass; passports, plane tickets and travelers' checks were all safely tucked away in her purse. Everything was done except for the last-minute things that needed to be packed into her overnight case.

She caught sight of her reflection in the mirror and couldn't stifle an amused grin. Leaving from Wichita, she and Rook were making a stop in New York City to take care of unfinished business. What a stir they were going to make when they walked into Royal Publishing that afternoon and Hannah tendered her official resignation! She was wearing tight western jeans and boots, a pale blue chambray shirt and the fringed and beaded vest she'd bought at Cowtown. She couldn't begin to imagine the expressions on the faces of her friends and coworkers when they saw her—or, for that matter, when they saw Rook. For the first time, she considered the possibility that they would be envious. Without smugness, she hoped her good fortune would be a reminder to them that it paid to have a dream. Dreams sometimes had a funny way of coming true.

With nothing much left to do until Rook got there, Hannah began to feel a little fidgety. Buying a car and driving to Kansas seemed rather tame by comparison to the new adventure upon which she was embarking. If she dwelt on it too long, she was bound to get the traditional jitters. Recalling the lone can of Pepsi left after she had cleaned out the refrigerator yesterday, she decided to take a short break.

In the kitchen, Hannah leaned against the stone sink and drank the cola as she stared out the window at the hazy brightness of the August sunshine. So much had happened since she'd first entered the cottage that chilly spring morning and met the impudent cowboy who was going to change her life....

Engrossed in memories, she did not hear Rook until he called out her name and came striding into the room. She turned to move into his embrace, but he stopped short and warded her off with a broad grin.

"I remember what happened the last time you kissed me with a Pepsi in your hand—and I don't have time to change before we leave."

She nodded sagely, admiring his new jeans and the rust-and-navy plaid shirt he was wearing. Solemnly she set the can aside, her eyes resting on the firm curve of his mouth.

Rook drew her into the shelter of his arms, and she stood on tiptoe to accept his kiss. They indulged themselves with a slow, deliberate exploration of each other's mouths, as though they had been apart for days instead of hours. The kiss was deeply loving and filled with heart-meant promise.

When it ended, they simply held each other for a time, content to share a last quiet moment before what was certain to be a hectic departure.

Finally, with reluctance, Rook released her and stepped back. "You look great, honey," he said, "but I brought you something to complete your outfit."

He reached into his hip pocket and handed her a coil of tooled leather.

"A belt?" she queried, puzzled.

"Not just any belt, Hannah—one with a God-awful cowhead buckle."

They burst into laughter as he mimicked the words she had spoken to him on that long-ago day they'd met.

Hannah unfastened the plain brown belt she wore and let it drop to the floor. Then, arms slightly raised, she allowed Rook to thread the new one through the loops of her jeans and buckle it. Her hands shifted to his shoulders and she wordlessly expressed her gratitude.

"I've wanted to see you dressed like this since that first day," he confessed. "You look beautiful."

"And so do you. We're going to make quite a splash in New York."

"Speaking of which..." He placed a kiss on the tip of her nose. "The Boss and Aunt Maggie are waiting in the car. We'd better get going."

"I'm almost ready. Why don't you take the rest of my luggage out while I throw some cosmetics into an overnight case?"

"Don't be long. I'm anxious to get started."

"So am I," she said fervently.

When they had first begun making plans for their wedding Hannah had been in a daze, her head filled with visions of medieval wedding gowns and heather bridal bouquets. It had taken Rook's calm influence to finally convince her she wasn't dreaming. He had made plans for them to travel to Inverness to collect her wedding dress and the custom-made kilt he'd ordered, and then they would drive to the isolated castle on the west coast where his mother and aunts would meet them for the wedding. A leisurely honeymoon would last throughout the remainder of summer and into late fall. After all, Rook had told her, one of the advantages of being the boss was that once you had discovered romance you could be free to enjoy it. At last Hannah's life was outdistancing her daydreams!

And she sternly reminded herself, she was through with all that. She was no longer the old Hannah, an incorrigible dream weaver who couldn't bear to face reality. Instead, with determination, she was striving to become a new, mature Hannah, a wife Rook could be proud of. She intended to keep her feet firmly on the ground, saving any romantic flights of fancy for the book she planned to write. And maybe, she decided, after suddenly remembering Rook as the pirate—occasionally the bedroom.

No doubt this very room, she thought, closing the overnight bag and glancing about. They would be living in her grandmother's cottage until they could plan and build a house of their own, but Rook had already announced his intention of spending lots of weekends there throughout their married life. Hannah smiled, bid the cottage a silent farewell, then went out, shutting the green door behind her.

While he waited for Hannah, Rook had wandered into the backyard to stand gazing off across the prairie, fixing its beauty firmly in his mind until his return. He was keenly aware of a sultry wind and the sun-baked smell of cedars. Funny, the combination seemed to be having a strange effect on him. . . .

Rook guided the chestnut gelding through the tall blue-stem grass, his arm curved protectively around the little girl sitting in front of him. The child pointed into the distance and turned to look up at Rook with sparkling green eyes.

"Look, Daddy, that's a wheat field, isn't it?"

"It sure is. You're pretty smart for a four-year-old."

"Did you know I'm gonna be a farmer someday—just like you?"

"That makes me real proud, honey." Rook smiled and ruffled the girl's dark hair. "Real proud."

"Hey," the child exclaimed in delight. "There's Mommy—she's walking out to meet us!"

Rook's heart rocked in his chest the way it did each time he saw her anew. Hannah was beautiful . . . and never more so than now as she moved awkwardly toward them, her hand lying protectively over a very rounded tummy. She stopped to wait for them, her smiling, heart-shaped face tilted upward.

"Is anything wrong?" Rook asked, dismounting. He brushed a kiss on her mouth.

"Not a thing. The doctor told me to exercise, and that's what I'm doing. I just wish your son wasn't so fond of tap-dancing on my ribs!"

He laughed happily and draped an arm around her waist. They began to walk, Rook slowly leading the horse upon which his daughter was seated. Occasionally they stopped to watch a hawk circle overhead or discuss finishing touches for the house they had built.

All around them, the wind-whipped prairie grass undulated like the waves of a restless ocean. Rook paused, shoving the cowboy hat he wore back on his head, and let a prideful glance sweep the countryside.

"Someday, sugar," he said to the child, "all this is going to belong to you and your sisters and brothers...."

"Oh, brother!"

At the sound of Hannah's agitated voice, he blinked and quickly turned to face her.

"My gosh, look at the time," she said, pointing to her wristwatch. "We're going to be late. Don't you think we'd better get started?"

He grinned. "The sooner the better."

Rook and Hannah crawled into the back seat of Helen McAllister's maroon Mercedes, holding hands as the elegant vehicle lurched over the rough track across the pasture.

A large sign reading "Just About Married" and strings of tin cans adorned the back of the car, and as they rattled through the usually deserted barnyard Rook said, "Looks like we've got an escort."

Falling in behind them for the trip to the airport were trucks and cars containing all of Rook's hired hands and their families, friends and neighbors, and even a van from the boys' ranch, with familiar faces pressed against every window. Deeply moved by this show of affection, Rook and Hannah shared a misty glance.

I'm a lucky man, Rook thought, lost in her silvery gaze. For a while back there, he had understood something of Hannah's addiction to fantasy. Despite his hard-headedness, she had finally taught him to dream.

I'll never rely on daydreams again, Hannah was thinking. Why should I, when life with this man is sure to surpass my wildest imagination? She studied the contours of his beloved face. One last fantasy, she promised herself. One last one... and then no more.

She would have been surprised to know Rook was sharing the same vision.

Once there was an incredibly lonely girl from the big city who went out to the Midwest and met an impossibly arrogant Kansas cowboy. It was surely written in the stars that they were to be together, for all the elements combined to make it so. Their souls were tempered by earth, wind, water and fire, their love forged by fate. Each discovered that which he was lacking within the other... and they lived happily ever after.

* * * * *

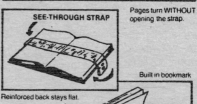
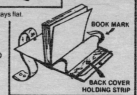